DEADLY BETRAYAL

A JANE PHILLIPS NOVEL

OMJ RYAN

1

Ordinarily he didn't kill women, but Victoria Carpenter was about to become one of the rare exceptions. After all, orders were orders. With his knee wedged firmly in the small of her back, she was trapped face-down against the cold concrete floor of the garage as he looped the nylon noose around her neck and pulled it tight. Her arms flailed as she attempted to grab the blue rope and loosen it from around her neck, but it was no good. She didn't stand a chance.

He jumped to his feet and handed the rope to his partner for tonight's job, who threw it up over the steel girder that held the small out-building in place before catching it again and expertly wrapping it around his gloved right hand. Standing together, they began to pull on the rope with all their might. Carpenter's head jerked up and she let out a stifled gasp as the noose tightened. She grabbed at the rope as they continued to pull, but within a few seconds her feet were off the floor, her body rising into the air. He watched in awe as she tried to scream, but no sound came out. Her eyes bulged and her face reddened as the blood began pooling in her head. Despite her obvious terror, he felt nothing other than a desire to get the job done quickly and efficiently, which meant leaving no evidence behind and enough clues to suggest suicide.

Carpenter's legs kicked out as she attempted in vain to find something solid to stand on. Holding her weight on his own now, his partner moved across the garage and secured the end of the rope in a thick knot against the heavy workbench that was bolted to the floor. All the time, her fingers manically clawed at the noose as her oxygen supply dwindled.

It won't be long now, he mused, watching her body jerk back and forth as she began to lose consciousness. Ten seconds later, and with one last desperate flurry of movement, Carpenter passed out. The garage fell almost silent, the only sound the rhythmic creaking of the rope against the steel girder as Carpenter's dying body swayed gently in the air.

Moving to stand underneath her, he used both hands to hold her body still, and stared up into her lifeless face. He felt nothing.

He checked his watch; it was 8.18 p.m. It would take at least ten minutes for Carpenter's brain to shut down completely and he would not leave until he was sure she was dead. His partner had been careless tonight, so he would use the time to clean up his mess and dress the space ready for the discovery of her body, which would happen later this evening. In the meantime, he returned to the main house to remove any evidence of their presence, and ordered his accomplice to get the car ready for a quick retreat.

Fifteen minutes later he returned to the garage, just in time to witness as Carpenter's body finally gave up the fight. A small puddle of urine had pooled on the concrete floor below her. Careful to avoid stepping in it, he moved closer and felt her pulse at the wrist as it faded away and stopped.

With everything in place, he surveyed the space one more time, then switched off the light and made his escape through

Carpenter closed his eyes and took a deep breath. 'I left just before it finished so I could get ahead of the crowds. There was a tram just about to leave as I got to the station, which got me back to Burton Road at about half-ten. Then I walked back here.'

'And what happened when you got home?'

'When I came in, I noticed the house was oddly quiet. I couldn't see or hear any sign of Vicky, so I called out to her. When there was no answer down here, I headed upstairs, but there was no sign of her. I couldn't figure out where she could be, so I came back down and called her mobile, which started ringing nearby. I found it on the kitchen table and started to panic – she never went anywhere without her phone. And that's when I spotted the back door was slightly ajar.'

'And is that unusual?'

Carpenter scoffed, 'Around here? Too bloody right. We make a point of locking the doors and windows all the time. People are always getting burgled; it happened to us a few months ago – although they didn't take much, just Vicky's laptop.'

Phillips continued 'So what happened then?'

'I went out to the garden to see if she was outside, but there was still no sign of her. That's when I thought to check the garage, and found...' Carpenter's voice trailed off and tears streamed down his cheeks.

'Did you touch Vicky at all?'

Carpenter nodded. 'I ran and grabbed her legs, trying to take the weight off her neck.'

'And when did you call the police?' asked Phillips.

'Immediately. I had my phone in my pocket, so I called 999. I stayed with her, holding her legs, but it was no use. I could see she was already dead...but I couldn't just leave her hanging there.'

'I understand, Mr Carpenter,' said Phillips. She allowed a

moment of silence before she asked her next question. 'Did Vicky ever talk about taking her own life?'

Carpenter recoiled. 'God, no. Never.'

Phillips glanced sideways at Bovalino, who discreetly raised an eyebrow. She continued. 'The uniformed sergeant told us that you think your wife was murdered. Why would you say that?'

'Because there was no way she would kill herself. Not Vicky.'

'You're certain of that?'

'One hundred percent,' said Carpenter.

'So she hadn't shown any signs of being depressed of late... anxious, even?'

'No. No. Not at all.'

'Are you sure? Mental health can be a silent killer,' said Phillips. 'Many people feel the need to hide it when they're struggling.'

'She wasn't *struggling*,' said Carpenter firmly. 'She was having the time of her life.' His voice was acidic now.

'What do you mean by that?'

Carpenter swallowed hard and waved away the question. 'Nothing. We just weren't getting on very well of late, that's all.'

Phillips eyed him for a moment. 'If your wife was murdered, Mr Carpenter, do you have any idea who might want to kill her?'

Carpenter took a gulp from his glass, then shook his head. 'No. I don't.'

'So what makes you so sure it wasn't suicide?'

'It's just not something that Vicky would do. It wasn't in her nature. She would consider killing herself as cowardly. She was a fighter, no matter what the issue.'

Phillips watched Carpenter for a long moment, attempting to read his body language.

3

Phillips took a seat in Dr Tanvi Chakrabortty's office in the basement of the Manchester Royal Infirmary in the heart of the city. She placed a cardboard tray holding three cups on the desk in front of her, and handed Chakrabortty her usual: a steaming hot soy latte. For the next few minutes they passed the time of day like colleagues in any one of the glass office blocks that filled the Manchester skyline might do. The difference for Phillips and Chakrabortty was that their immediate task was to examine the body of Victoria Carpenter to ascertain her cause of death. Thankfully, like Phillips, Chakrabortty was an early riser. The post mortem had been scheduled for 8 a.m. However, with the time approaching 8.10 a.m., they were still waiting for Detective Sergeant Jones, Phillips's right-hand man, to appear. He was ten minutes late, which wasn't like him at all.

Finally, at 8.15 a.m., a sheepish, unshaven and dishevelled-looking Jones appeared at the door to the pathology office. Phillips frowned. He looked skinnier than normal.

'Good of you to join us,' said Phillips, her tone sarcastic.

'Sorry, Guv. I hit some traffic,' Jones replied in his South London drawl.

Phillips stood and handed him his peppermint tea, then Chakrabortty led them out of the office and towards the mortuary.

As they waited for Chakrabortty to scrub up, Phillips and Jones stood next to the metal table that supported Carpenter's body, which was covered with a green sheet. Even with the strong smell of bleach and embalming fluid filling her nostrils, Phillips could detect Jones's body odour. She was sure she picked up the scent of stale alcohol on his breath. She made a mental note to deal with it later. For now, her focus was on finding out what had happened to Victoria Carpenter.

Chakrabortty appeared a moment later and peeled back the sheet to expose Carpenter's naked torso.

Phillips brought Jones up to speed on the previous evening. 'Victoria Carpenter, aged thirty-nine. She was found by her husband at approximately 10.45 last night, hanging by her neck from a steel beam in her garage. There were no signs of forced entry or foul play, and Evans's initial conclusion at the scene was that she likely committed suicide. However, Victoria's husband believes she would never consider such action and, therefore, that someone else must have killed her.'

'Based on *what* evidence?' asked Jones.

'That's just it. He had nothing to back up his theory,' said Phillips. 'Just said that it wasn't like her.'

Chakrabortty pulled back the green sheet that covered the body and prepared to start the examination. 'Well, let's find out for sure, shall we?'

Carpenter's torso, arms, legs and feet looked like she had just stepped out of a hot bath. Chakrabortty narrated her findings as she worked quickly, but methodically, through the different parts of the body. Carpenter's neck and throat bore the heavy bruising typical of ligature marks. Dark shadows surrounded her mouth and closed eyes, and, on closer inspection, the whites of her eyes were red from myriad burst blood vessels.

'This is interesting,' she said, sometime later, as she examined Carpenter's fingers.

'What is?' asked Phillips.

Scraping under the nail of the little finger, Chakrabortty lifted the small tool in her right hand towards the light. 'Looks like human tissue. That could suggest the victim might have scratched someone before she died.'

'Maybe her husband was right and she tried to fight off an attacker?' said Jones.

'Maybe. Or it could be her own skin,' said Chakrabortty. 'What's more interesting, though, is the fact that the rest of the hands have been thoroughly cleaned. I can't tell if that was pre or post mortem, but it's almost as if this little finger was missed.' Chakrabortty continued her examination of the other fingernails, then placed the tissue sample in a small petri dish and set it to one side.

A few moments later, she removed the green sheet completely, exposing the whole body, as she turned her attention to Carpenter's genitals. 'Her vagina shows some signs of bruising,' she said in a low voice.

'Consistent with sexual assault?'

'Or very rough sex, yes,' said Chakrabortty. 'And there are traces of semen inside too,' she added, as she collected samples.

Phillips locked eyes with Jones, who appeared glad of the distraction. 'Maybe Aaron Carpenter was right, then?'

Jones nodded. 'Maybe, yeah.'

Finally, Chakrabortty shifted her focus to Carpenter's neck.

'Why didn't you start there?' Philips asked.

'An old habit,' Chakrabortty explained. 'My old professor at medical school vehemently believed that any pathologist worth their salt should look at the most obvious injuries last. That way, their view wouldn't be skewed by a significant find early on, meaning every part of the body receives the same attention. He often reminded us that many a killer had been identified by the most innocuous of injuries found about the victims' bodies.'

Phillips nodded her approval, and watched on in silence as Chakrabortty spent the next fifteen minutes giving Carpenter's neck a thorough examination, which included taking a number of X-rays. Chakrabortty was never one to offer a cause of death without all the facts, so Phillips knew to stay quiet until all the external examinations had been done. She also hoped that both she and Jones would be able to take their leave before the buzz saws came out.

One of the pathology assistants arrived with the developed X-rays and passed them to Chakrabortty, who attached them to the lightboard fixed to the wall. She scrutinised them for a minute before turning to face Phillips and Jones. 'It'll need final sign-off from the coroner, but from what I can see in these X-rays, I'm quite confident that someone else killed Victoria Carpenter.'

Phillips stepped around the steel table to stand next to the doctor.

'See here,' said Chakrabortty, as she pointed at the negative image with the index finger of her right hand. 'This is the C2 vertebra. Essentially, one of the large bones at the top of the spine. If the victim had jumped from a chair in order to hang herself, the C2 vertebra would be displaced or fractured. As you can see here, it's fully intact, but the hyoid bone is severely crushed at the point where the rope was attached. That would suggest to me that Victoria Carpenter was slowly strangled.'

'Could she have strangled herself?' asked Phillips. 'You know, hung herself from the rope without her body actually dropping?'.

'It's certainly possible, but if that *were* the case, the bruising on her neck would be localised to a single contact line where the rope was attached.' Chakrabortty directed Phillips back to the body. 'As we can see, the bruising follows a gradient pattern, getting darker at the top, just under her jaw. That suggests to me that she was dragged upwards until she was hanging, when she finally died.'

'Jesus,' whispered Phillips, the terrifying last moments of Victoria Carpenter's life running through her mind.

'Like I said,' Chakrabortty continued, 'the coroner will make the final decision, but taking into account the evidence we've seen so far, I'd suggest you're looking at a homicide or an assisted suicide. Based on that, I'll pull some favours to run the tissue samples and semen through the DNA database as a priority, and see if we can find a match.'

'Thanks, Tan. As ever, you're a star.' Phillips checked her watch. It was approaching 10.30 a.m. 'We'd better get back to Ashton House and brief the team, then update Fox.'

Chakrabortty picked up the buzz saw, and a wicked grin appeared on her face. 'What? You're not staying to see the internal?'

'I'm happy to leave that to you,' said Phillips, returning the grin. 'I think we've had enough fun for one day, don't you, Jonesy?'

Jones nodded vigorously, and needed no encouragement to get moving as Phillips ushered him towards the door.

'Suit yourself,' said Chakrabortty from behind them, then activated the saw. The unmistakable sound of the high-speed ultra-sharp blades echoed around the examination room.

4

Phillips called ahead to let Bovalino and Entwistle know what time they could expect her and Jones back in the office. Considering Chakrabortty's verdict, she was keen to get started on the background checks for Victoria and Aaron Carpenter, and there was no time like the present. As she walked into her office followed by Jones, Bovalino and Entwistle were already sat down and waiting. As ever, Entwistle was sharply dressed, his chiselled mixed-race features giving him the look of a model rather than a young Detective Constable. She hung her mid-length grey coat on the back of her chair, took a seat, and wasted no time in bringing them up to speed with the results of the post mortem.

'So,' Bovalino said once she was done, 'what's your take on it, Guv? Murder or assisted suicide?'

Phillips tapped her fingers on her desk for a moment as she considered. 'We'll need to do a lot more digging, but from what her husband says, suicide seems unlikely.'

'Unless *he* was the one that helped her?' said Jones.

'It's certainly possible, but he claims he was at the cricket all night.' She pulled Aaron's ticket from her pocket and laid it on the desk. 'Let's check the CCTV at the ground, as well as the trams from Old Trafford to Burton Road – see if we can find him.'

'I can do that,' said Bovalino.

'So what did you find out about the Carpenters so far. Who are they?' asked Phillips.

Entwistle shifted forwards in his chair. 'Victoria Carpenter worked for the Council as the deputy leader of the Planning Department.'

'Really?' asked Phillips. 'That'll kick up a bit of a stink within the Town Hall.'

Entwistle continued, 'Yeah. She was there six years and earned forty-five grand a year. Aaron is a chartered surveyor and works for Shotten Construction Ltd. He's only been there just over a year, and is on 40K a year. They got married in Bali seven years ago, have no kids, a joint mortgage on the house in Withington which is worth £450,000...they also have combined savings of ten thousand pounds and a small amount of credit card debt. They're pretty much unremarkable.'

'So why the hell would someone want to kill her?' asked Jones.

Phillips remained silent for a moment as she digested the information. 'Why indeed. Anything else? Any health issues for Victoria, or large insurance policies?'

'I'm still working on those, Guv,' said Entwistle.

'And what about problems in the home? Any reports of domestic incidents?'

'I checked that,' said Bovalino. 'Both clean as a whistle.'

'Right. Well, keep looking. There must be a good reason someone would go to all the trouble of killing her – or helping her commit suicide.'

Each of the team nodded. They knew the drill.

'In the meantime, I need to get upstairs and brief Fox before she hears it from within the Town Hall,' said Phillips.

'Rather you than me, Guv,' joked Bovalino.

Phillips forced a thin smile, 'Well actually, Bov, as you were first on scene, I can take you with me if you like? You know, so you can share your thoughts on the case?'

Bovalino's face fell and he jumped up from the chair in a hurry. 'No, you're all right, Guv. I've got plenty to do down here.'

Phillips stood, smiling wryly, 'Funny. I thought you might say that.'

When Phillips was shown into the large office by Fox's assistant, Ms Blair, she found Fox in her usual position behind her large smoked-glass desk.

'What do you know about Chief Superintendent Broadhurst?' Fox asked, even before Phillips had taken her seat.

Phillips raised her eyebrows. Usually Fox made her wait until she was squirming before engaging in conversation of any kind. She sat down. 'Er, not much, other than people say he's a good copper and a fair boss.'

Fox nodded in silence for a moment. 'And what do they say about *me*?' she asked – with no hint of irony.

Phillips swallowed hard. She didn't like lying, but telling Fox the truth could be the end of her career in Major Crimes. 'Well, er...they say...' she stuttered as she attempted to find the right words.

Fox continued to glare at her.

'...they say you're tenacious, determined and ambitious,' said Phillips, lying through her teeth. What she really wanted to say was 'You're a sociopathic narcissist who would sell your own children to get ahead.'

Fox seemed satisfied with Phillips's verbal answer and nodded her approval. 'I've just found out it's between him and me for the Chief Super's job.'

'I had heard Morris was retiring,' said Phillips, trying to play down the fact Chief Constable Morris was leaving. It was, in fact, all anyone was talking about within the halls of Ashton House. Pretty much every copper, to a man – or woman – wanted Broadhurst to get the top job because he was so well-liked and respected, whereas *everyone* feared what a future under Fox's leadership would be like. Her ambition knew no bounds, and most people worried that could easily lead to drastic budget cuts and seriously jeopardise the safety of officers on the streets of Greater Manchester.

'The final interview is at the end of the month,' Fox said, without emotion.

'I'm sure you'll get it, Ma'am,' said Phillips – with mixed emotions. She would really love to see the back of Fox, but there were no guarantees any successor would be an improvement. Fox was a bitch, but Phillips had learnt how to play her to get what she needed. Better the devil you know, she thought.

Seemingly tiring of the discussion around the soon-to-be-vacant Chief Constable position, Fox turned her full attention back to Phillips. 'Ms Blair said you wanted to see me urgently?'

'Yes, Ma'am,' said Phillips. 'I landed a case last night that I thought you'd want a heads-up on.'

'Really? Why so?'

'Well, initially it looked like a suicide by hanging, but the victim's husband – who found the body – claims there was no way she would kill herself. And in the PM this morning, Chakrabortty confirmed that it looks like she was either strangled or someone helped her commit suicide. We also found tissue under one of her fingernails, and there were signs she may have been sexually assaulted.'

'I see,' said Fox, her brow furrowed. 'And why is this so urgent?'

'Well, Ma'am, the thing is, she also worked quite high up in the Town Hall as part of the City Council.'

'Really? What was her name?'

'Victoria Carpenter. She was deputy leader of the Planning Department.'

'Vicky? Good God, I know her,' said Fox. 'She's on one of the committees I chair regarding the regeneration of the inner city suburbs. Or, should I say, *was* on one of the committees.'

'I figured, based on her high profile within the business community, her death will make the news pretty quickly, so I wanted you to be aware of it.'

'You did right, *Jane*. Well done.'

Fox must be pleased. She rarely called Phillips by her first name.

'So, what's your opinion on the case?' Fox continued. 'Did someone help her kill herself, or was she murdered?'

'Well, it's a bit too early to say, but I have a strong feeling in my gut she was killed. Call it a hunch, but the stats show that women rarely commit suicide by hanging. Plus, with the tissue under the fingernails and the potential sexual assault, it feels to me like a homicide.'

'When will you know for sure?' asked Fox, eagerly.

'Well, Chakrabortty has fast-tracked the samples found on the body through the DNA database. We'll know more once we can figure out who was with her in the last hours of her life.'

Fox's eyes were fixed on a point behind Phillips in a trance-like gaze.

'What's on your mind, Ma'am?'

Fox's trademark Cheshire Cat grin spread across her face. 'If Victoria Carpenter was murdered, but it was made to look like suicide, this could be a supremely high-profile case for Major Crimes. If we can get a quick result on it, this is exactly the kind of investigation I need to get me ahead of Broadhurst and into the Chief Constable job.'

Phillips sat in silence. After working for Fox for so long, Fox's self-serving approach to the investigation shouldn't

5

Later that evening, Phillips took a seat at a table in a quiet corner of the Bull's Head pub just outside the leafy – and highly desirable – Cheshire village of Prestbury. It was almost 8 p.m. and she was waiting for the renowned Manchester investigative newspaper reporter, Don Townsend, to show up.

Earlier that afternoon, he had called Phillips on her mobile. Based on his reputation for always being first to the big stories – not to mention her own experiences with him – she had fully expected a barrage of questions regarding Victoria Carpenter's death. Instead, the complete opposite had happened. Sounding quiet and withdrawn, he'd admitted he *did* want to talk about Carpenter's death, but not to get the scoop; rather, that he had information about her *murder* that he felt Phillips needed to hear. If Don Townsend wanted to share information, it had to be worth hearing.

As Phillips waited for him to arrive, she checked Facebook on her iPhone. Since connecting with her ex-boyfriend from Hong Kong, Dan Lawry, through it late the previous year, she had started to post and share content on her page semi-regularly – but only a very small group of connections, which included Jones, Bov and Entwistle. She still couldn't make up her mind whether it was acceptable or foolish to be Facebook friends with your direct reports, so was always careful with what she posted.

Scrolling through her feed, she saw yet another post from Entwistle. She marvelled at his ability to plough through mountains of digital data during the day, and still have the energy to share funny videos, pictures and memes in the evening. Next up was a post from her niece, Grace – her brother's eldest, who he often described as 'fifteen going on thirty'. Her birthday was coming up in a week's time, and Phillips had no idea what to get her. Grace was a girly-girl who loved makeup and the latest fashion trends – in other words, her complete opposite. Phillips smiled at Grace's pout in the selfie, which had clearly been taken in her bedroom. She chuckled when she found herself trying to imitate the picture, puckering her lips and tilting her head to one side.

'You look like you're having a stroke,' said a deep male voice from above her head.

Phillips recoiled and blushed as she cast her eyes up towards a dour-looking Don Townsend. 'Sorry,' she said, closed the app and placed her phone face-down on the table.

Townsend, holding a pint of Guinness in his right hand, took a seat. His tanned face carried a thickly wrinkled brow, and his gelled-back dark hair gave him the appearance of an American TV show gangster. 'Thanks for agreeing to meet with me, Jane,' he said, his voice low.

'I must admit I was intrigued, Don. It's not like you to give me information, is it? It's usually the other way round.'

Townsend took a long drink from the Guinness, and wiped his top lip as he set it down. 'I'll get straight to the point.'

Phillips folded her arms. 'Ok.'

'You're leading the investigation into Victoria Carpenter's death, right?'

'I am.'

Townsend scanned the surrounding tables, as if checking to see if anyone was listening, then looked back at her. 'Well, I'm *certain* she was murdered.'

Phillips nodded. 'Yeah, you said that on the phone earlier. What makes you so certain?'

'Because *I* know who did it.'

Phillips raised an eyebrow. 'And who might that be?'

'Her husband, Aaron.'

'And why do you think that?'

'Because he threatened to kill her a few months ago.'

'Says who?' asked Phillips.

'Says me, and *said* Vicky.'

Phillips's ears pricked up. 'Vicky? You knew her as Vicky, as opposed to Victoria?'

'Yes.' His shoulders suddenly sagged.

'Just how well *did* you know Victoria Carpenter, Don?'

Townsend took a moment to reply. 'Very well.'

'Go on.'

'We were in love.' His eyes glistened. He was clearly fighting back tears.

Shocked, Phillips pushed an imaginary wisp of hair behind her ear. She had never pictured a man like Townsend ever uttering those words. They just didn't suit him. 'As in, you were having an affair?'

Townsend nodded. 'That makes it sound sordid, but yes.'

'How long for?'

'Just under a year. We met at a charity function and hit it off immediately. We swapped numbers on the night, and I genuinely never expected to hear from her again. I mean, she was ten years younger than me and gorgeous, and, well, I'm...' His words tailed off as he tapped his bulging belly.

'So, had Aaron found out about you two?'

Townsend took another drink. 'Yeah. He must have had his suspicions, because he went through her phone one night when she was asleep. He found text messages I'd sent, telling her how much I loved her and wanted to be with her. The crazy bastard even called me in the middle of the night to confront me!'

'And then what happened?'

'I hung up, of course, and tried to call Vicky, but she didn't answer. Apparently, when I ended the call, he made his way into the bedroom and started screaming at her. She didn't deny it, and under pressure she told him who I was – and where I lived. Why she ever thought that was a good idea, I'll never know. He went ballistic, jumped in his car and raced over to my house in the early hours of the morning. Vicky called me to warn me, and the next thing I knew, there was a brick through my front door. I went outside onto the drive to try and calm him down, only to find he'd scratched the word "cunt" across my white garage door with his keys. That pissed me off, so I told him to grow up. Then he took a swing at me. I ducked out of the way and ran back inside before Vicky showed up and persuaded him to go home with her.'

'And was that the end of it?'

'No. According to Vicky, when they got home and she managed to speak to him, he told her that she had to stop seeing me. And that if she didn't, he'd kill her, and then he'd kill me.'

'Did she believe him?' asked Phillips.

'Considering the fact he was holding a 12-inch carving knife in his hand at the time, yes, I'd say she did.'

Phillips took a sip of her own drink. 'Look, Don. We both know people make threats to kill their partners every day. That doesn't mean they actually go through with it.'

'True,' said Townsend, 'but the fact is, we didn't stop seeing each other. Not completely.'

'So the affair continued?'

'After a short break, yes. Deep down she still had feelings for Aaron and wanted to make a go of it, but that didn't last long. Neither of us could bear to be apart, so we started seeing each other again. But as far as Aaron was concerned, Vicky was committed to their marriage.'

'But she wasn't?' asked Phillips.

'No. Once she realised she only wanted to be with me, she took legal advice from a solicitor. Once we were ready, and her finances were all in order, she was going to file for divorce and move in with me.'

'I'm guessing he found out about you two again, then?'

'Yes, he did,' said Townsend. 'Apparently he got an anonymous call one night from a woman who told him we were still having an affair, then hung up.'

'Really? That's a bit Machiavellian, isn't it?'

'That's what we thought.'

'Any ideas who might have made that call?' asked Phillips.

'None. We wracked our brains, but couldn't think of anyone who would benefit from doing it.'

Phillips took a moment to think. 'Look, Don. I get the whole jilted husband, and the attack on you and your house in the heat of the moment, but I'm not sure that translates into Aaron Carpenter strangling his wife and making it look like a suicide.'

'But who would want her dead other than Aaron?'

'I don't know. I mean, was she sick?'

Townsend's eyes narrowed and he shook his head. 'No. Why do you ask?'

Phillips chose her words carefully. 'I have to consider all possibilities, and that includes the fact that she may have died from assisted suicide, Don.'

'Don't be ridiculous!' Townsend scoffed. 'She had absolutely no reason to want to kill herself. She had everything to live for. We were going to start a new life, maybe even a family.'

Phillips felt a pang of sorrow, knowing Vicky had been carrying an unborn child. Now wasn't the right moment to bring it up, so she blocked it out of her mind. 'What about work?

'What about it?'

'Were there any issues at work she may have been keeping from you? They can soon build up for people,' said Phillips.

'Vicky loved her work. She lived for it, in fact. I mean, sure, she had some challenges with the politics of working in the public sector, but she accepted that as an occupational hazard.'

Phillips's mind was drawn to Fox. 'I know the feeling.'

'Seriously, Jane, it wasn't work. She was totally dedicated to the job. Especially just recently, with the proposed St John's Towers Development decision looming.'

'St John's what?'

'Towers Development.'

'That's news to me. What is it?' asked Phillips.

'It's a twin-tower development of commercial and residential units. The proposed site is where St John's Gardens and Tranquil Park currently sit, just off Deansgate.'

'Really? I would have thought that place was green belt and protected from developers.'

'It is,' said Townsend eagerly, 'but it's worth £700 million to the development company, and would bring in thousands of jobs to the city. A lot of people inside the Town Hall want the area rezoned so the development can get the green light.'

'Was Vicky one of those people?'

'No fucking way. She was *totally* against it. That's why she was working so many hours lately. She had teamed up with local conservationists and protest groups to help them stave off the development through the courts.'

Phillips frowned. 'So, how was she able to do that without upsetting her bosses in the Town Hall?'

'Very carefully. It was all done on the QT, and I helped where I could. She did all the background work that demonstrated how the development went against various planning laws and regulations. Then I met with the groups and their key members to pass on the information, which they used to block the proposed changes each time they returned to the Planning Department.'

'So her bosses had no idea what she was doing?'

'Not that I'm aware of, no,' said Townsend, taking another drink from his glass.

Now Phillips had reached the point in the conversation she had been dreading. She shifted in her seat and fiddled with her glass as she prepared to change tack. 'Don, I'm sorry to have to ask you this...'

'Ask me what?'

'Did Vicky like rough sex, at all?'

Townsend swallowed hard and closed his eyes momentarily. 'What makes you ask that?'

'Just something in the post mortem. It might be nothing, but it could be something.'

Townsend remained silent, his eyes fixed on Phillips, then nodded softly. 'Yes, she did.'

'How rough?'

'Rougher than I'd done it before I met her.'

'Did she ever scratch your back during sex?'

'Occasionally,' said Townsend.

'So, when was the last time you slept together?'

'The evening she died.'

'And what time was that?' asked Phillips.

Townsend appeared deep in thought for a moment before he answered. 'Aaron left for the cricket at about 6.30 p.m., and I was waiting round the corner from her house. She called me and I rushed round. We'd not seen each other for about a week, so we couldn't keep our hands off each other.'

'Did she scratch your back on that occasion?'

'Not that I can remember, but to be fair it was all over pretty quickly. We never even made it to the bedroom.'

Phillips took a sip of her drink. 'And what time did you leave?'

'About 7.15 p.m. I had a story to follow up on and she had a pile of work to get through. It was only meant to be a quickie. I could never have imagined it would be the last time I'd ever see her.'

Knowing what she was about to ask next, Phillips took a long, silent breath, then let it out and made a conscious effort to soften her voice. 'Don, did you know Vicky was pregnant?'

Townsend didn't react at first. Instead, he just stared at Phillips's face. Eventually he broke down, dropping his chin to his chest as he closed his eyes tightly. After a long moment, he lifted his head. A single tear fell down his cheek.

'It might not have been yours,' Phillips said, reaching out to touch his hand. 'It could have been Aaron's.'

Townsend straightened his posture and took a deep breath in through his nose. 'How far gone was she?'

'Four weeks.'

'It was mine,' he said with confidence. 'She told me they'd not had sex since he first found out about us. Aaron was struggling with that side of things.'

'Oh Don, I'm so sorry.'

Townsend forced a weak smile. 'Don't worry about me,' he said, his voice cracking. 'I'll get over it.' Another tear streamed down his cheek.

Phillips pulled her hand back and picked up her phone. 'Do you *really* think it was Aaron Carpenter who killed Vicky? Or is he just an easy target for you?'

Townsend rubbed his hands down his face, causing his

cheeks to redden. 'Oh, I don't know, Jane. I really don't. All I can say for sure is that it wasn't suicide in any way shape or form. She just wouldn't do that. No way.'

'Ok, Don, I hear you. Look. Because you and Vicky were intimate the night she died, I'm going to need to take some DNA. You know how these things work. It's purely for elimination purposes.'

'I get it,' said Townsend, and nodded once.

'You can either come to Ashton House tomorrow, or I can take some tonight?'

Townsend's eyes widened. 'Tonight? Where?'

'In the car park. I have a mobile sample kit in the car. It's up to you, mate.'

Townsend wiped his damp cheeks with his sleeve and drained the remainder of his pint. 'Let's do it now. Ashton House has way too many nosey bastards who'll try to find out what I'm doing there.'

Phillips smiled softly. 'You know it well, then?'

Townsend nodded as Phillips stood up to leave.

'Look, Jane,' he said from his seat. When he looked at her, his eyes, surrounded by dark shadows, were filled with sadness. 'God knows you don't owe me any favours, but promise me you'll find out who did kill Vicky.'

Phillips smiled softly. 'I'll do everything I can, Don. I can promise you that.'

Townsend stood up now, his tall frame almost dwarfing Phillips's.

'You ready?'

'Yeah. Let's get it over with. I just wanna go home, now.'

6

The following morning, when Jones, Bovalino and Entwistle filed into the offices of the Major Crimes Unit at Ashton House, Phillips shared Don Townsend's surprising revelations from the previous evening.

A couple of hours later, at 11 a.m., she and Jones arrived at the Carpenters' Withington home to hear Aaron's version of events from the night he threatened to kill his wife.

After a few minutes of constant bell ringing from Jones, an unshaven Carpenter finally answered the front door. Wearing sports shorts and a T-shirt, and staring at them with bloodshot eyes, he led them into the open-plan kitchen, where he took a seat at the breakfast table. He reeked of booze and, as Phillips cast a cursory glance at the array of empty whiskey bottles perched on the kitchen bench, it was clear he'd been drinking heavily.

'Do you mind if we sit?' asked Phillips.

'Do what you like,' Carpenter replied without conviction.

Once seated, Jones took out his notepad and Phillips took the lead. 'How are you holding up, Aaron?'

'Peachy,' he replied, his tone sarcastic.

'Are you feeling up to answering a few questions about Victoria?'

'Have I got any choice?'

Phillips glanced at Jones, then forced a thin smile as she locked eyes with Carpenter. 'I promise it won't take long.'

Carpenter nodded.

'Look. I'm sorry to have to ask this, but I'm afraid I must. Is it true your wife was having an affair?'

Carpenter's jaw clenched and his nostrils flared. 'How do you know about that?'

'We're detectives, Mr Carpenter. It's what we do.'

Carpenter breathed heavily, then raised his chin. 'She told me it was all over, but they were still at it behind my back.'

'*When* did she tell you it was over?'

'About three months back, when I first found out about it.'

'And how did you discover the affair?' asked Phillips.

Carpenter looked at the table for a long moment. 'It was something she said in bed one night. It got me thinking.'

'What was that?'

'That she "didn't deserve me."'

Phillips frowned. 'That seems a fairly innocuous statement.'

'Maybe so, but for some reason it stuck in my head. She'd been a bit distant and working late a lot at the time, so at first I figured she was referring to that. But when I mentioned it to a mate of mine who I go to the cricket with, he jokingly said that maybe she was having an affair. He reckoned he'd said the same thing to an ex-girlfriend he'd cheated on when he was feeling a bit guilty. He was just having a laugh at the time, but it rankled me and I couldn't get it out of my mind. Then, with that thought in the background, for the next week or so it did start to look to me like she was having an affair: text messages at all times of night, going into the garden to take so-called work calls, and making excuses as to why she had to work late. So one night, when I couldn't sleep for thinking about it, I brought her phone down here to the kitchen and had a look through her messages. That's when I found them from that slimy cunt Townsend.'

'Did you know who he was at the time?'

'No,' said Carpenter, 'and I couldn't believe my eyes when I went round to his house. The guy's old, fat and wrinkled, with a perma-tan. He looks like a melted candle, for God's sake. I couldn't understand why she would choose him over me?'

'Love can do strange things to people,' said Phillips.

'It wasn't love!' scoffed Carpenter. 'It was lust.'

'So what happened then?'

'Once I'd calmed down, she told me it was all a mistake and promised me it was over. She said she wanted to make another go of our marriage – but that was just bullshit too.'

'So when did you realise the affair was still going on?' Phillips already knew the answer, but wanted to check if Carpenter's version of events matched with what Townsend had said.

'I got a call to the house one night, on the landline. Vicky was out, and when I answered, a woman just said, "Your wife is still having an affair with Townsend. I thought you'd want to know", and then hung up.'

'Did you recognise the voice at all?' asked Phillips.

Carpenter shook his head. 'No.'

'What about the accent? Was it distinctive in any way?'

'No. Just a regular Mancunian. I tried dialling 1471 to check where the call had come from, but it was listed as unknown.' Carpenter exhaled loudly. When he spoke again, his voice cracked. 'Jesus. I thought it hurt the first time I found out she was cheating on me, but that second time... When I asked Vicky if it was still going on and she said yes, it crushed me. I couldn't believe she had lied to me again.' He shook his head and burrowed his palms into his eye sockets, fighting tears.

Jones continued to make notes. Phillips remained silent for

a long moment, allowing Carpenter to regain his composure. When he appeared ready, she continued.

'If you knew the marriage was over, why did you continue living together?'

'Money,' said Carpenter. 'I was pretty sure she had started talking to a divorce lawyer, so I did the same. He told me in no uncertain terms not to leave the house or it would be much harder for me to get my fair share of our assets. Believe me, the last thing I wanted to do was see her every day, knowing she was with him, but I wasn't going to let her fuck me over on the money too.'

Phillips nodded. 'I know this isn't easy to talk about, but when were you last intimate with your wife?'

'Sex, you mean?'

'Yes.'

'Before I found out about the affair.'

'The first or second time you found out?' said Phillips.

'The first. Knowing he'd been there, inside her, touching and kissing her all over...I couldn't bring myself to be with her in that way. I had hoped that, in time, I could come to terms with it, but maybe I was kidding myself. Once the trust has gone, intimacy is very difficult. Why is that important, anyway?'

'Oh, just standard procedure,' Phillips lied, and quickly changed tack. 'Do you know anything about what she was working on before she died?'

Carpenter shook his head. 'No. Vicky never talked about her work, and now I know why. She probably wasn't there half the time she claimed to be.'

'She never mentioned anything about the St John's Towers Development?'

'No. Like I say, we never discussed her job.'

'Can you think of anyone who would want to hurt Victoria?' Jones asked.

'Apart from me, you mean?' he said with a wry chuckle, but

his grin quickly disappeared and his mouth fell open. 'I'm joking of course.'

Jones didn't react. 'Did anyone ever threaten her?'

'Not that I know of. Having said that, there's been a few odd things that have happened over the last month or so.'

'Like what?' said Jones.

'Her car was damaged when it was parked on the drive. Someone threw acid over it. I thought it must be vandals, so I checked the CCTV we have that covers the front of the house. The wire had been cut! That freaked me out, I can tell you.'

'Did you report it to the police?' Jones asked.

'Yeah, but nothing came of it. A couple of uniformed officers came round, took a statement, and I never heard from them again. Anyway, I got a guy in to repair the CCTV and a few weeks later, as I told you the other night, we were burgled. They came in through the kitchen door.'

'And did you get that on CCTV?' Phillips asked.

'No. The camera on the back is a dummy.'

Phillips did her best to hide her frustration. She'd lost count of the number of CCTV cameras pointed at crime scenes that had turned out to be dummies. 'Anything else?'

'I'm not sure if it's relevant, but not long after that, our cat went missing. It turned up on the drive a few days later with a broken neck. We figured it must have been hit by a car and one of the neighbours had found it and put it on the drive, but when I asked them about it, no-one had seen anything. It was really weird. Vicky got very upset about that. She loved that stupid cat.'

'And you didn't?'

'It was her cat from before we met. I'm more of a dog man myself, but Vicky wouldn't entertain the idea.'

Phillips stared in silence at Carpenter for a long moment, watching for any signs he may be lying, but he appeared genuine enough. She eventually smiled and signalled to Jones it was time to leave. 'Thank you, Mr Carpenter. You've been very helpful. We'll leave you in peace now.' She passed him her card. 'If you think of anything else, please call me, any time, day or night.'

Carpenter examined the card in his hands as Phillips and Jones stood. 'When can we bury her, Inspector?'

'We'll need the final sign-off from the pathologist, but I'm hopeful it won't be too long now. Someone will be in touch as soon as that happens.'

'Thank you,' Carpenter said.

'We'll see ourselves out.'

'Why didn't you tell him Victoria was pregnant?' asked Jones a couple of minutes later, as they arrived at the car.

'You heard him. They'd not had sex for three months, and she was only four weeks gone. Some things are better left unsaid.'

Jones appeared agitated. 'I think he deserves to know, Guv. It doesn't seem fair to keep things from him about his own wife.'

'Do *you* want to tell him?' snapped Phillips.

Jones shook his head.

'Well, in that case, shut up and get in the car.'

7

Manchester Town Hall, a gargantuan example of Victorian Neo-gothic architecture located in the centre of Manchester, had taken nine years to build and was completed in 1877. Everything about the design was intended to be grand, but as time passed and repairs and upgrades became dependent on public funding, large parts of the interior had fallen into disrepair. As Phillips and Jones waited to see Eric Jennings – leader of the Council Planning Department, and Victoria Carpenter's former boss – Phillips was also struck by the contrast between the original building materials and the relatively cheap-looking furniture that adorned Jennings's personal assistant's office. She also noted that the young assistant's eyes were red and puffy, as if she'd been crying.

'Are you ok?'

The young woman sniffed hard and smiled. 'Yes, thank you. I'm just a bit upset about Vicky. It's come as such a shock.'

'You mean, Victoria Carpenter?' asked Phillips.

'Yes.'

'Did you know her well?'

'Fairly. I was her personal assistant as well as Mr Jennings's. I worked for her for almost a year.'

'And you are?'

'Cindy Shaw.'

At that moment, the large oak door to Jennings's office opened and a thin man with stark features appeared. He had a wispy ginger beard and small metal-framed glasses. Phillips guessed he was in his late fifties.

'DCI Phillips, DS Jones?' said Jennings. 'Please come in.'

The furniture in Jennings's office matched Shaw's in its cheapness, and the large room, with its vaulted ceiling, had the unmistakable smell of an ancient, untouched building.

'How can I be of help to the Greater Manchester Police?' asked Jennings as he sat behind his desk.

Phillips and Jones took seats opposite.

'We'd like to ask you a few questions about Victoria Carpenter, if you don't mind?'

Jennings's brow furrowed, 'A terrible shock to us all. I must say, I feel terrible. I never had any idea she was depressed, let alone suicidal.'

Phillips decided to keep the true nature of Carpenter's death to herself for the moment. 'It's come to our attention that Victoria was very busy with her work, and in particular the proposed development of St John's Gardens and Tranquil Park.'

Jennings flinched slightly. 'How do you know about that?'

'It's our job to know these things, Mr Jennings. What can you tell us about that particular development?'

Jennings sat back in his chair and folded his thin arms across his pigeon chest. 'There's not much to tell you, to be honest. The site is currently classed as green belt and protected, and there is a proposal going through the planning process currently that is looking to rezone it so it can be built on.'

'And who is the proposed developer?'

'I'm afraid that's confidential at this stage, Chief Inspector.' Jennings gave her a forced smile. 'I'm sure you understand.'

Phillips resisted the temptation to threaten him with a formal interview at Ashton House – for now. She would keep that one in her locker for later, just in case. 'Is it correct that Victoria was against the rezoning?'

Jennings raised an eyebrow. 'Who told you that?'

'That's confidential at this stage. *As I'm sure you understand?*'

'Touché, Chief Inspector,' replied Jennings. 'Well, I suppose one could say that Victoria had some reservations about the St John's development *initially*, but she soon changed her mind.'

'So, you're saying she supported it?' asked Jones.

'Yes.' Jennings nodded his head vigorously. 'In fact, I actually spoke to her the day she died and she told me what a great opportunity it would be for the city. It will, after all, create hundreds of jobs and bring millions of pounds-worth of investment into Manchester.'

'What time was that? When you spoke to her?'

Jennings reclined in his chair and stared up at the ceiling for a moment. 'Sometime after lunch...about two-ish, I'd say. I popped into her office to drop off some paperwork and she mentioned it then.'

'That doesn't seem to tally with what we've heard about Victoria and how she was passionately against the rezoning,' said Phillips.

'Well, I can't speak for anyone else, but she had no issues with it when we spoke. Quite the opposite, in fact. She was all in favour of it.'

'Really? That's odd, because as we understood it, she was actively feeding protest groups legal documentation in order to help them block the rezoning.'

Jennings's lip curled into a slight snarl. 'I don't know who's giving you that information, Chief Inspector, but I know nothing about it, nor do I believe it.'

'You wouldn't have any emails or written confirmation that testify to her support, would you?'

'I'm afraid not. Like I say, she told me face to face in her office.'

'Was anyone with you at the time? Ms Shaw, for example?'

'No,' said Jennings firmly. 'It was just the two of us.'

At that moment, Jennings's phone buzzed. 'Will you excuse me? I should take that.'

'Go ahead,' said Phillips. She glanced at Jones. They'd worked together for so long she could tell what he was thinking from the expression on his face. And he was in clear agreement with her thoughts: Jennings was lying.

'Thank you, Ms Shaw,' said Jennings, and replaced the receiver. 'Is there anything else I can help you with? If not, then I have an appointment on the other side of town and I'm afraid I need to leave now or I'll be late.'

'Don't let us keep you, Mr Jennings,' said Phillips. She stood up and ushered Jones out of the room.

As they passed through Cindy Shaw's office on the way to the main stairs, Jennings's assistant was notable by her absence.

'Was it something we said?' joked Jones, nodding in the direction of the empty chair.

Phillips grinned, and continued walking. When they reached the stairs and she was sure they were alone, she stopped Jones in his tracks. 'Jennings is lying, isn't he?'

'One hundred percent, Guv.'

'If Townsend's telling the truth, there's no way Carpenter would have changed her mind on the rezoning,' said Phillips.

'So why say that she had?'

Phillips set off down the stairs, and Jones followed. 'I dunno, Jonesy. But I think it's time to check Jennings's version of events with Townsend, see what he has to say.'

'Good idea, Guv.'

'And in the meantime, let's dig into Mr Jennings's background, see if he's got anything to hide.'

'On it,' said Jonesy as they stepped onto the ground floor and walked briskly towards the exit.

As THEY MADE their way back to the car, Phillips called Don Townsend on her mobile. He answered promptly. *'Jane, have you got an update for me?'*

'Nothing of note as yet, Don.'

'Oh.' Townsend sounded deflated.

'Look, it's probably wise not to expect too much too soon. In terms of the investigation, it's still very early days yet.'

'I know, I know. I'm just struggling to get my head round it, that's all. I need to know what happened to her.'

'And you will, in time. You have my word on that.'

'Thanks, Jane. So, what can I do for you?'

'What can you tell me about Vicky's boss, Eric Jennings?' asked Phillips.

'That useless prick? He's a total wanker.'

'And what makes you say that?'

'Because of how he treated Vicky,' said Townsend. *'He's a fucking bully and a snake.'*

'What do you mean he's a bully? How so?'

'Look, I can't prove anything because he's far too slippery to leave a paper trail, but he was trying to force Vicky into supporting the rezoning of St John's Square.'

'And how was he doing that?'

'Emotional blackmail, saying that by being so vocal about her opposition to the development, she could cost the city hundreds of millions of pounds and deny thousands of people the chance to find work. You see, she was honest with him about how she felt – too honest at times, and very clear on where she stood regarding the

rezoning: vehemently against it. Her stance was widely known within the Town Hall, and Jennings didn't like it because A, it made him look bad. In his eyes, his assistant should be toeing the department line, and Vicky just wouldn't. And B, she was casting doubt in the minds of senior officials who were tasked with reviewing the proposals.'

'Are you sure he didn't know about her helping the protest groups?'

'Well, I can't be a hundred percent sure, but we were very, very careful. She used her own private laptop to do all the research, for example—'

'The same laptop that was stolen?' Phillips cut him off.

'Come to think of it, yeah. Shit! You don't think Jennings was behind the burglary, do you?'

Like all reporters, Townsend had a vivid imagination, and Phillips knew better than to feed it. 'I think burglary might be a bit out of Jennings's league, Don. It's probably just a coincidence,' she said.

Walking beside her, Jones turned and raised an eyebrow. She knew instantly what he was thinking. Like the rest of the team, he was well aware of the fact Phillips did not believe in coincidences. In truth, the stolen laptop could yet prove to be connected to Carpenter's murder, but she wasn't ready to let Don Townsend know that.

She changed the subject. 'Jennings said that Vicky had had a change of her heart regarding the rezoning and fully supported it.'

'Utter bollocks,' spat Townsend.

'He reckons she spoke to him on the day she died, offering her full support.'

'He's lying. There is no way in hell she would have changed her mind. The night she died, she was drafting the next set of instructions for the planning protest groups. The leaders of the group were planning on presenting at the next public hearing regarding the

rezoning. If she was supposedly supporting it, why would she be doing all that work?'

'That's a very good point.'

'Plus, if she had changed her mind, she'd have told me. I was in it with her. There's no way she'd keep something like that from me.'

'Ok, Don. I had to ask and look into what he said.'

'If you want to look into anything or anybody, look into Jennings. He's as bent as a nine-pound note. Vicky was convinced he had a vested interest in the development going ahead,' said Townsend.

'How do you mean, a vested interest?'

'I can't be sure because, like I said, he never left any trails, but she was convinced he was taking kickbacks from developers coming into the city.'

'And why did she think that?' asked Phillips.

'Just the way he was with certain projects and developments. There was a number of them in the last year alone that he seemed to obsess over, and they were always the most contentious – and always approved. That's not in line with the culture within the Town Hall, which is "don't rock the boat", and Jennings is not the kind of man to stick his neck out unnecessarily. He never did anything unless there was something in it for him. He's on the take, Jane. I'm sure of it.'

'Maybe he is,' said Phillips, 'but can anyone prove it?'

'God knows I've tried to find evidence, but so far I've not been able to come up with anything. I'll just have to keep on looking.'

Phillips and Jones arrived at their car.

'Look, Don, I appreciate you want answers, but I think it's best you leave the digging to us now, ok? I promise I'll keep you updated as and when I find something I can share.'

Townsend remained silent on the other end of the line for a moment. When he finally spoke, he sounded resigned. *'Whatever you say, Jane.'*

Phillips hoped he would do as she asked, but, knowing Don

Townsend as she did, she wasn't convinced he could stay away from the case even if he wanted to.

'I'll be in touch, Don' said Phillips, and ended the call.

'What's he saying, Guv?' asked Jones.

'What we're *thinking*. That Jennings is lying about Carpenter's view on the St John's Towers Development.'

'So what now?'

'Now, Jonesy? Now we need to find out why, because I'm pretty sure that when we do, we'll find out why Carpenter was killed.'

'Back to Ashton House, then?'

Phillips nodded, opened the car door and jumped into the passenger seat.

A moment later, they were making their way back to headquarters.

8

A couple of hours later, back in the offices of the Major Crimes Unit, Jones, Bovalino and Entwistle eagerly opened the hot cardboard boxes of freshly delivered Chinese food.

'What's yours, Bov?' asked Jones, peering into one of the containers as Phillips emerged from her office.

'Singapore chow mein with a double portion of chips and some salt and pepper ribs.'

'It's a good job Fox is relaxed about the budget on this case,' said Phillips with a warm smile. 'We need most of it just to feed Bov.'

The big Italian grinned as Jones passed over three large boxes of steaming food. She'd asked the team to work late to try and get ahead on the case, and as a thank you had ordered in dinner. Like most hungry men presented with food, there was an initial flurry of movement as they each went in search of their quarry before a contented calm descended and they began to fill their bellies. Phillips chuckled to herself as she picked up her special fried rice, a pair of chopsticks and a diet coke, then headed back to her desk.

She had not realised how hungry she was, and it wasn't long before she had reached the bottom of the box and drained the can. A satisfied belch exploded from her mouth, drawing looks and grins from each of the team outside.

'Did you enjoy that, Guv?' said Jones.

'Just a bit,' said Phillips, laughing.

At that moment, Phillips's iPhone began to vibrate on the desk next to her. Chakrabortty. Phillips wiped her mouth and hit the green answer icon on the screen. 'Tan?'

'Sorry to call you so late, Jane,' said Chakrabortty, *'but I thought you'd want to hear this.'*

'Hear what?' said Phillips, noting the time on her laptop: 8.18 p.m.

'The DNA results are back from the lab. We have a match on the skin sample.'

A shot of adrenaline coursed through Phillips's body as her pulse quickened. 'Who?'

'The name's Jimmy Wong.'

'Jimmy who?'

'Wong. He's a Chinese national arrested on suspicion of rape last year. The case fell apart and he was never charged, but his details are still on the database.'

'And what about the semen? Is that Wong's, too?' asked Phillips.

'I'm afraid not, no. That matches the sample you sent over yesterday from Don Townsend.'

Phillips nodded into the phone. 'So you're saying she wasn't raped, then?'

'Not unless Wong had sex with her after Townsend and used a condom.'

'Which is not impossible, but rather unlikely,' said Phillips.

'I'd say so, yes.'

Phillips said nothing for a moment as she mused over

something that had been bothering her for a few days. 'Tan, would you be able to do me a favour?'

'As long as it's not tonight, yes. I've been on my feet all day and I really need to get home,' said Chakrabortty.

'Don't worry, it's nothing urgent – just something as and when you have time,' said Phillips.

'In that case, what do you need?'

'A paternity test on the foetus. I'd like to know if the father was Aaron Carpenter or Townsend.'

'Why?'

Phillips let out a sigh. 'Something Jonesy said to me the other day. I haven't told Carpenter that his wife was pregnant – and I still won't if it wasn't his. But if he was the father, then he probably should know the truth.'

'Leave it with me,' said Chakrabortty. *'I've got a crazy week ahead, but I'll get it sorted for you when I get some time.'*

'Much appreciated, Tan. Now go home and get some rest.'

'Don't you worry. I'm leaving now,' said Chakrabortty cheerfully, as she ended the call.

Phillips sat for a moment in silence, thinking of the mess made by Carpenter and Townsend's affair. Still resolutely single, she wondered if she would ever have the courage to trust someone with her heart. Occasionally she found herself longing for someone to talk to besides the team and her cat Floss – a partner to share things with – but then something like the Carpenters-Townsend love-triangle would show up and scare her half to death. What a mess they'd all made of everything. Still, it didn't help to dwell on things, so she jumped up from her chair and made her way out to the main office. 'Entwistle, I need you to find me an address for a Jimmy Wong. He'll be on the database for an alleged rape last year.'

'Of course,' said Entwistle, as he began typing.

Jones and Bovalino gazed at Phillips, their eyes wide and expectant.

'Wong's DNA was found under Carpenter's fingernail.'

'Jesus, really?' Bovalino sounded more than a little surprised.

'He's now our number one suspect,' Phillips continued. 'Jonesy, book a uniform team in for the morning. We'll raid his place at dawn.'

Jones nodded and picked up the phone.

'Once that's done, let's all get some rest. It's gonna be an early start and a big day tomorrow.'

9

News travels fast in Chinatown, especially when it comes to the activities of outsiders.

As soon as he had received the message from one of his trusted sources, he had travelled through the empty streets of Manchester city centre to his current position, less than forty feet up the street from the entrance to the old building. Despite it being the early hours of the morning, he had made the short journey on foot without being seen. Standing in the shadows of the doorway, he watched on as a number of uniformed police prepared to make a dawn raid through the main entrance of the apartment block. The speed at which they had found his associate's address had both surprised and infuriated him. He knew his accomplice had made some rookie errors on the night of the kill. Precisely because of that, he had gone to great lengths to remove any trace that they had been there that night. Clearly he had not gone far enough. He cursed himself for allowing such an amateur into his world and vowed that, from here on in, he would only ever work alone.

Up ahead, the uniformed officers made ready their weapons as a woman in a long, dark coat emerged from a side street with three men in tow. He was too far away to hear any of the conversation, but from the way she moved and the reactions of the men when she spoke, it appeared that she was in charge of the operation. A moment later, a number of the uniformed officers headed towards the rear of the building at pace, and the remainder of the crew turned their attention to the main entrance.

He continued to stare out from the shadows as he considered his options. Tempted as he was to watch the entire operation unfold, he knew it was too much of a risk. That was just not his style.

The police finally gained access through the large glass front door of the apartment block, and began to file into the reception area. As they did, he stepped out from the doorway and slipped away silently down the adjacent alley.

10

Wong's apartment was located in the city centre, just a minute's walk from Chinatown, in an old clothing factory that had been repurposed as part of the city's redevelopment in the early noughties.

With the sun casting a hazy glow on the horizon as dawn approached, Phillips stood on the street outside the block with Jones, Bovalino and Entwistle, waiting to raid Wong's apartment. Each of them wore a stab vest as they stood alongside the uniformed tactical firearms unit, all of whom carried MP5 semi-automatic machine guns. Because of the time of day, the procedure was further complicated by the lack of a concierge to let them into the building. Instead, one of the TFU officers had been forced to call a number of Wong's neighbours in the hopes that one of them would open the main door. After a few false starts, and expletives from residents who clearly did not believe they were speaking to the police, one neighbour did finally agree to give them access.

A second TFU team was stationed at the rear of the building in case Wong tried to make his escape through one of the metal fire exits attached to the apartment block.

Once inside the ground floor lobby, the team split, with the TFU taking the stairs while Phillips and the team used the elevator. A moment later, huddled on the small landing outside Wong's address, Phillips gave the order for the lead member of TFU to smash open the door with the small battering ram he held in his hands. A couple of deafening blows followed, and as the door gave way, the TFU charged into the apartment, each shouting 'Armed police!' as they fanned out, weapons engaged and trained on any potential targets. Phillips and the team followed them in to hear shouts of 'Clear!' from every room.

'He's not here, Ma'am,' said Sergeant Rhodes, the TFU senior officer.

'Shit!' said Phillips as her frustration boiled over.

Jones and Bovalino disappeared into the bedrooms whilst Phillips scanned the lounge. The place was sparsely decorated, with just a small sofa, an IKEA armchair and an old TV on a stand beneath the large window.

Jones reappeared. 'There's nothing in the main bedroom to indicate where he's gone, and the wardrobe is empty apart from a couple of metal hangers on the rail.'

A moment later, Bovalino walked into the lounge holding a small piece of paper in his hand, which he passed to Phillips. 'There's an address written on here, but it's quite hard to read. The handwriting is shocking.'

Phillips squinted as she attempted to decipher the scrawled words. 'Looks like somewhere in London. Jonesy, you're our resident cockney. What part of the city is the W1 postcode attached to?'

Jones stepped forwards, took the piece of paper and inspected the address for a moment. 'Er, if my memory serves me right, I think W1 is Soho, or Chinatown way,' he said, then began typing the sequence of letters and numbers into Google on his phone. A second later, he found what he was looking for.

'Yep, that address is coming up as the Golden Flower restaurant, just a few doors down from the Chinatown Gate.'

'Anyone fancy a Chinese?' grinned Bovalino.

Phillips shot him an agitated look and his face straightened.

'I've got a friend in the Clubs and Gangs Unit of the Met, DI Ben Walsh. I could call him and see if that address is known to them?' said Jones.

Phillips checked her watch; it was just after 5.30 a.m. 'Will he be up yet?'

Jones smiled. 'One way to find out.' He opened up the contact list in his phone and walked back into the main bedroom.

'What would you like us to do, Ma'am?' asked Sergeant Rhodes.

Phillips released a frustrated sigh. 'Nothing. You and your guys can get back to base.'

Rhodes nodded, and signalled to his team that it was time to leave.

For the next five minutes, Phillips, along with Bovalino and Entwistle, milled about the apartment looking for anything that might give them a clue as to Wong's location, but found nothing.

Then Jones returned to the lounge room.

'Was Walsh awake?' asked Phillips, as Bovalino and Entwistle gathered next to her.

'No, but he is now,' said Jones, with a grin. 'It turns out that address is well known to the boys in CGU.'

Phillips eyes widened. 'Go on.'

'It's an apartment above the Golden Flower restaurant. From the outside it looks legit, but Walsh reckons it's used as an illegal gambling den by Chinese nationals. They keep themselves to themselves and don't involve tourists, and because the CGU don't have enough people to shut them down, the Met turns a blind eye.'

'So could Wong be there?' said Phillips.

'Possibly. He's known to Walsh and CGU,' said Jones. 'He used to run with one of the Triad gangs down in the capital, but as far as they were concerned, he had moved up here a couple of years ago. He's not been seen in London since.'

Phillips mulled the information over for a moment.

'What you thinking, Guv?' asked Bovalino.

Phillips smiled and turned to face him. 'I'm thinking it's time you took a little trip to London, Bov, with your Cockney mate over here,' she said, nodding in Jones's direction.

'London?' said Bovalino, clearly aghast. 'I fucking hate London. It's full of arseholes.'

'Oi!' said Jones, with a grin, as he punched Bovalino on his arm. 'I'm one of those arseholes, thank you very much.'

'You know what I mean, Jonesy,' said the big Italian. 'Can't Entwistle go instead? He's a flash git, he'll fit right in down there.'

Entwistle's brow furrowed. 'Are you deliberately trying to offend everyone today, Bov?'

Phillips cut in before he could answer. 'I need Entwistle here with me, so it has to be you and Jones. I'll speak to Fox this morning to get her approval to set up a joint operation with the Met to raid that place. See if we can flush Wong out.'

Bovalino nodded reluctantly and his shoulders sagged, which gave him the appearance of a freshly chastised teenager.

'Don't worry, Bov,' said Jones, playfully. 'I know you get a nosebleed whenever you leave Manchester, but I'll look after you, big man.'

'Piss off!' said Bovalino, half-smiling now.

'Right. Let's get back to Ashton House and get organised,' said Phillips. She made to leave the apartment. 'Get forensics in here ASAP. I want every inch of this place checked for anything that might connect Wong to Carpenter's murder.'

Jones nodded. 'Guv.'

Phillips continued, 'And I want you and Bov on the train to Euston this afternoon.'

Entwistle and Bovalino followed her out as Jones brought up the rear, jokingly singing a famous old London song in a thick Cockney accent, thumbs tucked into his stab vest. It was clearly for Bovalino's benefit. "Knees up Mother Brown, knees up Mother Brown, under the table you must go, Ee-aye, Ee-aye, Ee-aye-oh..."

11

After returning from the raid on Wong's apartment, Phillips debriefed Fox, who wasted no time in ensuring that a joint operation was agreed between the MCU and the Met's Clubs and Gangs Unit. The plan was to raid the address above the Golden Flower at midnight.

As the time approached 6 p.m., Jones and Bovalino found themselves on the 17.55 train to London Euston as it rolled steadily out of Manchester Piccadilly. Sadly for Bovalino, it was rush hour and the carriages were packed to the rafters. Huddled into his tiny seat in standard class, he was forced to stick his huge thighs out into the aisle, which had already proved problematic with other passengers struggling to get their luggage through. Conversely, Jones, who was at least six inches shorter and about half as wide, sat comfortably in the window seat next to him.

'So why do you hate London so much, Bov?' asked Jones.

Bovalino flinched as a passenger, making his way down the aisle on his way back from the buffet car, clattered into his protruding knee. Bovalino shot him a frustrated look.

'Sorry,' said the man with a sheepish expression, then continued back to his seat.

'Like I said, it's full of arseholes,' said Bovalino, 'and it's just too damn busy for my liking.'

'How often have you been, then?'

'Often enough,' said Bovalino, as he adjusted his weight in a vain attempt to get comfortable.

'Come on. How many times?'

'It's not important, Jonesy. Just leave it, will you.'

Jones stared at his partner for a long moment before a large grin spread across his face. 'You've never been, have you?'

'Yes I have,' replied Bovalino indignantly.

'Bollocks! I know you, Bov, and I can tell when you're lying. And you're definitely lying now. You've never been.'

Bovalino attempted to change the subject. 'Is there a drinks trolley on here?' He leaned out into the aisle and looked left and right.

Jones chortled. 'You're a bloody idiot, Bov. Thirty-five years of age and you've never even been to London.'

Bovalino turned back to face Jones now. 'All right, all right. You've made your point. Can we just drop it, please?'

Jones grinned, and tapped Bovalino on his left thigh. 'A bit touchy, aren't we? What's the matter? You scared what might happen to you in the Big Smoke?'

'Oh piss off.'

Jones giggled. 'Don't you worry, big man. I'll keep you safe and get you back to your beloved Manchester in one piece.'

Bovalino didn't respond. Jones turned to the view out of the window. When Bovalino finally spoke, his voice was low, almost a whisper. 'If you must know, I *am* scared.'

Jones spun round to face Bovalino, eyes wide. 'You what?'

Bovalino's chin dropped to his chest. 'I'm scared, Jonesy.'

Jones shifted in his seat. 'Is this a wind-up?'

Bovalino took a deep breath. 'No, no it's not. Since my accident on the Hawkins case, I feel like I've lost my nerve. I came so close to losing everything. Everything. What if I'm not so lucky next time?'

'Don't be daft, mate. That was a complete one-off. That won't happen again.'

'But what if it does? What if *next time* I end up in a wheelchair, for good? Or get killed, even? What would that do to Izzie? I can't stop thinking about it.'

There was a long pause before Jones responded. 'Have you spoken to the Guv about this?'

Bovalino shook his head. 'I haven't even told Izzie.'

'Jesus, Bov,' said Jones. 'The Hawkins case was over six months ago. How long have you been feeling like this?'

'Since the dawn raid we did on the Fizle case, when he pulled that knife.'

'Fizle? But that was in your first week back.'

'Yeah. I know.'

'Mate, you should have said something sooner.'

'I wanted to, but I felt stupid,' said Bovalino. 'I mean, how would it look? A big guy like me, scared of the action? They'd kick me out of MCU, and I couldn't bear that.'

'Well, you're gonna have to do something. You can't carry on like this.'

Bovalino nodded. 'I know, I know.'

'Look, maybe you shouldn't come on the raid tonight, hey? I can make an excuse to Walsh and the Guv, say you were sick or something, and you can head back to Manchester. I'll take care of things from our end.'

Bovalino forced a thin smile. 'You're a good mate, Jonesy.'

'I just want to help, big man.'

'You already have,' said Bovalino. 'I appreciate the offer, but I'm your oppo. I go where you go, no matter how hard it might be.'

'You really don't have to, you know.'

'Yes I do, Jonesy.' With that, Bovalino pulled his large frame out of the seat and stood. 'I need a piss.' He headed for the toilet at the end of the carriage.

Nothing else was said for the remainder of the journey. As the time approach 8.10 p.m., the train pulled into London Euston and came to a stop. Jones and Bovalino waited for the bulk of their fellow passengers to make their exit before they stepped up out of their seats and left the carriage. Jones led the way to the taxi rank situated under the station concourse, where they discovered an enormous queue of people waiting for cabs.

'This could take a while,' said Jones.

'I told you it was too bloody busy down here,' said Bovalino with a gentle smile.

'Scotland Yard is close to Embankment. We can always get the tube?'

Bovalino shook his head. 'No way. I'm not going on that thing. If we were meant to travel underground, God would have given us claws instead of fingers.'

Jones chuckled and checked his watch. It was approaching 8.25 p.m. They were due to meet Walsh at 9.30 p.m. 'Come on, we can walk it in forty-five minutes, and I can show you the sights on the way.'

Bovalino smiled. 'I like the sound of that.'

Jones turned and headed back upstairs towards the station exit.

12

Back at Ashton House, Phillips returned to the MCU office from the canteen, carrying a pre-packed sandwich and a cup of tea she'd bought from the vending machine. She cursed herself for missing the hot food that was served until 7.30 p.m. but, as was often the case, she had been so engrossed in her work that she had lost track of time. Spying Entwistle at his desk, she wandered over to see what he was doing.

'You still, here? It's gone 8.30,' she said as she dropped into Bovalino's seat opposite him.

'Yeah,' said Entwistle, stretching his arms out for a moment. 'I'm working my way through the CCTV footage from Old Trafford to see if Aaron Carpenter was actually where he claimed to be the night his wife was killed.'

'And?' Phillips took a bite of her ham and cheese sandwich.

Entwistle turned his laptop screen to face Phillips. 'He was indeed.' He pressed return and a video started to play.

Phillips leant forwards to take a closer look as Entwistle narrated. 'Once we knew his seat number, it was fairly easy to locate the various cameras that cover his route in and out of the ground. This piece of video shows him leaving five minutes before the end. There's a bunch more that capture him arriving half an hour before the match too, then getting a drink at the bar and buying some food, etc. He was there all night, without a doubt.'

'And what about the cameras on the tram?'

'Yep, he's on them too. We have footage of him getting on the tram at Burton Road heading to Old Trafford before the match, and then getting off again at the other end at 10.30 p.m., just as he claimed he did. Unless he's got an identical twin or a doppelgänger, he's not our killer.'

Phillips swallowed the piece of sandwich in her mouth and slurped her hot tea. 'Well, at least that's one person we know definitely *didn't* kill Victoria Carpenter. Which leads me nicely on to someone who probably did; what have you got on Wong?'

Entwistle grinned. 'Now, there is someone a lot more interesting.' He picked up a Manila folder from his desk and handed it to Phillips.

She placed her remaining food on the desk and began leafing through the pages.

'According to immigration records, Jimmy Wong is a Chinese national born in Hong Kong, who entered the UK via London Heathrow almost two years ago. Initially his work visa was attached to the Golden Flower restaurant in Chinatown, London, where he worked for six months as a waiter – or at least, that's what his paperwork said he did.'

'A likely story,' said Phillips.

Entwistle nodded. 'Then, about eighteen months ago, he left London and moved to Manchester, working for the Belmont Casino chain as part of their security team. Belmont is owned and operated by the Red Dragon Trading Company, a subsidiary of Gold Star Trading in Hong Kong.'

'And what do they do?'

'Obviously, since the Brits handed Hong Kong back to

China, we no longer share data with the Royal Hong Kong Police, but a quick Google search tells me they're into all sorts of ventures: shipping and mining in mainland China, as well as owning a number of casinos and hotels in Macau.'

'So how many casinos do they have over here?'

'Three in Manchester – one near Chinatown, another on Portland Street and a third in Spinningfields.'

'And do we know which one Wong worked for?'

'Sorry, Guv, no.'

Phillips checked her watch; 8.45 p.m. 'Jones and Bov should be arriving at Scotland Yard soon.'

'What are the chances of finding Wong, do you think?'

Phillips let out a frustrated sigh. 'Slim, I'd say. If he *did* kill Carpenter then I think, it's more than likely he's gone to ground. But it's always worth a look. You never know, we might get lucky for once.' She passed the Manila folder back.

'If it's ok with you then, Guv, I think I might head home?' said Entwistle.

Phillips dropped the remaining sandwich in the bin next to Bovalino's desk and stood up. 'Good idea,' she said, and patted his shoulder. 'There's nothing more we can do tonight. It's up to Jones, Bov and the CGU now.'

13

DI Ben Walsh walked briskly across the main reception of Scotland Yard, a wide grin across his friendly face. Of medium height, he had the appearance of a man who had once worked out regularly, but had since added weight to his midriff.

'Jonesy!' he said, and offered his hand. 'It's been too long, mate.'

Jones smiled and accepted the firm handshake. 'It has Walsh, it has.'

DI Walsh turned his attention to Bovalino now, and once more offered his hand. 'You must be Bov?'

'Pleased to meet you,' Bovalino said, applying a firm grip.

'So, you're looking for that scumbag Jimmy Wong?'

'We are indeed,' said Jones.

'I'd thought we'd seen the last of him when he moved up north,' said Walsh as he ushered them in the direction of the lift. 'The team is in the briefing room upstairs. Come on, I'll introduce you to the guys.'

A few minutes later, they found themselves walking down a

long corridor that had windows on either side and offered views into the offices of the Metropolitan Police.

'The place must have changed a bit since you were last here, Jonesy?' asked Walsh.

Jones's eyes remained fixed on the offices to his left as they continued walking. 'I hardly recognise it.'

'How long have you been in Manchester now?'

'Too bloody long,' joked Bovalino, which caused Walsh's grin to return.

'Well, Rebecca's coming up fifteen,' said Jones,

Walsh recoiled slightly. 'No way! Little Becky?'

'Yeah, I know, and she was three when we moved up, so it must be twelve years now.'

'Jesus. Time flies, hey?'

Jones blew his lips and ran a hand through his thinning hair. 'Doesn't it just.'

A moment later, they approached what appeared to be a large briefing room. The door was open, and Jones could hear the familiar sound of a team waiting for a briefing; a mixture of laughter and fierce banter.

Walsh led the way into the room.

'Right, you lot,' said Walsh, in a loud, confident voice, 'let me introduce you to DS Jones and DC Bovalino.'

Jones smiled and nodded along with Bovalino as all eyes turned on them.

Walsh continued, 'These guys have come all the way from Manchester to see us this evening—'

'Did thar bring theee whippet?' shouted one of the team in a mock northern accent before Walsh could finish, drawing guffaws from the rest of the team.

'Very funny, Sergeant Parker,' said Walsh. 'As I mentioned to you all in the briefing this afternoon, they've come down from Manchester looking for Jimmy Wong, a guy we all know very well from his time as a gang enforcer in Chinatown.'

'Check the sewers,' someone else shouted from the back of the room, but Jones couldn't see who.

For the next few minutes, Walsh formally introduced each member of the Clubs and Gangs Unit as well as the Tactical Firearms Unit, headed up by Sergeant Farmer. Jones tried his best, but struggled to keep up with all the names and who did what. In the end, he comforted himself with the fact it didn't really matter, because he and Bovalino would essentially be passengers on the raid. This was Met Police territory, and CGU would take the lead.

Walsh soon began the full debrief of the plan for the evening. They would strike at midnight. The operation would involve the firearms team, who would go in first, followed by CGU and then Jones and Bovalino. There would also be three uniformed teams in three locations on the perimeter of the Golden Flower, ready to arrest anyone who tried to make a run for it.

As Walsh delivered the specific details of each team member's responsibilities for the raid, the room remained respectfully silent. These boys know what they're doing, thought Jones as he watched on.

When the briefing was complete, Walsh signalled for Jones and Bovalino to follow him back out onto the corridor. When he spoke, his voice was almost a whisper. 'Look guys, I'm more than happy for you to come along tonight, but I think it's best you watch from the sidelines. The people Wong hangs around with are nasty bastards, and not afraid to use extreme force when cornered. If Wong's in there, we'll find him and he's all yours, but you should leave the rest of them to us, ok?'

Jones glanced at Bovalino, who closed his eyes for a split second. He could tell his partner was relieved to be out of the firing line. 'That's fine by us, Walsh,' he said, patting the DI on his shoulder.

Walsh checked his watch, then clasped his hands together.

'Excellent. We've got about forty-five minutes before we move out, so let's grab a brew and you can tell me all about "how grim it is, up north."'

THE GOLDEN FLOWER restaurant was positioned on the corner of Gerrard and Macclesfield in Soho's Chinatown. Thankfully, the entrance to the target location and first floor flat was located to the side of the building, meaning the TFU and CGU could avoid a noisy entry through the now-closed restaurant on the ground floor. The uniformed officers took up their positions along the perimeter.

As Jones and Bovalino exited the unmarked squad car, the TFU's Sergeant Farmer reiterated Walsh's instructions from earlier. 'So, my boys will go in first, then Walsh's lot, then you guys. We're fully expecting weapons of some sort inside, so keep your wits about you and make sure your stab vests are secure. Got it?'

Jones and Bovalino both nodded.

The strong aromas of Chinese food lingered in the air. 'I could murder a crispy duck right now, couldn't you?' said Walsh, flashing his trademark grin.

'I'm more of a chow mein man myself,' said Bovalino, with a nervous chortle.

'Right, then,' added Walsh, as he secured the straps on his own stab vest. 'Let's see if we can find Wong for you, shall we?'

A couple of minutes later, with the TFU – each carrying the ubiquitous M5 machine gun – in place, Walsh gave the order to go in. The officer at the front thrust his hand-held battering ram into the top hinge, and the dilapidated door gave way with one hit.

Shouts of 'Armed police!' filled the space as the team rushed in and straight up the staircase. Walsh was next in, followed by his team, then Jones and Bovalino brought up the rear.

From above came the shouts of the firearms officers, and the unmistakable sound of furniture being displaced.

'Put the weapons down!' Sergeant Farmer shouted just as Jones reached the entrance to the cigarette-smoke filled flat.

The scene that greeted him was surreal: armed police on one side of the room, weapons trained on three Chinese targets that stood on the opposite side of the room, each holding an unsheathed machete. A Mah-jong board, and its pieces, lay scattered at their feet. The target's eyes were wide with a mixture of fear and adrenaline.

It was Walsh's turn to shout now. 'Put your weapons down and get on the floor!'

None of the men flinched.

'I won't tell you again,' said Walsh. 'Put your weapons down and get on the fucking floor, now!'

Jones stared at the faces of the three targets, but did not recognise any of them as being Wong. 'He's not here,' he shouted across to Walsh, who nodded.

Farmer took a step forwards and pointed his rifle towards the floor several times. 'Get down,' he repeated with each movement of his weapon. This finally drew a response from the targets, who conversed briefly in Chinese, then, as one, nodded. Slowly they dropped their machetes and got down on their knees.

'Flat down,' said Farmer, again using his weapon to make his point.

One by one, each of the men complied and lay down with their faces turned to one side against the filthy carpeted floor. As soon as they were in the desired position, Farmer's men moved in and secured their hands behind their backs with plastic cuffs.

Walsh moved in above the men now. 'Where's Jimmy Wong?' he said in a loud voice.

The men remained silent.

'Jimmy Wong, where is he?' Walsh repeated.

Once again, the men said nothing.

'This is classic Triad bullshit,' said Walsh as he turned to Jones, 'pretending they don't speak English.'

'So what do we do now?' asked Jones.

'Take them in,' Walsh said, and turned to Sergeant Parker. 'Caution them for harbouring a fugitive and get them back to the nick. Let's see what an interpreter can get out of them.'

Parker nodded and, along with other members of the CGU, yanked the three men to their feet and began reading them their rights.

14

Jones sat alongside Bovalino in the observation suite, staring at the large flat-screen monitor on the wall, which showed the feed from Interview Room Four. He checked his watch; it was just after 5.30 a.m. He yawned as he took a sip of cold coffee from the plastic cup in front of him. The raid had gone like clockwork, and they'd returned to Scotland Yard at 1 a.m. Each of the three men arrested had then been processed and placed in custody within forty-five minutes of their arrival, ready to be interviewed by 2 a.m. However, it had taken an age to find a Cantonese-speaking interpreter, who had turned up fifteen minutes ago. With him now in place next to the man named Tian Qing in Interview Room Four, Walsh entered and took a seat, then placed a folder on the desk between them. He explained the use of the DIR – digital interview recorder – as well as the fact that the discussion was being filmed by a small camera fixed to the wall behind his head, which information the interpreter passed on to Qing. The formalities out of the way, Walsh got to work.

'Where is Jimmy Wong?' he asked.

The interpreter relayed the question to Qing, who shrugged his shoulders and spoke briefly.

'He doesn't know a Jimmy Wong,' said the interpreter.

Walsh pulled a blown-up black-and-white image of Wong's passport photo from the folder and passed it across the table. 'This is Jimmy Wong. Ask him when he last saw this man.'

The interpreter did as requested, but got the same response: Qing did not know of anyone called Jimmy Wong.

'Bullshit,' said Walsh. 'They're both Triads and they've both spent time at the address where we arrested him.'

The interpreter relayed these facts to Qing, who denied both points. He insisted he was just a waiter and an innocent man, trying to earn a living so he could send money home to his family in Hong Kong.

Walsh grabbed Qing's hand and pulled it across table, then yanked up his shirt sleeve to expose the man's intricately tattooed wrist.

'Ask him where he got this, then?' said Walsh, 'Looks like Triad ink to me.'

Qing pulled back his arm and scowled at Walsh as he spoke.

'It is his daughter's name,' the interpreter said a few moments later. 'He has it there to remind him of why he lives apart from his family: to make a better life for them.'

Walsh pulled another image from the folder and passed it across the table. 'Looks an awful lot like this tattoo, which belongs to a Triad enforcer named Cheng, currently doing fifteen years in Wormwood Scrubs for attempted murder.'

'He says all Chinese symbols look the same to you,' said the interpreter.

And so this cat-and-mouse approach continued for the next thirty minutes, with Qing insisting, through very short bursts of conversation with the interpreter, that he did not know of, and had never heard of, anyone called Jimmy Wong; he was not, and never had been, a Triad, or involved in crime of any kind; he was an innocent man who did not understand what he had done wrong.

Finally, and clearly frustrated, Walsh returned the images to the folder and paused the DIR. He then pushed back his chair and left Interview Room Four.

A moment later he entered the observation suite, where he slammed the folder down on the table in front of Jones. 'Bloody Triads do this every time,' he growled. 'Claim they don't speak English and pretend they're not gangsters at all. Just "poor put-upon migrant workers". They're a bloody nightmare.'

'He has an answer for everything, doesn't he?' said Jones.

'Exactly. Which is why I know he's lying to me.'

'So what's next? Do we try the others and see what they have to say?'

Walsh exhaled loudly and rubbed his eyes with both hands. 'We may as well, but I'm pretty sure we'll get the same response.'

'You never know; one of the others might let something slip,' said Jones.

'Yeah, maybe.' Walsh cast a glance at the monitor, on which Qing and the interpreter could be seen talking. He turned his attention back to Jones and Bovalino. 'There's no point me doing anything without a fresh coffee. Either of you two want one?'

'I could murder one,' said Bovalino as he stepped up from the chair and stretched his arms and back.

'Me too,' said Jones.

Walsh led the way up to the canteen, and the three men eagerly huddled round the coffee machine as it processed their hot drinks one by one.

'They'll be serving food from 7 a.m.,' said Walsh. 'I'll buy you both a bacon roll, courtesy of the Met.'

'Now you're talking,' said Bovalino, cheerfully.

Just then, a voice called out from behind them. 'Guv, we've got something on Wong.'

All three men turned to see Sergeant Parker stood in the doorway to the canteen.

'What it is?' asked Walsh.

'Before the raid last night, I circulated Wong's file to the airports, the ferries and Channel Tunnel—'

'And?' said Walsh sounding impatient.

'The Aviation Team at Heathrow have just called through, Guv. It looks like Wong's passport was used on a flight to Hong Kong three days ago.'

Walsh let out a frustrated growl. 'Bollocks!'

'Bloody hell, he's scarpered,' said Bovalino. 'The Guv's not gonna be happy.'

'No, she's not, and neither is Fox,' said Jones, as he pulled his phone from his pocket and checked the time on the screen. It was 6.15 a.m. 'Phillips'll want to know straight away. I'd better call her and give her the bad news,' he added as he walked out of the canteen.

15

Later that morning, the landline phone rang on Phillips's desk. It was the call she'd been waiting for.

'This is Phillips,' she said.

'Chief Superintendent Fox will see you now,' said Ms Blair. 'You have twenty minutes before she's due in another meeting.'

'I'm on my way,' said Phillips.

She jumped up from her desk. Two minutes later, she made her way towards Blair, seated behind her desk.

'You can go straight in,' said Blair without looking up.

Inside Fox's office, the Chief Superintendent stood by the window behind her desk, looking down at the street. She took a sip from a mug. Phillips could smell fresh coffee in the air.

'DCI Phillips,' said Fox as she turned to face her. 'What's so urgent you needed to see me so early this morning?'

Phillips didn't consider 9.10 a.m. to be early, but then she was at her desk by half-seven most mornings. 'Well, Ma'am. I received a call from Jones in London earlier this morning. They've located Wong.'

'The suspect in the Carpenter case?'

'That's him.'

'And?'

'He's fled the country, Ma'am, back to Hong Kong.'

Fox's expression remained stoic as she took a longer drink from her mug. She took a seat. 'You'd better sit down.'

Phillips sat, and continued, 'We raided the target apartment in Soho last night, alongside the Clubs and Gangs Unit, and apprehended three Chinese nationals. Wong was not among them, but DI Walsh from CGU believed the men were his former associates and brought them into custody for questioning. During their interrogation, the operational team received information from the Aviation division at Heathrow, who confirmed Wong's passport was used to board a flight to Hong Kong two days after Carpenter was killed.'

'That is unfortunate,' said Fox. 'I was rather hoping for a good result on this one, especially so close to the final interview for Chief Constable.'

'That's what I wanted to speak to you about, Ma'am. Where do we stand on jurisdiction here?'

'How do you mean?'

'Well, are we in a position to extradite Wong back from Hong Kong?'

Fox chortled. 'In the old days, when it was governed by the British, maybe, but now it's under Chinese rule, it would most likely take forever.'

Phillips had been afraid that would be the case, and frustration built in her gut. Carpenter's killer was going to get away with murder just by jumping on a plane. Surely that couldn't be allowed to happen?

Fox took a moment to drain her remaining coffee, and her eyes narrowed. 'Are you one hundred percent sure Wong killed Carpenter?'

'We found his DNA under her fingernails, Ma'am, which indicates she scratched him, plus some of his blood at the scene.'

'Could there be any other explanation for that evidence?'

'Such as?'

'Well, for example, could Wong have been involved with Carpenter? You know, intimately? That could potentially explain those away.'

'Not unless she was having *two* affairs at the same time.'

Fox raised an eyebrow. 'What do you mean by that?'

'She was already having an affair,' said Phillips.

'How do you know?'

'Because her lover came forwards and told me.'

'Really? Why did he do that?'

'Because he's known to the police and has his own theory on who killed Carpenter,' said Phillips.

'So who is this lover?'

'Don Townsend, Ma'am.'

Fox recoiled, eyes wide. 'The newspaper hack?'

Phillips nodded. 'They'd been together earlier in the evening, about two hours before Carpenter died. We've checked his DNA and his alibi, and both stand up. He's not our killer.'

'Jesus. I would never have put those two together. I mean, Victoria was a very attractive woman, and Townsend...well, there's n*othing* attractive about him, is there?'

Phillips chose not to answer the question. 'They'd been together for almost a year, and it would seem it was serious. So much so, she had taken legal advice regarding a divorce.'

'Well, "there's nowt as queer as folk," as they say.' Fox placed her mug on her desk. 'So, who did Townsend suggest had killed Carpenter?'

'Her husband, but we've checked his alibi and he was across town at Old Trafford, watching the cricket game, when she died. He's all over CCTV from the moment he left home to when he got back and found the body. It *wasn't* him.'

'So why was Townsend so sure it was?' asked Fox.

'Because, when Aaron Carpenter found out about the affair, he threatened to kill Victoria if she continued seeing Townsend. But as we know, death threats in the heat of the moment rarely come to fruition, and at the time Aaron made the threat, he had literally just found out his wife was sleeping with another man. Hardly makes him a prime suspect.'

Fox nodded, and reclined in her leather chair as she cast her gaze towards the ceiling for a long moment.

Ms Blair buzzed through on the intercom. 'Your next appointment is due in five minutes, Ma'am.'

'Move it,' said Fox firmly.

'Of course, Ma'am,' said Blair.

'And find out how much flights to Hong Kong are,' said Fox. 'Bring them in as soon as you have them,' she added, and closed the connection.

Phillips frowned.

'You used to live in Hong Kong, didn't you?' said Fox.

'Yes, Ma'am. I was born there and left when I was fifteen.'

'Good, you'll need that local knowledge if you're going to track down Wong and bring him back here.'

'You want me to go to Hong Kong?'

Fox sat forwards in her chair and linked her fingers together on the desk. 'Victoria Carpenter was a rising star in the Town Hall, and the mayor himself was a great admirer. I promised him we'd do everything we could to find her killer, so I'm not in a position to let this one go. Not if I'm to stand any chance of becoming Chief Constable. His opinion of the candidates will have a big bearing on who gets the job. I want Wong brought to justice – preferably in front of the media. And I know that if anyone can catch him, Phillips, it's you.'

Phillips was stunned; had Fox just given her a compliment?

Fox continued, 'We may not have always seen eye to eye over the years, but I'd have to be an idiot not to acknowledge you get results, which is exactly what I need now: results.'

There was a knock at the door and Ms Blair entered, carrying a print-out in her hand. 'I have the flights information you asked for.'

Fox took the sheet and inspected it as Blair explained what she was looking at. 'I've given you two options, business and economy.'

'Economy will be fine,' said Fox. 'We're not made of money.'

Blair continued, 'Depending on which day you want, you're looking at between £900 and £1,300, each way, flying from Manchester via Heathrow. There are no direct flights, I'm afraid.'

Fox passed the sheet back to Blair. 'Fine. Once DCI Phillips has made the necessary arrangements, I'd like you to book her and DS Jones on the next flights to Hong Kong.'

Phillips couldn't believe what she was hearing. 'You want Jones to come, too?'

'Of course,' said Fox. 'You may get results, Phillips, but you also have a knack for getting yourself into trouble, which is something DS Jones seems particularly adept at getting you out of. I need someone to keep an eye on you.'

With that, Ms Blair left the room.

'I must admit, Ma'am, I'm a little confused. I thought you said extradition would take forever?'

'It would, if we wait on the Chinese to do it on our behalf. However, if we find our suspect ourselves, we can go through the British Consulate and bring him back a lot quicker. You'll need to liaise with the Royal Hong Kong Police, of course, and make sure they're aware of your operation.'

'Of course, Ma'am,' said Phillips, trying her best to conceal her excitement; she was going back to Hong Kong for the first time in twenty-five years, *and* she was going after Wong.

'Is there anything else?' asked Fox.

'No Ma'am.'

'Very well. In that case you'd better get packing, hadn't you?'

Phillips allowed a smile to creep across her face. 'Thank you, Ma'am.'

'Don't thank me, Phillips. It's not a holiday, and I want a result on this one.'

Phillips nodded and headed for the door.

'Oh, and Phillips,' said Fox after her.

Phillips stopped and turned. 'Yes?'

'Try not to get yourself killed, will you?'

'I'll do my best, Ma'am,' said Phillips as she stepped out through the door.

16

Phillips called Jones straight after her meeting with Fox. He and Bovalino were just outside Macclesfield, making their way back to Manchester on the train. Judging by his reaction to the news of their impending visit to Hong Kong, he was just as surprised as her. With their flights already booked for late that evening, she sent him home to pack, then meet her at Manchester Airport. She told Bovalino to take the rest of the day off.

Next, she called her contact at the Royal Hong Kong Police, Senior Inspector Billy Li. His and Phillips's fathers had been colleagues during her father's thirty years as an officer on the Island. She had made Li's acquaintance a few years previously, when he had travelled to the UK for a convention. They had swapped emails, and remained in touch.

Phillips checked her watch; it was just after 1 p.m., which meant it was 9 p.m. in Hong Kong. She keyed in Li's mobile number and hit the call icon. She hoped Li would be ok to speak at this time of day. A second later, she heard the unmistakable sound of an international phone ringing, and waited. It seemed to ring for an age before it finally connected.

'Hello?'

'Senior Inspector Li?'

'Yes?' Li's tone was suspicious.

'This is Detective Chief Inspector Phillips, from the Greater Manchester Police.'

There was a pause on the line; Phillips assumed Li was processing the information.

'As in Jane Phillips?' said Li.

'Yes, Billy, it's me. Sorry to call so late.'

'Don't be sorry, Jane, it's lovely to hear from you. To what do I owe the pleasure?'

'I'm coming to Hong Kong, Billy.'

'Really, when?'

'Tonight,' said Phillips.

'You should have told me sooner. I could have made arrangements to show you round.'

'It's all been a bit last minute, to be honest.'

'So is it business or pleasure?' asked Li.

'Business. I'm looking for a murder suspect by the name of Jimmy Wong – potentially with links to the Triads. Do you know him?'

'I'm sorry, I don't. As you know, there are a lot of Wongs on the Island.'

'Of course. We believe he landed back in the country a few days ago,' said Phillips.

'And he's wanted for murder?'

'Yes. We suspect he strangled a woman in her own home two days before he left the UK and flew to Hong Kong. It's very important that we find him.'

'Give me his name again,' said Li. *'I'll see what I can dig up.'*

'He goes by the name Jimmy Wong, or Wong Heng.'

Phillips could hear Li scribbling a note at the other end of the line.

'I'll run him through the database in the morning.'

'Thank you, Billy,' said Phillips. 'And what can you tell me about the Gold Star Trading Corporation?'

'Why do you ask?'

'I believe they could be somehow connected to Wong,' said Phillips.

Li chuckled into the phone. *'I very much doubt that, Jane. The Gold Star Trading Corporation is one of the most respected names in business in Hong Kong and China. They would have no reason to get involved with low-lifes and murderers.'*

'You're probably right,' said Phillips. 'They just came up during our investigation. I thought it was worth a look.'

'By all means look, Jane, but I think you'll be wasting your time,' said Li.

'And there's one more thing I was hoping you might help with?'

'Oh, what's that?'

'I'm going to need a liaison officer within the RHKP—'

'Let me guess – you want me to do it?'

'If you're not too busy, Billy.'

Li laughed. *'Never too busy for you, Jane. And besides, if my father found out Chief Superintendent Phillips's daughter was in town and I didn't look after her, he'd have my head.'*

'Thanks, Billy.'

'When do you land?'

'We'll be in Hong Kong early afternoon tomorrow.'

'Call me when you get to your hotel and we can make arrangements to meet.'

'Great.'

'Well, I must go. I'm just about to eat dinner,' said Li.

'Oh, God. I'm sorry. I didn't realise.'

'Not a problem, Jane. You take care and I'll speak to you tomorrow.' Li ended the call.

Moving her focus back to her laptop, Phillips could see it was approaching 1.30 p.m. She would need to leave soon to get packed and to the airport for the hop to London. Before she did, though, she had one more thing to do.

Opening up a new email, she entered 'Daniel Lawry' into the address box, which auto-filled with his email address.

Hi Dan.

Short notice, I know, but I'm flying to Hong Kong tonight, arriving tomorrow afternoon. It's work-related, so I can't give details on email. I'd really like to meet up and pick your brain on a few things if you don't mind? I'll call you when I get to the hotel.
In the meantime, can you give me the local view on the Gold Star Trading Company? I'll explain why when I see you.

Take care, Janey. x

As a journalist, she hoped he might have the low-down on the company. She pressed send, then shut down her laptop and packed it away into her briefcase. It really was time to go if she was going to make her flight. A few minutes later, she strode across the car park.

'Hong Kong, here we come,' she whispered to herself.

17

When Phillips met up with Jones at the Manchester Airport check-in, she was taken aback by his hangdog demeanour. He looked exhausted. Dark shadows framed his bloodshot eyes, and his skin was almost grey in colour. He noticed her looking at him.

"Lack of sleep," he muttered.

Phillips frowned. She wasn't sure she believed him. He hadn't been himself for several weeks now; unusually short-tempered, tardy, and lax in his personal hygiene. She was also surprised to see that he didn't seem particularly pleased about the trip to Hong Kong.

'What's going on with you, Jonesy?' Phillips asked as they approached the British Airways check-in desk.

'Nothing Guv, I'm fine,' he said, but his tone lacked conviction.

'You don't look fine.'

'Well, I am! Ok?' he challenged her, which was not like him at all.

Phillips raised her hands. 'All right mate, don't bite my head off.'

Jones's shoulders softened. 'I'm sorry, Guv. It's just been a long couple of days, that's all.'

Phillips nodded. 'Well, it's not going to get any easier, I'm afraid. Have you ever flown long-haul?'

'Does five hours to Egypt count?'

Phillips chortled. 'No.'

As they reached the desk, Phillips produced her passport and ticket, and Jones followed suit.

The smiling assistant made small talk whilst she processed their boarding cards. 'Business or pleasure?'

'Business, I'm afraid,' said Phillips.

'And what line of work are you in?'

'We're police, detectives.'

The assistant looked up from her computer screen, her interest evidently piqued. 'Really?'

Phillips produced her warrant card and showed it to the assistant, who inspected it with eyes wide. 'Wow, I've never met a real detective before. It must be a really exciting job.'

'It has its moments,' said Phillips with a wry smile.

For the next few minutes, the assistant tapped away into her computer, Phillips and Jones waiting in silence until it was time to place their bags on the belt. After what felt like an age, the assistant handed back their passports and then purposefully placed their boarding cards in front of them on the counter and drew a circle in pen across each. 'It's a quiet flight, so I've upgraded you to business class,' she said, with a twinkle in her eye. 'Can't have you stuck in coach for twelve hours now, can we?'

'Oh? Thank you very much,' said Phillips, feeling a rush of excitement as she picked up the boarding cards and passed one to Jones.

Suddenly he appeared full of life. 'I've never flown business before.' A huge grin spread across his face. 'That's amazing, thank you.'

'You're so very welcome,' said the assistant. 'I hope you have an enjoyable flight.'

'We will,' said Jones, as he stood, holding his boarding card like a Willy Wonka Golden Ticket.

Phillips smiled at his childlike grin, then nodded towards the departure gates. They set off towards them.

The short internal flight from Manchester to London Heathrow took less than an hour, which gave them plenty of time to enjoy the British Airways business lounge at Heathrow before their departure to Hong Kong. As a seasoned long-haul traveller, Phillips was keen to minimise the effects of jet lag, so stuck to soft drinks. Jones, on the other hand, took the 'kid in a sweetshop' approach and sampled as much of the free food and alcohol as he could manage during their hour-long stay in the lounge.

Finally, with their flight called, they made their way onto the A380 and into the opulent surroundings of business class.

As Phillips took her single seat next to the window, she marvelled at the large TV screen angled to her right and the vast amount of leg room. Jones was in the seat next to her but facing in the opposite direction. With the screen between them retracted, she watched as he made himself comfortable, a huge grin on his face.

At that moment, a stewardess approached and presented him with a glass of champagne. He appeared reluctant to accept it.

'It's free,' said Phillips.

Jones's eyes sparkled as he grabbed at the glass and took a long, greedy swig, then announced, 'This is the life, hey Guv?'

Phillips smiled and nodded.

The stewardess then offered a glass to Phillips.

'Not for me, thank you. I'll have orange juice.'

'Of course, madam,' said the stewardess, and set off in search of her drink.

A few moments later, with an orange juice in hand as the plane taxied to the runway, Phillips stared out of the window and wondered what awaited them in her old stomping ground of Hong Kong. She hoped to God she could find Wong and bring him to justice, but she had a gnawing feeling in her gut that it would be anything but easy.

Just then, the engines revved, and Phillips was pushed back into her seat as the plane began to pick up speed.

There was no going back now.

18

Just after 2 p.m. local time, Phillips and Jones checked into the Empire Hotel located in the Wan Chai district of Hong Kong Island. They both needed to freshen up after the long flight, so agreed to meet back in the lobby at 3 p.m.

Phillips took a quick shower, and was soon dressed and ready for work. As the time approached 2.45 p.m., she pulled out her phone and dialled Daniel Lawry's number.

He answered promptly. *'Janey, how are you?'*

'I'm good, Dan. A little groggy from the flight.'

'That's long haul for you.'

'Indeed. So, are you still free to meet up tonight?'

'Yep. I should be done at work by about 7. How does 7.30 sound?'

'Perfect,' said Phillips. 'Where were you thinking?'

'We can go to my club. It's The Foreign Correspondent Club on Lower Albert Road.'

'Sounds very colonial.'

'It does the job for us hard-working journalists,' Lawry said playfully. *'Somewhere to rest our weary souls and enjoy the odd refreshment after a hard day at the office.'*

'Hard work? That doesn't sound like the Dan I used to know.'

'Like a dagger to my heart,' said Lawry, feigning upset. *'A man can change you know, Janey.'*

Phillips chortled. 'I don't believe a word of it. So anyway, this club of yours, can I walk to it?'

'Where are you staying?'

'The Empire in Wan Chai,' said Phillips.

'Oh God. They've hardly pushed the boat out with that place, have they?'

Phillips cast her eyes around the uninspiring room. 'I'll grant you it's a little basic, but at least it's clean. Anyway, back to your club. Is it walkable from here?'

'Good heavens no. It's well over thirty minutes from there, and all up hill. The humidity will kill you and you'll look like a drowned rat by the time you get here. No, jump in a taxi. It'll only be a few dollars. I'll text you the address in Cantonese, as most of the taxi drivers don't speak English. You can just show him the message.'

'Whatever you say. I'm bringing my number two with me, is that ok?'

'More the merrier. In fact, I've invited a colleague mine along too – Jonny Wu. He's somewhat better versed on Gold Star Trading than I am. He'll be able to give you far more information than I can.'

'Sounds great.'

'Excellent. Look, I've got to go. My editor wants a word and it doesn't pay to keep her waiting.'

'I know the feeling,' said Phillips as Fox sprang to mind. 'Ok, in that case, I'll see you later, then.'

'Looking forward to it, Janey,' said Lawry, and ended the call.

Next up, Phillips called Li.

'Wai,' he said, using the traditional Chinese greeting as he answered a moment later.

'Billy, it's Jane. How are you?'

'Chief Inspector Phillips,' said Li. His tone sounded very

formal in comparison to their last conversation. *'What can I do for you?'*

'Any news on Wong?'

'Nothing concrete as yet. We traced his passport to the airport, and we have a visual on him leaving the terminal building, but he got into a taxi and disappeared. We're trying to locate him as we speak, but as I said last night, there are a lot of Wongs on the Island.'

Phillips couldn't put her finger on what it was, but something about Li's tone suggested he really wasn't happy having this conversation. 'Ok, well, can you tell me anything about Lui Genji?'

'Why do you want to know about Ms Genji?' asked Li, sharply.

'Well, like I say, the Gold Star Trading Corporation came up in my investigation as a potential connection to Wong, and I was wondering if you knew anything about her and the organisation that might help me?'

Li's tone was stern now. *'Like I said last night, the Gold Star Trading Corporation is a very respectable business. Their Vice President, Lui Genji is very well respected and incredibly well connected within the Hong Kong business community. I can assure you, she will have no connection to Wong.'*

'Maybe not, but it can't hurt to ask her, can it?' said Phillips.

'Look, Jane,' said Li. *'There is nothing to be gained from asking Lui Genji about a man wanted for murder. Do yourself a favour and leave the likes of the Luis alone. I'm happy to help you find Wong, but my bosses won't like a guest of the RHKP harassing prominent business leaders on the Island.'*

'I have no intention of harassing anyone, Billy,' said Phillips. 'I just want to ask her a few questions, that's all.'

'Well don't. She's off limits. Ok?'

Phillips said nothing for a moment as she tried to understand the obvious change in Li's behaviour.

'Did you hear me, Jane?'

'I heard you, Billy,' said Phillips. 'Look, I'd better go. I said I'd meet my colleague in the hotel foyer in a couple of minutes.'

'Going anywhere nice?' asked Li, his tone softer now.

'No, not really. Just for a walk. We could do with stretching our legs.'

'Well, enjoy the rest of your afternoon and I'll see you tomorrow. Why don't you come to the office when you're ready? We can share what we have on Wong.'

'I'll do that,' said Phillips, and ended the call.

With Li's words ringing in her ears, she considered her next move. Phone in hand, she typed 'Gold Star Trading' into Google Maps and soon located the head office. It was less than fifteen minutes' walk from the hotel.

'Why don't you want me to speak to Lui Genji?' she murmured as she stared at the screen. 'And what would be so bad about me asking her a few questions?'

Phillips walked over to the window and stared out at the bustling street below as she wrestled with the growing feeling that Li was deliberately keeping her in the dark. Then she looked back at the map on her phone.

'Fuck it,' she said out loud. 'One conversation can't hurt,' she added as she turned away from the window and headed for the door.

19

On the walk across town, Phillips brought Jones up to speed on her conversations with Lawry and Li.

'I think you're right, Guv,' said Jones. 'It does sound like Li was warning you off. But why?'

'I don't know, but he couldn't have been more different just now compared to when I spoke to him last night. He was all smiles then,' said Phillips, as they reached the lavish main entrance to the Gold Star Trading Tower, a fifty-storey skyscraper located next to the iconic Bank of China building, a staple of the Hong Kong skyline. 'Lawry was right about this humidity,' she added as she pulled the damp collar of her shirt away from her soaking neck.

'It's unreal, isn't it?' said Jones, pulling his own polo shirt, which was already dark and wet with sweat, away from his chest.

'Right. Let's see if we can get some answers, shall we?' said Phillips, as she stepped towards the revolving door.

Jones's hand locked onto her arm, stopping her in her tracks. 'Are you sure this is the right thing to do, Guv? If Li's dead against it, shouldn't we listen to him?'

'Something's not right with this picture, Jonesy, and I want to know what.'

'I know you do, Guv, and back home I wouldn't have a problem going after someone like Genji. But here? It's not our jurisdiction, and we have no idea what kind of shit might come back on us.'

Phillips stared Jones in the eye for a long moment as she considered his words. He was right, of course. They had no idea what they were getting themselves into. But at the same time, she couldn't sit back and do nothing. Li was keeping her from Genji for a reason, and she wanted to know why. 'I hear you, Jonesy, but it's not as if I'm gonna arrest her, is it? I just want to ask her a couple of questions, that's all.'

'I know, Guv. I've got a bad feeling about it, that's all,' said Jones, his expression grave.

'Like I said, it's just a few questions. Nothing more, I promise,' said Phillips. 'Look. If you really feel that strongly about it, you can stay out here. I'll go in on my own.'

'Don't be ridiculous,' said Jones. 'I'm here to watch your back. I'm not letting you go in there on your own.'

Phillips grinned. 'Come on, then. It won't take long. I can take you for a drink and some dinner afterwards.'

Jones offered a reluctant nod before Phillips stepped into the revolving door.

Inside, the lobby was mercifully air-conditioned, but the dampness of their clothes made them shiver.

'You can't bloody win, can you?' said Jones as he rubbed his bare arms, trying to generate some heat.

Phillips shook her head, then strode with purpose across the polished marble floor to a large reception desk manned by two smart-looking receptionists. The one to the right looked up and made eye contact.

Phillips presented her police ID. 'I'm Detective Chief Inspector Phillips from the Greater Manchester Police, and this is Detective Sergeant Jones.' She attempted to sound as officious as possible.

The receptionist flashed a smile and her perfect white teeth seemed to glisten in the light. 'And how can I direct you today?'

'We'd like to see Lui Genji please.'

'And do you have an appointment?' asked the receptionist.

'No. It's a police matter. I don't need an appointment,' said Phillips firmly.

The receptionist smiled again. 'I'm afraid Ms Lui does not meet with people without an appointment.'

'Well, if you could ask her to make an exception, I'd be very grateful.'

'I'm sorry, that is not possible.'

'Please call her and let her know we're here. It's very important that we speak with her,' Phillips said.

The receptionist shook her head. 'I'm afraid that won't be possible.'

'Well, we're not going anywhere until you do, so why not save us all a lot of time and trouble and make the call.'

Jones glanced at Phillips. His body, half turned back towards the exit, betrayed his uncertainty.

At that moment, the receptionist spoke in Cantonese to a man sitting behind a smaller desk to the rear of the lobby. He was dressed in a security uniform and made his way over to the desk.

'What seems to be the problem, madam?' he asked, his English almost perfect.

'There's no problem,' said Phillips as she flashed her ID in front of his face. 'I'm a police officer and wish to speak to Lui Genji regarding the whereabouts of a murder suspect.'

The guard inspected her credentials for a long moment. 'You are *not* Hong Kong police?'

'No, British,' said Phillips.

'Well, in that case you have no authority here,' said the guard.

'We are on attachment with the Royal Hong Kong Police,' Phillips lied, drawing yet another nervous look from Jones, 'and it is a matter of great urgency that we speak with Ms Lui.'

'That is not possible,' said the guard. 'Ms Lui is not available,' he added before speaking Cantonese into the radio attached to his chest.

Phillips pressed, 'Look, I'm sure she's very busy—'

At that moment, a door behind reception opened and three more uniformed men appeared and walked round to where Phillips and Jones stood.

'I'm going to have to ask you to leave, please,' said the guard, gesturing towards the exit.

Phillips looked at Jones, who stared back at her, unflinching. She could tell he was in favour of an exit. Placing her ID back in the pocket of her trousers, she raised her arms in mock defeat. 'Very well, if that's the way you want it. But this isn't over.'

The guard remained silent, his open hand still pointing towards the way out.

Phillips cleared her throat. 'Come on, Jones. Looks like it's time for us to go,' she said as she headed for the exit.

Jones followed, and a moment later they were back out in the oppressive humidity; their senses further assaulted by the bustle of late afternoon traffic all around them.

'Well, that went well,' said Phillips.

'Didn't it?' said Jones, blowing his lips with relief.

Phillips took a step away from the building and craned her neck as she took it in the scale of the glass structure.

'So what now?' said Jones.

Phillips returning her gaze to Jones. 'Let's get out of this heat and have that drink I promised you. According to Google, there's a place in the building opposite called Sevva,' she added as she set off across the road.

ON THE TWENTY-FIFTH floor of the Prince's building, Phillips and Jones came across the bar they were looking for. As they stepped out of the lift, a small neon sign promised ice-cold beer and ice-cold air. It didn't disappoint on either score.

Taking a seat alongside each other on a large sofa in a quiet, darkened corner next to a designer bookcase, Phillips offered her frosted glass to Jones. 'Cheers, then.'

Jones clinked his glass against hers and took a long swig before wiping the beer from his top lip. Phillips allowed herself to relax back into the comfortable seat.

'Without Li in tow, we're powerless over here aren't we, Jonesy?' said Phillips.

Jones nodded. 'I don't think I've ever truly appreciated the power of a warrant card until just now.'

'Me neither. So we'd better hope Li's in a better mood tomorrow and will actually help us, otherwise this trip will be a bloody expensive waste of everybody's time. Fox was clear we needed a result on this one. If we go back empty-handed, she'll go ballistic.'

'And that's all we need.'

Just then, Phillips's phone, on the table in front of her, began to ring. Leaning forwards, she picked it up and showed the screen to Jones. 'Speak of the devil.' She answered and switched it to speaker. 'Senior Inspector Li.'

Li didn't waste any time with pleasantries. *'Did I, or did I not, tell you to stay away from the Gold Star Trading Corporation?'*

'Yes, of course. Why?' said Phillips, feigning surprise.

'You know damn well why!'

'I'm not following you.'

'I'm not a bloody idiot, Jane,' said Li, almost shouting now, *'I know you've been to their offices this afternoon.'*

Phillips looked at Jones and grimaced. 'Look, I can explain—'

'Don't bother. May I remind you, you are a guest in this country, and as such you must follow our rules and protocols. If I tell you someone is off limits, then that's exactly what they are. Is that clear?'

'Crystal,' said Phillips.

'I expected better from you of all people, Jane,' said Li, sounding like a scolding father.

Phillips felt herself nodding. 'I know, Billy. It was a mistake. I promise it won't happen again.'

'It had better not,' said Li, and rang off.

Phillips placed her phone back on the table. 'How the hell did he know about us going to see Genji?'

'News obviously travels fast in Hong Kong,' said Jones.

'So it seems,' replied Phillips as she took a drink of beer.

'Well, let's hope we have more luck getting information out of Lawry and his mate tonight,' said Jones.

Phillips nodded, but remained silent. The gnawing feeling she'd had on the plane had returned. She had expected that finding Wong would be difficult, but from where she was sitting now, it appeared almost impossible.

20

The Foreign Correspondent Club interior is a strange mix of the colonial British heritage of the island and the new world order of modern Chinese Hong Kong. Clusters of smart leather chairs and mahogany tables lined the walls of the main bar, whilst diners and drinkers perched on high stools at the large rectangular bar in the centre of the room. Above their heads, flat-screen TVs showed 24-hour news and business channels.

After meeting Phillips and Jones at reception in order to sign them in, Lawry led the way to a quiet table in one of the far corners. 'It'll give us a little more privacy,' he said over his shoulder.

Watching him walk in front of her now, Phillips was impressed with how well he had aged. He appeared effortlessly chic in his flannel shirt and khaki shorts. His thick, curly blond hair was brushed casually back against his head. As they reached the table, a short Asian man stood and offered his hand.

Lawry made the introductions. 'Jonny Wu, this is Jane

Phillips and...sorry, I've forgotten your name?' he said, as he looked at Jones.

'Jonesy. Everybody just calls me Jonesy.'

Lawry produced a wide grin. 'Jonesy it is.'

As everybody took seats, Lawry beckoned a waiter over, who appeared in a flash, smartly dressed in black trousers, white shirt and black waistcoat, complete with bowtie.

'Choose your weapons,' said Lawry, cheerily.

'I'll have a glass of pinot,' said Phillips.

'Beer for me, please,' added Jones.

'Excellent,' said Lawry. 'And we'll have the same again.'

As the waiter took his leave, Lawry turned his attention back to the table. 'So, how are you finding Hong Kong so far? Pleased to be back?'

Phillips bit her top lip for a moment. 'We've had better days, haven't we, Jonesy?' she said.

'You could say that,' said Jones with an ironic chuckle.

Lawry raised his eyebrows. 'Oh really? What's been happening?'

'Well, we made the mistake of trying to get an impromptu meeting with Lui Genji this afternoon, which, you could say, didn't exactly go according to plan.'

Lawry laughed now. 'Turfed you out, did they?'

'Pretty much, yeah.'

'Sounds about right. No appointment, no business. That's the Chinese way,' said Lawry.

At that moment, the waiter returned and passed around the drinks before he stepped away to a safe distance, ready for his next order.

Lawry took a long drink from his gin and tonic, prompting everyone else to do the same.

A moment later, Phillips placed her glass down on the table. 'And if that wasn't bad enough, our chaperone in the RHKP found out about our impromptu visit. He wasted no time in calling me to make it very clear he wasn't happy about it, pointing out just how well connected Genji was and how she's off limits.'

Lawry's eyes widened. 'That *is* interesting.' He turned to Wu now. 'That certainly backs up your thinking, doesn't it, Jonny?'

Wu nodded. 'I'm sure Dan mentioned it to you both already, but I'm an investigative journalist. My focus in the last couple of years has been on the infiltration of Triad families and gangs into legitimate business across Hong Kong, Macau and overseas. Your friend Genji Lui is a big part of that.'

Phillips sat forwards now. 'Genji's a Triad?'

Wu smiled warmly. 'Not quite, but she is closely connected to them. On the quiet, of course.'

'How?'

'Her father, Lui Lok Yu, is the head of the Lui Triad family,' said Wu. 'There's no actual proof – there never is with the Triads – but word is he's pulled together a consortium of sympathetic and like-minded families who have bankrolled the Gold Star Trading Corporation. It's their way of setting up a legitimate business enterprise. Hong Kong is changing, and the new hardline rule from the mainland has the gangs looking to find alternative ways to launder their money. Behind closed doors, everyone knows China's corrupt, but it also has a very different external perception it's trying to create. Long term, it cannot allow the old-school Triad gangster image to tarnish the country's carefully manufactured "Brand China".'

'So, where does Genji fit in with this consortium?' asked Jones.

'She's the public face of it, as Vice President of the Gold Star Trading Corporation. She was educated in Oxford, she's young, charismatic, beautiful and ambitious: exactly the image the business needs,' said Wu. 'Plus, she's "Daddy's little girl", so she's loyal to the consortium and completely untouchable when it comes to outside influence.'

'And untouchable to the police, it seems,' said Phillips. 'It took less than ten minutes for our chaperone, Senior Inspector Li, to find out about our visit and warn me off.'

'Again, there's no proof, but it's widely known that the RHKP turn a blind eye to what's happening with the gangs' infiltration of big business,' said Wu.

Phillips recoiled. 'Are you saying the cops are corrupt?'

'Some, yes, but not all of them.'

'What about Inspector Li? Could he be corrupt?'

Wu shrugged his shoulders. 'The way the force is run since the British left is far more in line with the policing in mainland China. These days, there's a lot less autonomy and even the most senior ranks follow the "party line". If Li *was* told to keep you away from Genji, that order could have come from any one of the ranks above him.'

'That would explain why his attitude suddenly changed towards our visit,' said Phillips.

'How do you mean?' asked Lawry.

Phillips took another drink. 'Well, When I called him from the UK and told him I was coming over, he seemed pleased, but by the time we arrived on the island, it was like we were dog shit on his shoe.'

Lawry chuckled.

'So, what else is known about Genji?' asked Phillips.

'She's the driving force behind Gold Star Trading's overseas investment,' said Wu. 'She's very skilled at buying failing companies and making them profitable.'

Phillips nodded. 'Yeah. As I understand it, they've already acquired a chain of casinos in Manchester that was going bankrupt.'

'Yes. It's all part of Gold Star Trading's careful strategy to build their overseas brand and portfolio. You see, Manchester, with its world-famous football clubs, the music scene, the media hubs, the regeneration of the city, etc., it presents the perfect backdrop for their overseas ambitions and looks great in investment prospectuses. In fact, in less than a month, Genji is due to present their latest UK development opportunity to investors here in Hong Kong: an enormous twin tower construction in Manchester City centre.'

That sounded familiar. 'That wouldn't be St John's Towers, would it?'

'I'm afraid I don't know the name of it. They're keeping that under wraps until the big launch.'

Phillips said nothing for a moment as she processed the information. 'This is all very interesting stuff, Jonny, but we're here looking for a murder suspect. None of this helps us find him.'

'You're talking about Jimmy Wong?'

'Yeah. Do you know him?'

'No, I don't, but Dan mentioned earlier that he works for the Red Dragon Trading Company, in Manchester. That means there's a *very good* chance he could have been working for Lui Genji's cousin, a guy by the name of Zhang Shing, who recently moved over there.'

Wu had Phillips's full attention now. 'Now that is an interesting connection.'

Lawry's grin returned as Wu continued. 'Zhang Shing and Genji grew up together, and are as close as brother and sister. When they both turned eighteen, *she* went to study at Oxford, whereas Zhang Shing went to work for Genji's father, joining the Triads. Shing is considered a very, very dangerous man – an enforcer. Again, there is no proof of any of this, but some even suggest he's an assassin. In fact, that's rumoured to be the reason why he was shipped off to the UK.'

'What happened?' asked Jones, taking a drink.

'Shing supposedly killed a high-ranking government official who was making a big stink about the Triad gangs across the island, telling all and sundry that they should be shut down for good. They say Shing silenced the official: tortured him, then cut his head off with a butcher's cleaver.'

'Jesus,' mumbled Phillips.

Wu continued, 'Anyway, it was a step too far for the government, and they had to be seen to act in order to protect "Brand China". The subsequent murder investigation brought a lot of unwanted attention to the Triad families, so, about a month after the official's body was found, Shing flew out to the UK to oversee Gold Star Trading Corporation's interests in Manchester.'

'Bloody hell,' said Phillips. 'This is starting to make sense now.'

Wu nodded and took a drink.

Phillips continued, 'You see, we have good reason to believe that our victim was actively working to block the re-zoning of the St John's development in Manchester. If that *is* the same development Genji is about to launch over here – then, without realising it, Vicky Carpenter could have got herself into a fight with the Triads—'

'Which is why Wong killed her,' Jones cut in.

'It's certainly the sort of thing the Triads would do,' said Wu.

'This is unbelievable,' said Jones, shaking his head.

Phillips drained her glass and set it back down on the table. 'So, all we need to do now is find Wong, which is like hunting for a needle in a haystack over here.'

'And I'd suggest that time really is of the essence,' pressed Wu. 'If Wong *did* kill your victim and him coming back to Hong Kong has brought unwanted attention to the Gold Star Trading company, then the Triad consortium will not take kindly to it.'

'What exactly do you mean by that?' asked Phillips.

'That Wong could well be a dead man walking,' said Wu.

'My day's just getting better and better, isn't it?' replied Phillips, sarcastically.

Lawry smiled. 'Well, whilst you figure out how you're going to find Wong before the Triads do, shall we have another round?'

Phillips nodded. 'Same again, please.' She stood and pulled her phone from her pocket. 'I'll be back in a minute,' she added, and made her way outside onto the veranda.

21

'Guv?' Entwistle sounded surprised. *'I wasn't expecting to hear from you. How's things?'*

'Complicated,' replied Phillips.

'Any luck finding Wong?'

Phillips let out a deep sigh. 'Sadly not. What time is it with you?'

'Coming up to 2 p.m.'

'Is Bovalino with you?' asked Phillips.

'Yeah. He's sat opposite me now, devouring what looks like half a pig wrapped in a bread roll.'

'Late lunch, is it?'

'Not sure to be honest, Guv,' said Entwistle, with a chuckle. *'You know what he's like; he's always eating.'*

'Well, when he's finished, I want you both to start looking into a couple of things for me.'

'Sure. What do you need?'

'We think Wong may have been working for a guy in Manchester called Zhang Shing. We're led to believe he's in charge of the Red Dragon Trading Company, which owns the Belmont casinos.'

'Ok,' said Entwistle.

'I want to know when exactly he landed in the UK and who signed off his visa paperwork. We need all his addresses since he moved over, and I want to know how many times he's been back to Hong Kong or China during his time in the UK.'

'Anything else?'

'The usual: known associates, any convictions or cautions, and see if you can find any connection between him and Wong.'

Phillips could hear Entwistle scribbling notes on the other end of the line.

'Oh, and send me a picture of his passport photo. I wanna know what this guy looks like.'

'Consider it done, Guv.'

'How soon can you have something for me?'

'I'll get straight onto my contact in immigration and see what she can dig up for me. She's usually pretty efficient, but it'll probably take twenty-four to forty-eight hours, I reckon.'

'Right, well, I'd better leave you to it, then.'

'No worries, and say hi to Jonesy for us. Tell him not to spend too much time in the strip clubs,' said Entwistle playfully.

'I will,' Phillips chortled. 'Chat tomorrow.'

Standing for a moment in the heat of the night, she listened to the sound of the city around her; the buzz of cars honking their horns on the nearby Wyndham Street and Ice House Street, the roar of planes coming in to land above her head, the distant sirens somewhere in the mass of buildings surrounding her, juxtaposed the polite chatter coming from inside the club. The warm breeze dancing across her cheeks reminded of her teenage years on the Island. She had loved this city and the untold excitement and possibilities it had offered back then. She'd been devastated when her parents had announced they would be leaving once the territory was handed back to China in July of 1997. Phillips recalled the heartbreak of saying her farewells to all her friends – as well as her first true love, Daniel Lawry. Turning, she glanced back into the club to see him gesturing to her now, indicating that fresh drinks had arrived. She nodded and held up her index finger. 'One minute,' she mouthed, then dialled Li.

After what seemed like an eternity, the call eventually went to answer machine. Phillips ended the call and tried again, with the same result. This time she left a message. 'Billy, it's Jane. If you get this, can you call me back? I have some information I need to share with you on Wong. Thanks.'

Staring down at the phone, she wondered if she had done the right thing calling him. Was Billy Li corrupt, or was he, as Wu had suggested, most likely toeing the party line. Whichever one it was, the reality was that the clock was ticking and she needed a reaction from him one way or another. If she was going to find Wong before the Triads killed him, she needed to know if Li was on her side or not.

Closing her eyes, she took a deep breath and soaked in the atmosphere one more time before she pushed her phone into her pocket and headed inside.

IN THE TAXI back to the hotel, Jones was unusually quiet as he stared out of the window. For most of the evening he had chatted comfortably with Lawry and Wu, and had seemed more like his old self. Then, as the conversation drifted onto the details of Carpenter and Townsend's affair, he had become quiet and reserved again. He had hardly spoken a word since.

As the cab pulled onto Queen's Road East, Phillips decided it was time they had a proper talk. 'What's going on with you at the minute, Jonesy?'

Jones flinched and spun his head to face her. 'Sorry?'

'I've worked with you long enough to know when something's not right, and you aren't yourself. What's up?'

'Nothing. I'm fine,' he said, without conviction.

'Bullshit, Jonesy. Something's not right.'

Jones said nothing for a moment as the cab stopped at a set of red lights.

'Come on, mate. If there's something wrong, then maybe I can help.'

'I doubt it,' said Jones.

'So there is something?'

Jones nodded.

'Is it the job?' asked Phillips.

'No, no. Well...maybe.'

'Look, we all get stressed, and God knows we see things most people should never have to see. That can take its toll. I know that better than most.'

'The job's not affecting *me*. The problem is what it's doing to *Sarah*.'

Phillips was taken aback. 'I don't understand.'

'She says she's had enough of being an MCU widow, and thinks we need time to figure out what we both want from life.'

'Oh, God. I'm sorry.'

'Apparently I'm never at home and she never sees me.'

'That's my fault,' said Phillips. 'I've been working you guys too hard. Look, if I'd known, I would never have asked you to come all the way out here.'

'It's nothing to do with you, Guv. I choose to be available. I'm the one that works on weekends when there's no need. It's on me – and besides, I wanted to come to Hong Kong. Beats being at home pretending everything's ok in front of the kids, when inside I'm dying.'

'Ok, but that said, we need to do something about this. I'll ask Fox for more support.'

'I think it's too late for that,' said Jones.

'Come on, don't say that.'

Jones sighed loudly. 'Sarah told me she's been for coffee a couple of times with a bloke from work; a younger guy who's been paying her a lot of attention.'

'She's been having an affair?'

'No. At least I hope not, but she says she's been tempted, and that's enough for her. She's suggested we have a trial separation; get some space and give ourselves time to think about what we want.'

'And what do *you* want?' asked Phillips.

'I just want my wife back,' Jones's voice cracked. 'For my marriage to be ok.'

Phillips blew her lips. 'God. No wonder you went quiet when we started talking about Carpenter and Townsend's affair.'

'You noticed?'

'Yeah, mate. It was like your batteries died. You just clammed up.'

'Sorry, Guv. This case has been tough.'

'I'm the one who should be sorry,' said Phillips. 'I knew there was something going on and I should've said something sooner.'

Jones didn't reply.

The cab came to a stop outside their hotel. Phillips paid the driver, and they got out and headed for the main entrance.

A few minutes later, they stepped into the elevator and the doors closed.

'When you get back, I want you to take some time off. Fix your marriage,' said Phillips as the lift began to ascend.

'But what about the case?'

'Leave the case to me and the guys. We can live without you for a week, ok?'

Jones smiled softly and nodded. 'Thanks, Guv.'

'It's the least I can do,' said Phillips.

A moment later, they arrived at their floor. The doors opened onto the empty corridor and they stepped out.

As they reached their adjacent rooms, Phillips placed a soft hand on Jones's shoulder. 'Now get some sleep, ok?'

'I'll try, Guv,' Jones replied as he unlocked the door. 'I'll try.'

22

The next morning Phillips woke at 5 a.m., and was unable to get back to sleep thanks to jet lag. So she decided to get up and get busy, and took breakfast in her room. Now dressed and ready for the day in lightweight flannel trousers and yet another white shirt, she heard movement coming from Jones's room, so knocked on the adjoining door to see if he was up and about.

A moment later, Jones released the lock and opened the door.

'Morning,' he said. He was dressed in a white hotel robe, his eyes bloodshot and lifeless. 'You couldn't sleep either, then?'

'No. I've been awake since about five,' said Phillips.

'Me too. I've been watching shit TV for the last hour. This bloody jet lag is a total bastard, isn't it?' His south London drawl made it sound like *barstard*.

Phillips nodded. 'The good news is, it'll be easier going home because you get the time back. It's always much harder coming out east.'

'D'you fancy heading down for breakfast?' asked Jones.

Phillips felt a pang of guilt that she'd not thought to check on him earlier. 'Sorry, I've had room service already. I woke up ravenous.'

'Not to worry,' said Jones. 'I'll call down and order something up myself. What time are we going to see Li?'

Phillips checked her watch; it was 6.50 a.m. 'I'd like to get in there as early as possible, but I have no idea what time he gets to his desk. I'm gonna call him in about an hour or so and check the lay of the land.'

'Well, in that case, I'm going to treat myself to a long hot bath and a full English.'

'Oooh, check her,' said Phillips playfully, 'pampering herself.'

'Piss off,' Jones said with a chuckle, then closed the door.

Phillips smiled. It was good to see him laughing again.

Just over an hour passed, and as the bedside digital clock display changed to 08.00, Phillips could wait no longer. She picked up her phone and dialled Li. Once again it seemed to ring for an eternity at the other end, but this time he did eventually answer.

'Jane?'

Phillips wasted no time. 'Did you get the message I left last night?'

'I did, but not until I checked my phone just now. What's your information on Wong?'

'I have reason to believe he, and the murder of Victoria Carpenter, are both connected to the Triads, and that unless we find him before they do, they'll simply make him disappear.'

'And where did you get this information from?' asked Li, sounding suspicious.

'I still have friends on the Island, Billy.'

'Could you be more specific?'

'Not at this stage, no,' said Phillips. 'For their own safety, I'd prefer to protect their identities.'

'Are you saying you don't trust me?' said Li, sounding affronted.

'No, that's not what I'm saying, at all,' Phillips lied, 'but I've seen and heard what the Triads can do, and I'd prefer not to take any risks with the identities of my sources. Ok?'

Li paused for a moment. *'And this intel you have, is it solid?'*

'I believe so, yes. And because of that, I really need your help to find Wong before anyone else does.'

'Well, in that case, you're in luck, Jane,' said Li. *'We've identified an address in Kowloon where we believe Wong is holding up.'*

'Fantastic!' said Phillips, as her pulse quickened.

'It's just off Nathan Road, about twenty minutes in the car. I'll pick you up from your hotel in an hour and we can check it out. Be waiting in reception, Jane, and be prepared; it's not a place for the faint-hearted,' said Li, then hung up.

~

'Do you know where you are, Jane?' Li, at the wheel of an unmarked squad car, asked as they entered the ludicrously busy shopping district. The time was approaching 9.30 a.m.

'Tsim Sha Tsui, or TST for short,' she replied from the passenger seat. Jones watched on from the rear.

'This is Nathan Road,' Li said over his shoulder towards Jones, 'one of the busiest shopping streets in all of Hong Kong. Fine for tourists during the day, but somewhere to take extra care at night. It has enough neon lights to put Las Vegas to shame.'

Phillips had little interest in a guided tour. She knew these streets well enough from her time on the Island. 'So where exactly are we headed?'

'An apartment on the eleventh floor of the Chungking Mansions.'

'Chungking Mansions? Jesus, I remember my dad talking about that place. Is it still a shit-hole?'

Li nodded. 'Like I said earlier, it's not a place for the faint-hearted.'

Phillips looked out of the window at the myriad shops with their bright neon signs and colourful frontages. 'One of my dad's squad was killed in there, cut to ribbons with a cleaver.'

'Sergeant Cai Yang,' said Li. 'He is still talked about whenever Chungking Mansions comes up in active operations, like a mythical warning to every officer to watch their backs within its walls. Only Yang's murder is not a myth; it really happened.'

'That must have been almost thirty years ago. Surely it's not as bad as that now?'

'The world may have evolved, Jane, but Chungking Mansions has not. It's still a place where drugs, crime, rape and murder thrive.'

'Well, in that case, aren't we a little light-handed?' Phillips asked, turning to look at Li's profile.

Li shrugged his shoulders. 'As this is not an official investigation for the Royal Hong Kong Police, I'm afraid resources are limited, so you just get me.'

Phillips exhaled silently and bit her lip as Fox's words came to mind: *Try not to get yourself killed, will you?*

The rest of the journey passed in silence until Li took a right onto Mody Road and brought the car to a stop. He killed the engine and swivelled in his seat to face them both. 'Ok. Chungking Mansions is split into five blocks, each lettered A, B, C, D or E, and each containing seventeen stories. The bottom two floors are open to the general public, and the residences start from floor three. Wong is reportedly staying in block D; apartment 44, which is on the eleventh floor. This place is like the Wild West at times, and if you go looking for trouble, you'll find it. So the best way to go in is quietly and with little fuss, ok?'

Phillips nodded, suddenly nervous.

'Ok,' said Jones from the back seat.

Li continued. 'I am not permitted to carry a weapon unless given express permission from the Commissioner, so we'll be going in unarmed.'

'This just gets better,' said Phillips, her tone sarcastic.

Li shot her a look, his brow furrowed. 'Do you want this guy or not? Because I really don't need to be here.'

Phillips raised her hands in mock defence. 'I'm sorry. That was out of order. We really do appreciate your help.'

Li nodded. 'Ok. Let's go.'

Out of the car, Li lead the way back onto Nathan Road and through the main entrance to block D, which was helpfully signed in both English and Cantonese. Stepping inside the dimly lit shopping mall that lay in front of them, they were hit by the powerful aroma of curry houses and the sounds of the bustling shops around them. They ducked down a small walkway and through a set of battered old double doors, beyond which they found an elevator.

'Shouldn't we take the stairs?' asked Phillips.

'I don't think that's wise,' said Li as he pressed the call button.

The elevator motors kicked into action and the digital display above the metal doors counted down from 7 to 0. The doors opened, and Li ushered them inside.

Phillips had never been a fan of tight spaces, and was not used to entering a suspect's address without back up. In fact, the last time she had done that, she had almost been strangled to death. As the lift began to ascend, the butterflies began to dance in her gut. She made eye contact with Jones, who swallowed hard and held her gaze. He was clearly as nervous as she was. Li, on the other hand remained calmness personified, which further unnerved Phillips. A terrifying thought jumped to the front of her mind: does he know what's waiting for us up there?

The lift arrived with a bump at the eleventh floor, and as the doors opened, Phillips held her breath. Mercifully, the small lift lobby was empty. Li stepped out, and Phillips and Jones fell in behind him. The trio quietly moved along the darkened corridor. Once more, the numbers on the doors were helpfully painted in Cantonese and English, and within a minute, they found themselves outside number 44.

A TV was playing within the apartment, loud enough for them to hear the show as if it were being piped directly to them. Li pressed his ear to the door and listened intently for a long moment. Then, pulling back, he signalled for Phillips and Jones to back up, away from the view of the spy hole. Once they were sufficiently out of range, Li rapped on the door and shouted something in Cantonese. He got no answer, so he repeated the process. Still no one appeared, but it was clear that the TV had been turned down significantly; someone inside was listening. Li knocked and shouted again, but this time, with no answer forthcoming, he stepped back from the door, took aim, and thrust his boot into the lock. The old door must have been forty years old and gave way in an instant, wood splintering around the battered frame. Li rushed into the tiny apartment with Phillips and Jones just behind. A man with his back to them grabbed a baseball bat from on top of the bed. He spun and took a wild swing at Li, who deftly ducked and continued running forwards, catching the man in the chest and knocking him to the floor. Li crashed down on top of him a split second later.

The force of the impact caused the man to release the bat, which Phillips picked up as Jones moved in to help Li restrain the man. When the melee finally came to an end, Phillips stepped up next to Li and Jones. She stared down at the man; he was Jimmy Wong.

She smiled and produced her warrant card. 'Jimmy Wong, aka Wong Heng, I'm DCI Phillips from the Greater Manchester Police. I'd like to talk to you in connection with the murder of Victoria Carpenter on the 11th of August.'

Wong stared at her with a blank look on his face. Li rolled him onto his back and placed him in handcuffs, then lifted him to his feet. 'I'll take it from here, Jane. Just so we're legal.'

Phillips nodded and stepped back.

Li continued. 'Wong Heng, I am arresting you in connection with the murder of a British National. Do you wish to say anything? You are not obliged to say anything unless you wish to do so, but what you say may be put into writing and given in evidence.'

He then repeated the caution in Cantonese.

When he was finished, Wong locked eyes with Phillips. 'It not me,' he said in broken English.

'Of course it wasn't,' said Phillips.

'It not me,' Wong repeated.

'We have your DNA, mate, from under her fingernails when she scratched you.'

Wong stared at her blankly before Li translated.

'It not me,' Wong repeated.

'Bullshit, mate. DNA doesn't lie. We know you killed her.'

Li relayed the message, and Wong replied in Cantonese, evidently agitated.

'He says he was there when the woman died,' said Li, 'but *he* didn't kill her.'

'So who did?' asked Phillips.

Li did the honours and once more translated Wong's response. 'He says he cannot tell you or he will be killed.'

'By whom?' asked Phillips.

'He's talking about the Triads,' said Li.

'Well, tell him that if he doesn't give me the name of the

killer, he's going to be spending the rest of his days in a maximum security prison in the UK.'

Li related what Phillips had said.

Wong shrugged his shoulders for a moment, as if he couldn't care less.

'That does not scare him,' said Li.

Phillips could feel her frustration building. 'We'll soon see about that. Let's get him into custody as quick as we can. We need Mr Wong alive.'

Li nodded, and pushed Wong forwards and into the dark corridor.

Soon they were back in the lift, but with four people now filling the small space, Phillips could feel the walls closing in. As the elevator began to descend, she watched as the digital display counted down, her heart beating harder with each floor that passed. After what felt like an age, but had probably been less than a minute, they reached floor zero and the metal box shuddered to a halt. There was a slight delay before the doors opened and Li pushed Wong out. Phillips followed, but as she stepped out, she sensed someone rushing towards her from the left. She raised her arms to protect herself, but was too late. Something heavy smashed into her temple and everything went black.

23

As Phillips regained consciousness, she tried to open her eyes, but they were fixed shut by something pressing tight against her face. Although disorientated, a hard surface pressed against the whole of her left side. It took her a while to realise she was lying on that side. Her hands were tied behind her back and her mouth was filled with some kind of foul-tasting fabric. The hum of an engine, and the steady movement of her surroundings, confirmed she was in a vehicle; a faint echo led her to the conclusion she was in a van. She told herself not to panic, but with her mouth full and her heart racing, she knew she wasn't far away from a catastrophic anxiety attack. Trying desperately to distract herself, she forced herself to recall the last moments before she was attacked. Li and Wong had left the elevator first, and she had followed them out. She was sure Jones had still been in the lift. Had he managed to get away? Had he been seriously injured? Killed, even? Or was he in the same vehicle as her? She had no way of knowing.

With her airways partially blocked, she was beginning to feel light-headed. She was certain that, unless the gag was removed soon, she would suffocate. Myriad thoughts rushed through her mind. Her job had brought her close to death on a number of terrifying occasions, but she had always managed to survive. Now she wondered if she had been spared each of those times because her fate was to die in the place where she had been born: Hong Kong.

The van came to an abrupt halt, which helped draw her mind back into sharp focus. As the engine died, there was movement of feet around her and sudden chatter in high-volume Cantonese. They sounded agitated, but then, to her ear, everyone speaking Cantonese sounded that way.

Thick fingers gripped at her arms before she was dragged backwards until the floor of the van gave out and her feet dropped onto what sounded like concrete. As she breathed in and out, the fabric in her mouth seemed to move deeper and deeper. A second later, it touched the back of her throat and, doubling forwards, she retched.

A man on her left shouted in Cantonese and someone in front of her pulled her head back. Then their fingers entered her mouth, grabbed at the fabric and pulled it out. She gagged and retched as it was released, and hot, foul-tasting spittle dripped from her lips.

A scuffling sound coming from her right made her wonder if someone else was being held captive just as she was. Then muffled noises, followed by the sounds of someone gagging and retching, just as she had, confirmed her suspicions.

'Jesus Christ.'

Her heart leapt. 'Jonesy?'

'Guv?' he replied. 'What the fuck's going on?'

'I dunno, mate. I can't see anything. I'm blindfolded.'

'Me too.'

'What happened to Li and Wong?' asked Jones.

Before Phillips could reply, there were more orders – she could tell from the tone – in Cantonese, then something hard and thin was pressed against her, back forcing her to move forwards.

With no idea where she was headed, she took tentative steps whilst being continuously encouraged, by whoever was behind her, to speed up. Soon the acoustics changed and Phillips could hear her footsteps, along with many others, echoing around her. She figured they had entered a large building. A moment later, all movement stopped.

'Jonesy?' she said, hoping he was still with her.

'I'm here.'

Thank God, she thought.

Fingers pulled at her blindfold, and a few seconds later it was yanked free. The sudden rush of light forced her eyes shut. She blinked rapidly as her pupils adjusted. When she could finally focus, she took in her surroundings. Jones stood next to her, eyes closed as he too adjusted to the light. Then she turned to take in the wider room. Her stomach fell. Kneeling in front of her, hands tied behind their backs and blindfolded and gagged, were Wong and Li. Asian men stood at their shoulders, each wearing a red bandana pulled across their nose and mouth so only their eyes and the tops of their heads were visible. Each man held an enormous meat cleaver in their hands. Phillips's mind was immediately drawn to the murder of Sergeant Cai Yang, decapitated with a cleaver.

'Li, are you ok?' she managed to ask before a heavy blow landed on the backs of her legs. In agony, she dropped to her knees. More pain surged through her shins and knees as she landed on the battered concrete. A second later, Jones was on his knees alongside her.

Another man, short and stocky, arrived, his face also covered with a red bandana. Unlike the other men, who wore jeans and boots, he was dressed in suit trousers. His black, polished shoes almost sparkled as he walked slowly towards the group. Up close, Phillips noted the heavy gold jewellery on his thick fingers and wrists. She guessed this man was the leader.

The bejewelled man stood in silence for a moment, moving his gaze from Phillips to Jones, then to Li, and finally to Wong. 'It would seem that the actions of one have affected the many,' said the man, his English clear but his Cantonese accent heavy. 'It is unfortunate for you, Inspector Phillips, that you find yourself in this situation.'

'How do you know my name?' asked Phillips.

Jones shot her wide-eyed a look that urged her to be quiet.

'We know a great deal, Inspector. For instance, we know that this man's actions—' He pointed to Wong as he stepped next to him, positioning himself directly in front Phillips. '—brought you to Hong Kong, where you have made a nuisance of yourself asking questions about certain organisations and institutions. Something that cannot go unpunished.'

Phillips stared at Wong. He was shaking uncontrollably. Li was shaking too.

'I wanted you to see how we deliver justice,' said the bejewelled man, his voice ice-cold. 'Si wú duì zhèng!' he barked in Cantonese.

Wong instantly tried to make himself smaller as the foot soldier behind him – still holding a cleaver – stepped to within an inch of him. The man raised the huge knife high into the air with both hands, then brought it down, with lightning speed and immense force, onto the back of Wong's neck. The sickening sound of metal slicing through thick flesh and bone filled the air, and Wong's head fell forwards, half off. Phillips almost vomited as she stared at the macabre scene. Jones, beside her, was shaking too. Another heavy blow finished the job, and Wong's severed head dropped with a thud to the floor, followed a second later by his lifeless body. Dark blood, almost black in colour, spewed from the severed arteries in Wong's neck, and a dark pool formed around the shoulders.

Li wailed like a banshee in his mother tongue, clearly begging for his life.

'You have *your* justice, Inspector; we have *ours*,' the bejewelled man said as he walked past Phillips and moved to stand next to Jones.

Phillips locked eyes with Jones. His eyes were wide, his breathing shallow. One of the gang members stepped behind him, a huge cleaver held in his hands.

'The British ruled this territory, *our* territory, for over one hundred years, until we took back what was rightly ours. Yet, almost thirty years later, we find the British sneaking into our country, trying to tell us that how we operate – how we have operated for centuries – is wrong. Did you really think we would do nothing?'

Phillips didn't know what to say.

'Well, did you?' the man shouted, so loudly it made Jones flinch.

'We made a mistake,' said Phillips, trying to control the fear in her voice.

'Yes, you did,' said the bejewelled man. 'And now, like Wong, you must pay for it.' He shouted instructions in Cantonese.

The man behind Jones raised the cleaver high into the air.

'Please! I have kids!' begged Jones.

'You don't need to do this!' shouted Phillips.

The cleaver came down with a heavy thud, and Jones's whole body slumped forwards onto the floor.

Phillips screamed and tried to scramble to her feet, but was pushed back down. She stared at Jones, unable to take in what had just happened. But then she realised that his neck was intact and there was very little blood. As her mind raced, someone stepped into her peripheral vision. Phillips turned to face them, but something heavy struck at the base of her skull. For the second time in as many hours, her world went black.

24

'Jane. Jane.'

Phillips heard her name being repeated as she regained consciousness. Opening her eyes and blinking them into focus, she found that she was lying on her back and looking up at Billy Li. His face above her was full of concern, lips pursed, eyebrows drawn together.

'Are you ok, Jane?'

Phillips was suddenly reminded of Jones and sat bolt upright, her forehead just missing Li's chin. 'Where's Jones?' she said, reliving the horror of what had happened to Wong.

'He's alive,' said Li, moving to one side so Phillips could see Jones, still unconscious, lying face down next to her. They hadn't been moved. 'It looks like they hit him with the blunt side of the cleaver at the base of the skull. They did the same to all of us. I think they hit you and I at the same time. I remember Wong, and Jones, then I heard a thud and was knocked out cold.

Phillips lifted her hand to the back of her head, which throbbed worse than any hangover. It was then she realised her hands were no longer tied.

'It looks like they cut our bindings before they left,' Li commented, seeming to read her mind.

Phillips rubbed her wrists and flexed her fingers, then leaned across and felt Jones's pulse. To her relief, it beat strong in his thin neck. Next, she allowed her gaze to fall on the decapitated body of Wong. Her mind raced. 'They killed Wong, so why not *us*?'

'Wong led you to Hong Kong and into their world,' said Li. 'That was a huge mistake on his part, so they executed him in line with Triad protocol. *We* were given a warning of what would happen if we try to remain in their world. Those cleaver blades will be facing the right way round the next time, I have no doubt about that.'

Just then, Jones began to stir, groaning as he opened his eyes.

Phillips moved closer to him. 'It's ok, Jonesy, you're safe,' she said softly as she placed her hand onto his back.

A few moments later, he lifted himself slowly onto his hands and knees. 'What the hell happened?'

'Looks like they knocked us all out,' said Phillips.

Jones eyes widened. 'Jesus. I thought I was a goner.' He dropped down onto his bottom and reached up to check the back of his neck. 'When he lifted that cleaver above my head, all I could think about was Sarah and the girls.' Tears welled in his eyes.

'I know. When he brought it down on your neck and you slumped onto the ground, I...' Phillips couldn't bring herself to finish the sentence.

Each of them remained silent for a long moment.

Eventually, Phillips was the first to speak. 'So, what happens now?'

Li pulled out his phone. 'I'll call this in, and we'll begin an investigation into who was behind Wong's death.'

'What about the warning? What if they come after you

again?' asked Phillips. 'You said yourself, they won't hesitate next time.'

'I'll take my chances, and besides, I have the weight of the Royal Hong Kong Police behind me. There is no way they would attack a properly manned squad. It would bring too much attention to their activities. It's only because I was alone with you that I suffered your fate.' Li got to his feet, then helped Phillips to hers.

'I'm sorry about that,' Phillips said as she in turn pulled Jones up from the floor. 'It's a bad habit of mine.'

Li's brow furrowed. 'What is?'

'Getting myself and others into trouble. Hey, Jonesy?'

Jones nodded as he continued to rub the back of his neck.

'What about you?' said Li. 'Now Wong is dead, what will you do?'

Phillips let out a loud sigh and shook her head. 'Well, if possible, I'd like a tissue sample from Wong's body – just to be sure it matches with what we have on file.'

'I can arrange that,' said Li.

'And then? Well. Wong mentioned he was at Carpenter's house, but that someone else committed the murder. I guess that's our next avenue of enquiry – finding the accomplice,' said Phillips.

'And will you be pursuing that line of enquiry in Hong Kong or the UK?'

Phillips took a moment before answering. 'I'm still sure Wong was connected to Genji and the Gold Star Trading Company, but I can't prove it. At least not here, anyway. To do that, I need to be back in Manchester with my full team.'

A relaxed smile crossed Li's face. 'So you'll be leaving us?'

Phillips nodded. 'There's no need to look so bloody pleased about it, Billy.'

Li caught himself and straightened his face. 'Sorry. It's just my life has been less than straightforward with you here, and I'm not sure I could cope with any more excitement.'

Phillips stepped closer to Jones and put her arms around his shoulders. 'And besides, I promised Jonesy some time off, didn't I?' she said with a smile.

'Well, before you go anywhere, you'll need to be checked over by a doctor. I'll be stuck here for some time with the team, but I'll get one of my sergeants to take you to the medical centre. They'll make sure you're safe to fly.'

'Ok, that sounds like a plan,' said Phillips. 'I think we're both ready to go home, aren't we Jonesy.'

'Too bloody right,' said Jones.

'If you'll excuse me,' said Li, then pulled out his phone and got busy making calls.

Phillips pulled out her phone and searched through the contacts. 'Before we do anything, I'd better update Fox on this shit-show,' she said as she placed the handset to her ear.

'Give the old cow my love,' said Jones sarcastically.

Phillips grinned and flashed a playful V-sign.

A split-second later, Fox answered. *'I hope you're ringing with good news, DCI Phillips.'*

25

An hour later, and after they'd both received a clean bill of health at the medical centre located on Kennedy Road near Hong Kong Park, Phillips and Jones made their way out into the heat of another summer evening. With their flights back to the UK booked for the following day, they had some time on their hands.

'So, what do you wanna do for your last night in Hong Kong?' asked Phillips.

Jones blew his lips. 'After today, anything that involves beer, Guv.'

'Dan told me to check out a place on the other side of the Park. It's called The Upper House Bar,' said Phillips, and led the way down the street.

Ten minutes later, Phillips and Jones took stools at an open window in a bar overlooking the harbour, each with a frosted glass on the high table in front of them. Phillips had chosen a gin and tonic, and Jones, as ever, was enjoying an ice-cold beer.

After a long moment of silence, Phillips addressed the elephant in the room. 'So, how are you feeling about what happened today?'

Jones stared out over the water, eyes glazed. 'Shocked,' he murmured, then took a long drink from his beer.

'I'm so sorry I put you in that position, Jonesy. I had no idea it would go south so quickly.'

'But how could you know that would happen?' said Jones. 'I mean, I've seen some shit in my time – we both have – but nothing could have prepared us for today. They cut the guy's head off right in front of us, for God's sake.'

Phillips remained silent as the image of Wong's decapitated body flashed to the front of her mind.

'This place is so fucked up. It's insane.'

Phillips nodded. 'I just can't help wondering if Li knew what was coming.'

Jones recoiled slightly on his stool, an eyebrow raised. 'Li? Seriously?'

Phillips took a drink. 'It's possible. After all, he tried to warn us off speaking to Genji. What if he *is* corrupt?'

'I can't see it, Guv. If he *was* working with the Triads, then why not just give them Wong's address in the first place? Why take us along with him. That doesn't make sense.'

'No, I guess it doesn't. But then, nothing about this case makes sense, does it?'

'Not a bloody thing.' Jones drained his glass and slipped off the stool. 'Fancy another one?'

Phillips nodded. 'Yeah, I really do!'

A few minutes later, Jones returned with their drinks and retook his seat. Phillips drained the remnants of her first drink and pushed it to the side of the table.

Jones said nothing as he continued to stare out at the busy harbour below.

'It's weird being back here after so many years,' said Phillips.

'Do you miss it?'

'I thought I did until this trip. It was always in the back of my mind that I'd one day move back here, but I'm not sure I want to anymore.'

'After today, I can see why,' said Jones.

'It's not just today. So much has changed – which is hardly surprising. It was twenty-three years ago that I left.'

'That's a long time,' said Jones. 'Maybe it's not Hong Kong that's changed. Maybe you have?'

Phillips smiled. 'Check you out, getting all deep and meaningful on me.'

'Shut up,' Jones shot back playfully.

Phillips took another long drink of her gin and tonic, then set it down again. 'In all seriousness, though, I think you might be right, Jonesy. Maybe it is *me* that's changed.'

For the next few minutes, they sat quietly. Phillips attempted to process their time in the city she'd thought she knew. She really did understand very little about the place she used to call home.

'If you lived here for fifteen years, how come you never learnt the language?' asked Jones.

'We didn't need to. Everyone spoke English, and the British saw no value in speaking Cantonese or Mandarin back then. I mean, it's not as if China was ever going to become a superpower, was it?' she said with a wry grin. 'I really wish I had, though.'

Jones nodded.

With their drinks almost finished Phillips, decided it was time for a change of scene. 'Have you ever heard of Victoria Peak?'

'Sounds like a porn movie,' chortled Jones, more relaxed now thanks to the beer.

Phillips chuckled. 'Now you mention it, it does, doesn't it?'

'So, what is it?'

Phillips pointed an index finger upwards. 'It's the peak of the mountain behind us. It's got amazing views of the city.'

She checked her watch: 6.45 p.m. 'And if we set off now, we can probably get to the top in time for the symphony of lights.'

'What the bloody hell's that when it's at home?'

'You're a detective, take a wild guess?'

'A light show?' asked Jones.

'Bingo,' said Phillips as she slipped from the stool. 'Come on. The tram stop is just around the corner.'

Jones drained a last mouthful of beer from his glass. 'Lights and trams? This place is just like Blackpool.'

Phillips smiled and shook her head. 'You've never been much of a traveller have you, Jonesy?'

'That's not true,' he said in mock defence. 'When I was a boy, we used to go to Bognor Regis all the time.'

'Well, in that case, I stand corrected,' grinned Phillips as she turned and set off towards the door.

Thankfully, the queue for the Peak Tram was unusually small for the time of year, and they managed to get to the front and into a tram in just under thirty minutes. Phillips chose to stand at the rear of the last carriage for the amazing views as they ascended the mountain. It took less than ten minutes to travel from the bottom to the summit, and as the tram climbed over 1,200 feet, the beauty and scale of the city was steadily unveiled beneath them.

At the top, Phillips led the way to the main viewing platform, which offered uninterrupted views of the iconic city skyline and the harbour below; it was truly breathtaking, and warm air blew hard against their cheeks.

'This is how I remember Hong Kong,' said Phillips, and a huge smile spread across her face.

Just then, music filled the air, along with the excited chatter of tourists as they rushed to the barriers to secure the best view.

'Perfect timing; the symphony of lights,' said Phillips.

At that moment, lights began to appear on the sides of

many of the city's skyscrapers, and music boomed through the humid night sky.

'Bloody hell. It's like New Year's Eve on steroids,' said Jones.

'I know. It's amazing, isn't it?'

For the next ten minutes they stood in silence, enjoying the show. When the spectacle was complete, Phillips gestured for Jones to follow her to the other side of the viewing platform which, in contrast, overlooked forests and water, with hardly a building in sight. 'This is my favourite view in the whole of Hong Kong.'

'God. It's a bit different to the other side, isn't it?' said Jones.

'That's why I like it. It's so unspoiled and untouched.'

'What are we looking at?'

Phillips used her outstretched arm as a pointer. 'That land mass ahead of us is called Lama Island. The large inlet of water to the left, over there, is Repulse Bay and if you follow the coastline farther along, you come to Stanley. All little slices of the real China, compared to the neon monster that has grown out of Hong Kong harbour behind us.'

'Stanley?' said Jones. 'That's not very Chinese, is it?'

Phillips chortled. 'You do remember this place was ruled by the British for over a hundred years, don't you?'

'Funnily enough, I seem to remember someone mentioning that today when he was threatening us with a meat cleaver,' said Jones, his tone facetious.

The events of the day rushed up on Phillips again and she grabbed the handrail to steady herself.

'You ok, Guv?'

'I'm fine. I just still can't believe what we saw. It feels like it was a dream that happened to someone else.'

'I know what you mean. I can't get the image of Wong's severed head out of my mind, either.'

'Why do we do this to ourselves, Jonesy?' asked Phillips after a moment of silence.

'Do what?'

'*The job*. Why do we keep doing it? It's dangerous, depressing...horrifying at times. So why do we continue to put ourselves through it?'

'I've been asking myself the same thing a lot lately. I'm coming up on thirteen years in Major Crimes now, and I'm wondering how long I can carry on. It can't be good for any of us, witnessing the depravity of the world day in day out.'

'My mum wanted me to become a doctor, like my brother,' said Phillips. 'I had the grades to do it—in fact, mine were better than Damien's—but all I ever wanted to be was a copper like my dad. Nothing else ever entered my mind. But as time's gone on, I do wonder what life would have been like if I'd chosen that route instead of this. Maybe I could have had a husband, a family even?'

'There's still time,' said Jones.

'Pah,' scoffed Phillips. 'I'm not sure there's a man out there crazy enough to take me on.'

'What about Lawry? He seems to like you.'

'Dan?' Phillips recoiled. 'Dan would love a fumble in the hay for old time's sake, but it'd never be anything more than that. Plus, as good-looking as he is, I can't imagine being with him physically again. It'd just be too weird.'

'Me and Sarah haven't slept together for a very long time.'

'Really?' asked Phillips.

There was deep sadness in Jones's eyes. 'Don't get me wrong. I was never Don Juan or anything, but since the kids, it just kind of stopped. Then, over time, the job got in the way and I was never at home. I kept telling myself the victims and their families needed me, but I think I was running away.'

'What from?'

'I'm not sure,' said Jones, 'but whatever it is, I think I'm still running.'

Phillips placed a reassuring hand on Jones's shoulder. 'Even more reason for you to take some time off when we get home.'

Jones let out a loud sigh. 'Yeah, I guess so.'

Silence filled the air for a long moment as they stared out across the forests.

Finally, Phillips spoke. 'So, do you wanna get another drink or call it a night?'

Jones looked at his watch. 'No point going back to the hotel. The TV's shit and I can't sleep.'

'Soho it is, then,' said Phillips. 'I'll take you for a ride on the world's longest escalator.'

'The world's longest what?'

'Escalator. The bloody thing's massive and runs through the middle of the city.'

'Sounds exciting,' joked Jones.

'Well, there's pubs and bars all the way along it,' said Phillips.

Jones cracked a wry smile. 'Sounds perfect!'

26

The next morning, after another night of fitful sleep, Phillips made her way down to the lobby to check out. The smiling receptionist ran through what must have been her usual repertoire for departing guests. Phillips nodded and smiled along with the conversation without paying much attention.

Before going to bed, Jones had agreed to meet her in the lobby at 10 a.m., but was yet to show at 10.10 a.m. She wondered if he had finally got a proper night's sleep, and maybe even slept in.

'Will you be checking your bags in at the downtown terminal, madam?' asked the receptionist. The question drew Phillips's attention.

'Er, yes,' said Phillips.

Just then, the lift doors pinged open and Jones appeared, pulling his suitcase as he strode towards reception.

'Sorry I'm late, Guv.' I forgot to charge my phone last night, so my alarm didn't go off.'

'No worries. I've taken care of the bill,' said Phillips. 'Come on, there's a taxi waiting for us outside.'

Fifteen minutes later, they stepped out of the taxi at Hong Kong Airport Express train station near the central harbour and made their way inside to the British Airways check-in. Soon, with their bags safely en route to the airport, Phillips handed Jones his boarding card.

He grabbed at it excitedly, and then his face fell. 'This says *Economy*.'

'Yep.'

'But we flew out in Business?'

Phillips nodded. 'That was an upgrade. These are the seats we actually booked. It's very rare you'll get an upgrade both ways, Jonesy.'

'Will we still get champagne, though?'

'Of course...' said Phillips.

'Really?'

'...as long you pay for it, yeah.'

Jones's shoulders sagged and he looked like a dejected child.

'Sorry, Jonesy.' Phillips said she ushered him towards the trains. 'Look, to make it up to you, I'll buy you a beer in Departures, how does that sound?'

The journey to Hong Kong International Airport took just over thirty minutes, passing through a number of suburbs such as Lai Chi Kok, Tsing Yi, and Ma Wan, as well as stopping at Disneyland Hong Kong.

As they alighted at the airport, Phillips said, 'This efficiency is one of the things I miss about this place compared to home. Everything is so bloody easy.'

Jones nodded, but seemed less impressed.

Thirty minutes later, having passed through security and passport control, they made their way into the airport's sports bar. Jones was put in charge of drinks, while Phillips headed for the gift shop to buy a last-minute present for her niece, Grace. When she finally re-appeared with her shopping in hand, she found Jones sitting at a table with an already empty glass and a face like thunder.

'What's up? Expensive round, was it?' Phillips joked as she placed her bags on the floor against the table legs.

Jones's face remained locked in anger, nostrils flared, breathing heavy.

Phillips took a seat. There was clearly something wrong. 'What's happened?'

'I've just plugged my phone in to charge, and found this.' Jones pushed the handset across the table.

Phillips picked it up and read the open text message.

Hi you. I've tried calling but can't get through. I've decided to take the kids to my mum's for a week or so. It'll give us both time to think about what we want. Please don't be angry. It's for the best. Sarah. X

'Oh Jesus. I'm so sorry, Jonesy,' said Phillips.

'So much for me taking time off to sort things out with her.'

'Did she know that's what you were going to do?'

'No. I wanted to surprise her,' said Jones. 'Take her and the kids away. That's all gone to shit now.'

'Why don't you try calling her, tell her your plans?'

'She's already gone. She sent that message before she left last night.'

'I really am sorry,' said Phillips.

'So am I,' said Jones as he stood. 'And I need another drink.'

27

After yet another fitful night's sleep in her own bed, Phillips woke at 4 a.m. The jet lag showed no signs of abating, so she took a long hot bath before heading downstairs for her first coffee of the day. Taking a seat at the breakfast bar, she opened her laptop and scanned her email account. In just a few days, she had amassed over three hundred unread messages. She contemplated powering through them to get them out of the way, but curiosity got the better of her and, instead, she began to search Google for any updates on the hunt for the men responsible for Jimmy Wong's murder. To her surprise, she could find zero information. Surely a beheading in broad daylight deserved a mention in the news, somewhere? Evidently not in Hong Kong, she thought, and wondered whether Triad influence on the news outlets was in play.

Draining her mug of coffee, she made her way upstairs and dressed ready for the day ahead. Even though the time had just passed 6 a.m., she decided there was nothing to be gained from sitting around the house any longer and made her way out to the car.

Thirty minutes later, she unlocked the door to her office at Ashton House Police HQ and switched on the light. It felt good to be back in the safety and security of familiar surroundings, and as she dropped heavily into her high-backed leather chair, she took a moment to appreciate the space.

For the next couple of hours, Phillips worked her way through her inbox, realising, to her immense frustration, that almost none of the messages offered any information that was remotely helpful to any of her open cases. People love to cover their arses with a paper trail, she thought to herself.

Finally, with all her paperwork squared away, her attention was drawn to Bovalino and Entwistle as they walked into the squad room. Phillips waved them in.

'Hiya, Guv,' said Entwistle.

'Guv,' added Bovalino.

'Have you seen Jones?' asked Phillips.

'You didn't leave him over there did you?' joked Bovalino.

'Almost very nearly, yeah,' said Phillips.

Entwistle and Bovalino both laughed, but stopped when Phillips didn't join in. Her face was stern.

'Are you being serious, Guv?' asked Bovalino.

Just then, Phillips's desk phone rang.

'I'd better get it. This is Phillips,' she said as she picked up the receiver.

'DCI Phillips. Ms Blair. Chief Superintendent Fox will see you now.'

'Brilliant. I'm on my way.' Phillips replaced the handset and stood. 'Look, it got a bit hairy over there. I'll explain when I get back from Fox's office, but for the time being, will one of you give Jonesy a call and check he's all right? If his jet lag's as bad as mine, I'd have expected him to be in by now.'

Bovalino nodded before Phillips brushed passed him and made her way towards Fox's fifth-floor office.

The door was open when Phillips arrived, with Ms Blair

stood in the doorway, listening intently to Fox's instructions. With her task list complete, she turned, coming face to face with Phillips.

'You can go in,' said Blair without feeling as she made her way back to her desk.

Fox was already in her seat behind her expansive desk when Phillips entered. 'Sit down,' she said, sounding more than a little agitated.

Phillips followed the instruction and took a deep breath.

'Well, that was a total waste of tax-payers money, wasn't it?'

Phillips opened her mouth to respond, but Fox had other ideas.

'You were sent there to arrest Wong, not hand him over to his killers!'

Phillips found her voice now. 'With respect, Ma'am, Senior Inspector Li led us to that location and insisted the arrest was his, not ours. From what my sources in Hong Kong told me, some senior officers in the Royal Hong Kong Police are on the Triad payroll. For all we know, Li could have set us up.'

Fox glared at Phillips for a long moment, her top lip curled up into a snarl, before she exhaled loudly. 'Not exactly the result I asked for, is it?'

'No, Ma'am, it's not, but I'm now convinced Wong was working with someone else when he killed Carpenter.'

'You mean this Zhang Shing fellow?' said Fox, clearly recalling the details of the debrief.

'Him, yes, but I also think Lui Genji and the Gold Star Trading Corporation are somehow involved her death. It's just too much of a coincidence that Gold Star was hoping to announce a £700-million two-tower development opportunity in Manchester at the same time Carpenter was trying to block one being built. Surely they're connected?'

Fox sat forwards and linked the fingers of her hands on the desk. 'Say they are connected, how do you prove it?'

Phillips shook her head. 'That's just it. I don't know if I can. The woman was untouchable in Hong Kong, so I doubt there's anything I can do from here.'

'Well, that leaves you with Shing, doesn't it? So, what do you know about him?'

'At the moment, nothing much other than what I was told by my contacts on the Island. However, Entwistle and Bovalino have been looking into him whilst I've been away. I'm expecting a full debrief straight after this.'

Fox nodded. 'Well, he looks your most likely lead. I'd suggest you focus on him for now. You never know; if he is involved along with Genji, he may well put all the pieces together for you.'

'I'm never that lucky, Ma'am.'

Fox raised an eyebrow. 'Based on what happened to Wong and *didn't* happen to you, I'd say you were very lucky, Jane.'

Phillips had to admit Fox had a point.

'On that, has what you saw affected you?'

Phillips considered the question for a long moment. 'Well, yes, I guess so, but nothing that I can't handle.'

'And how about Jones?'

Phillips knew better than to open up her team to additional scrutiny from Fox. Nothing good would ever come from it. 'Like me, he was a little shaken up, but he's ok now.'

Fox's eyes narrowed. 'Are you sure? I can't have officers having mental breakdowns on the job.'

'Yes, Ma'am. I'm quite sure,' said Phillips, not willing to give an inch.

Fox exhaled loudly. 'Very well. In that case, you'd better see what Shing has to say for himself, and *quickly*. The final interviews for the Chief Constable's job are happening next week, and it's of the utmost importance that I have positive progress on this case by then.'

'I understand.'

'Good,' said Fox firmly. 'Off you go then.'

Phillips didn't need any further encouragement. She was desperate to get back downstairs and find out what Bovalino and Entwistle had dug up whilst she'd been away.

28

By the time Phillips made it back to the squad room, Jones had appeared and was at his desk, holding court with Bovalino and Entwistle. All three turned to face her as she strode towards them. 'Been filling you in, has he?' said Phillips.

'He has,' said Bovalino. 'Sounds bloody terrifying, Guv.'

Phillips sat down at the spare desk and blew through her lips. 'I really thought he was dead at one point, and that I was next.'

Entwistle leant forwards on his desk. 'Any ideas who was behind Wong's execution?'

'Not a clue. I had a good look online this morning, but found nothing. Not a single mention, which just seems odd to me.'

'I can have a look if you like?' said Entwistle.

'Yeah. You might have more luck than me, but I wouldn't be surprised if the Triads have ensured the story has been buried. They seem to be one step ahead of everyone over there.'

Entwistle made a note in his pad.

'So, how about Zhang Shing? What have you found on him?' said Phillips.

Bovalino passed across a Manila file. 'It's pretty thin, I'm afraid.'

'You're not kidding, are you?' said Phillips as she opened it. 'Two pages?'

Bovalino shrugged. 'That's all we could find.'

Entwistle cut in. 'Before he arrived in the UK, he's a virtual ghost. There's nothing on him anywhere. Maybe your contact at the Royal Hong Kong Police could offer more information?'

'Based on what we experienced over there, I very much doubt it,' said Phillips. 'And besides, I'm not entirely sure I trust Inspector Li.'

'What? Do you think he's bent?' said Entwistle.

'I can't make my mind up on that one, but if he's not, then I'm confident he's taking orders from somebody that *is*. Either way, if we want to say ahead of Zhang Shing, we're best off keeping Li out of it.'

'Fair enough,' Entwistle said as Phillips began reading through the brief notes.

Bovalino narrated what she was looking at. 'Zhang Shing arrived in the country just under six months ago. According to his visa paperwork, he is being sponsored by the Red Dragon Trading Company.'

'Which is the same company Wong worked for?' asked Phillips.

'Yeah, that's the one.' Bovalino continued, 'He's the general manager of the Belmont casinos, which Red Dragon acquired at the beginning of the year for a nominal fee. The chain was going bust, so it helped them avoid administration. Shing is spearheading an overhaul of operations, and Wong was part of his security team.'

'So, where does Shing live?' asked Phillips.

'He has an apartment in the Sky Tower on Deansgate,' said Bovalino.

'All right for some,' said Jones.

Bovalino grinned.

'What about his personal life? Any family with him, a wife or kids?' asked Phillips.

'Nobody,' said Bovalino. 'He's a lone operator, this guy.'

Phillips stared down at a copy of Shing's passport photo. His black, soulless eyes appeared to stare straight back at her. 'My contacts in Hong Kong said he's a nasty piece of work; that far from being a businessman, he's actually an assassin for the Lui Triad family and he's been sent here to keep him out of the reach of the mainland Chinese police.'

Bovalino recoiled. 'An assassin? Seriously?'

Phillips nodded. 'Yeah. Rumour has it he killed a government official who was bad-mouthing the Triads. Cut his head off with a cleaver.'

'Jesus,' said Entwistle.

Phillips continued. 'When we spoke to Wong just before he died, he admitted he *had* been at Carpenter's house that night, but that *someone else* had killed her.'

'And you think he could have been referring to Zhang Shing?' said Bovalino.

'I'm almost certain of it. I'm pretty sure Gold Star Trading is behind the St John's development, and Gold Star Trading is funded by a consortium of Triad families. Without realising it, by blocking the re-zoning of St John's, Carpenter got in the way of a £700-million investment by some of the deadliest gangsters on the planet. Gangsters who use this man as their gun for hire.' Phillips turned Shing's picture around so the team could see it. 'He has to be in the frame for her murder, but how do we prove it?'

'What about DNA? Maybe he left some behind at the scene?' said Jones.

Phillips shook her head. 'Evans went through that place with a fine-toothed comb. The only DNA he found was from the Carpenters, Wong and Townsend. Nobody else's.'

'Maybe a good-old police shake-down would do the trick?' said Bovalino. 'Get in his face and see if he reacts?'

'You know what, Bov? I think that's a bloody good idea,' said Phillips.

Bovalino grinned.

'Woah! Take it steady, big lad. You'll be needing a lie down soon,' joked Jones.

Phillips didn't engage and remained silent for a long moment before jumping up from the chair. 'Right, get your coat, Bov. You're coming with me. Let's see what Shing has to say for himself,' she added as she went in search of her car keys.

29

The Belmont Casino near Chinatown represented the largest of the chain, and Phillips had decided that it was the best place to start their search for Zhang Shing. After introducing themselves at the main reception, she and Bovalino waited a few minutes before they were approached by a petite Chinese woman wearing a suit and carrying a small leather pouch under her arm. Having experienced Chinese traditions over the last few days in Hong Kong, she was not surprised to see the woman approach Bovalino first.

'Are you from the police?' said the woman.

'Yes,' said Bovalino.

'My name is Clarisa Shuren. What is the problem? Our gaming licenses are all up to date,' she said as she tapped the pouch.

Phillips stepped forwards and presented her ID. 'Detective Chief Inspector Phillips. We'd like a word with Mr Zhang Shing.'

Shuren's focus turned to Phillips, and her face hardened, 'Mr Shing is not available.'

After everything that had transpired in Hong Kong, Phillips's patience for game-playing had run out. 'We are here in connection with a murder case and I'd like to speak to Mr Shing *immediately*. If he is not forthcoming, then I will return with a search warrant and a full team of uniformed officers within the hour to take this place apart. Is that understood?' she said – louder than was necessary.

Shuren looked left and right, then nodded. 'Please wait here a moment.'

A few minutes later she returned, this time without the leather pouch. 'Please, come this way,' she said, and ushered them towards a large set of double doors.

On the other side, Phillips and Bovalino found themselves walking along a cold concrete corridor, surrounded by breeze block walls and electric strip lights that ran along the ceiling above their heads. After being guided through a labyrinth of left and right turns, they went through another set of double doors and into a more opulent space fitted with thick-pile carpet and soft furnishings. Shuren led them to a large mahogany door emblazoned with the word *Manager*. She stopped outside, knocked, then entered, and gestured for Phillips and Bovalino to follow her through. Inside, Phillips came face to face with Zhang Shing, who sat in a high-backed leather chair behind a vast mahogany desk. The room was windowless and lit by a series of up-lighters fitted to the blue and gold papered walls. Shing's face was cold, his eyes black and expressionless. A chill ran up Phillips's spine.

Shuren took a seat on a plain office chair to Shing's left and pointed to two seats opposite the desk. 'Please, sit.'

Phillips and Bovalino sat down and Bovalino pulled out his notepad.

'Mr Shing speaks very little English, so I will interpret on his behalf,' said Shuren.

Here we go again, thought Phillips; more game-play. She

decided to get straight to the point. 'Mr Shing, can you tell me where you were on the night of the 11th of August?'

Shuren translated.

As Shing answered, only his mouth moved; his eyes remained locked on Phillips.

'He was here, working,' said Shuren.

'From what time?'

Shuren translated again and a moment later, answered. 'He was here from midday through to midnight that day.'

'Can anyone vouch for him?' asked Phillips.

'I can,' said Shuren without relaying the question to Shing.

'Do you have CCTV that can back that up?'

Once more, Shuren answered without speaking to Shing. 'On the casino floor, yes, but not in the offices.'

'Well, maybe Mr Shing was captured on camera during that time whilst out on the floor?' said Phillips.

Shuren shook her head. 'Mr Shing does not go out into the public spaces.'

Phillips raised an eyebrow. 'Really? Why's that?'

'It is how he prefers it,' said Shuren.

'I see,' said Phillips as she held Shing's gaze. 'Would you like to know why we want to know where Mr Shing was on the 11th of August?'

Shuren flashed a thin smile. 'I am just here to translate for Mr Shing, Inspector. The content of the conversation is none of my business.'

Phillips returned her smile. 'Would you ask Mr Shing if he knew of a woman called Victoria Carpenter, please?'

Shuren turned to face Shing as she interpreted. Keeping his eyes locked on Phillips, he answered quickly; his response sounded abrupt.

'He does not know anyone by that name,' said Shuren.

'What about Wong? Jimmy Wong? Does he remember him?'

The process was repeated, with Shing offering another staccato response. 'Mr Wong did work here for a while, but he now lives in Hong Kong,' said Shuren.

'Correction,' said Phillips. 'Jimmy Wong *used* to live in Hong Kong, but he was murdered last week.'

Shuren didn't flinch as Shuren relayed the statement. Shing's reply was the shortest yet.

'He says that is not his concern,' said Shuren.

'Tell me about Lui Genji?' asked Phillips.

'What about her?' said Shuren.

'You *do* know of her then?'

Shuren nodded. 'She is the owner of the business.'

'What can Mr Shing tell us about his relationship with his *cousin*?'

Shuren's eyes widened before she turned and tentatively interpreted the question.

Finally, Shing's face changed. He appeared to snarl as he turned to look at his assistant. His answer this time was far louder than the earlier ones, and he appeared agitated.

Shuren seemed to shrink in her chair slightly as she responded. 'Mr Shing says his relationship with Lui Genji is not of your concern.'

'Oh really? Because, as I understand it, it was his relationship with his cousin that brought him to Manchester – after he murdered a Hong Kong government official four months ago. So, I think that makes it very much my concern.'

Shuren reluctantly relayed Phillips's words to Shing.

Shing's soulless eyes locked on Phillips's once again as he spoke.

'Mr Shing has nothing more to say. He wishes for you to leave now.'

An awkward silence filled the room as Phillips held Shing's gaze for a long moment. She tapped Bovalino on the arm and signalled it was time to go. As they stood, Phillips delivered a parting shot. 'Will you let Mr Shing know that he'll be hearing from us again, very soon. And also, please tell him that if he has any ideas about leaving Manchester or heading back overseas, he won't get very far. We'll be watching him.'

Shuren shared Phillips's threat but Shing remained silent.

'Thank you for your time.' Phillips led Bovalino out of the office.

'I'll show you out,' said Shuren as she rushed out after them.

Back on the street a few minutes later, Phillips stopped.

'I think it's fair to say you rattled his cage, Guv.'

Phillips shook her head. 'I'm even more convinced he's involved, now. This whole thing about him being the casino manager is bullshit. I mean, what kind of a casino manager doesn't want to go into the casino? And as for not having CCTV behind the scenes, that's horseshit too. With all that money floating around, there has to be cameras.'

'Could we get a warrant to view them?'

'Not without more evidence, Bov, and right now – aside from the last words of a Triad gangster relayed on the other side of the world – we've got bugger-all on Shing.'

At that moment, Phillips's phone began to ring in her coat pocket. Fishing it out, she read Chakrabortty's ID. 'Hi Tan. What's up?'

'I thought you'd want to know that the DNA from the foetus in Carpenter's womb is a match for the semen found in her the night she died.'

'It's Don Townsend's?' said Phillips, drawing a puzzled look from Bovalino.

'Yes, it is. He was the father. Not the husband.'

Phillips sighed heavily. 'Ok, Tan. I guess I'll have to let him know, then.'

'I'll leave it with you, Jane. Oh and I should've said, Victoria

Carpenter's body can be handed over to the family now. We're all done with it.'

'Thanks. I'll pass that on.'

Chakrabortty rang off.

Phillips placed the phone back in her pocket.

'What's that about Don Townsend, Guv?' asked Bovalino.

'Turns out DNA proves that he was the father of the baby Carpenter was carrying. Not her husband.'

'Oh, God. Aaron Carpenter'll be devastated.'

'Not if he doesn't know she was pregnant, he won't,' said Phillips.

'You mean you haven't told him, yet?'

Phillips shook her head. 'Considering he lost his wife, I didn't think it was worth telling him – *if* it turned out the baby wasn't his. I didn't want to add to his suffering.'

'So what are you gonna do, now?' asked Bovalino.

'As for Aaron Carpenter, I dunno, Bov. But I am going to have to tell Townsend, and I know for a fact he's going to be heartbroken. Victoria was the love of his life. Then there's the funeral to consider. God, it's all such a mess.'

Bovalino blew his lips loudly. 'Nothing good ever comes from having an affair, Guv. Nothing.'

Phillips tapped Bovalino absentmindedly on his left arm. 'You're right there, Bov,' she said as she considered what to do for the best. 'Come on, let's get back to the car. I need to call Aaron and let him know he can make the arrangements.'

30

After finishing her call with Aaron Carpenter, Phillips decided it would be best to talk to Don Townsend immediately. She knew he wouldn't want to talk in front of Bovalino, so sent Bovalino back to Ashton House to update Jones and Entwistle on the meeting with Zhang Shing.

Now, standing on the corner of Deansgate and Peter Street, she waited patiently for Townsend to appear from the offices of the Manchester Evening News. He had sounded surprised to hear from her; even more so that she was waiting outside and needed to speak to him. Ten minutes after her call, he came into view as he pushed his way through the revolving door at the front of the office block. He lit a cigarette as he strode towards her.

'This is an unexpected pleasure,' said Townsend as he blew smoke from his nose. He looked exhausted, with dark shadows under his red eyes.

'Walk with me,' said Phillips.

Townsend fell in beside her as they made their way along Deansgate.

'So, how have you been?' said Phillips.

'Not great, to be honest. I'm ok one minute and then in pieces the next.'

'That's grief for you.' Phillips turned right down St John Street, where it was noticeably quieter than the main drag.

'So, why the surprise visit, Jane?'

Phillips took a silent breath. 'You know I told you that Victoria was pregnant?'

'Yeah.'

'Well, we now know who the father was.'

Townsend stopped in his tracks and stared at Phillips as he swallowed hard. His lips quivered. 'It's me, isn't it?' he managed to whisper.

Phillips nodded gently. 'Yes, Don. I'm so sorry.'

Townsend didn't answer. He continued walking in silence. Phillips followed.

Eventually they reached St John's Gardens and Tranquil Park, where Townsend dropped down onto the nearest bench. He flicked his cigarette to the ground and stubbed it out with his shoe before lighting another one.

'She loved this park,' said Townsend. 'We would meet here for lunch most days. Sit on the grass, laugh, cuddle, make plans for our future together.'

'I can't imagine what you're going through,' said Phillips, laying her hand on his wrist.

'Are you sure the baby's mine?'

'Yes I am. The pathologist called me in the last hour to tell me the DNA from the foetus was a match for your semen.'

Townsend closed his eyes and dropped his chin to his chest.

Phillips said nothing.

After a few moments, Townsend looked up again. 'Does Aaron know?'

'No. He didn't know she was pregnant – and until I knew for certain who the father was – I didn't think it was necessary to tell him.'

Townsend took a long drag from his cigarette, 'So, will you tell him now?'

'I honestly don't know what to do for the best, Don. I understand he has a right to know, but I keep thinking, if it were me, would I really want to know that my wife was pregnant with her lover's child? Wouldn't that be the last indignity?'

Townsend remained silent as he blew out cigarette smoke.

'Also,' Phillips said, 'Victoria's body is ready for burial. I thought you should know.'

Townsend shook his head. 'I can't believe it. I meet the woman of my dreams and she's having my child, and then *bam!* – they're both taken away. Just like that. I knew an arsehole like me could never get that lucky.'

Phillips watched him for a moment as he stared into space. 'Will you go to the funeral?'

Townsend let out an ironic chuckle. 'Why? Do you think I'll be welcome?'

'Maybe not.' Phillips produced a thin smile, then moved onto the main reason for her visit. 'Look, Don, I can't say too much, but I think Victoria was murdered because of *this* park.'

Townsend recoiled. 'You what?'

'I think she was killed because she was protecting this park from development; a £700-million development that I believe is being funded by Chinese mob money.'

'Are you serious?'

Phillips nodded. 'I'm afraid so. This last week I flew to Hong Kong on the trail of our main suspect in her murder, a guy called Jimmy Wong. I watched him being murdered right in front of me by what I suspect was a Triad gang. Retribution for him leading us into their world.'

'Jesus,' said Townsend. 'That's insane.'

'Tell me about it. At one point I thought I might be next.'

'What? They tried to kill *you too*?'

'No. But they could have, and I think that was the point. We got off with a warning to leave it well alone and get out of Hong Kong.'

'Who's *we*?'

'Me and DS Jones. He came with me. You see, the thing is, before Jimmy Wong was killed, he admitted to us that he was there at the house when Victoria was killed, but that someone else actually murdered her.'

'Did he say who?'

'No. He said he'd rather die in one of our prisons than reveal the name of his accomplice. His head was cut off with a cleaver about an hour later,' said Phillips.

'My God. That is so fucked up.'

'Look, Don. I have an idea who Wong's accomplice might have been, but I need proof.'

'Can you tell me who it is?' asked Townsend.

'Not at the moment, no, but I could really do with your help.'

'Name it.'

'Well, I wondered if Victoria had ever said anything to you about being threatened, or someone wanting to do her harm.'

Townsend dropped his cigarette to the floor. 'She never said anything like that, but if you think she was killed because of the development, then you need to speak to her boss, Jennings. She was convinced he was bent and taking back-handers to push through planning permission and re-zoning right across the city. He's a right piece of work.'

'I've met him.'

'She hated him. He gave her the creeps and she was convinced he was crooked.'

Phillips nodded. 'I must admit that when I talked to him, I got the impression he was keeping something from us.'

'Sounds like him. He's a slippery fucker.'

'So why did she think he was on the take?' asked Phillips.

'It was something her old PA, Claire Peacock, said when she

was kicked out: that Jennings wasn't to be trusted and that Vicky should watch her back.'

'Vicky's PA was fired? When did that happen?'

Townsend shrugged. 'I can't remember exactly, but at least six months ago, I'd say.'

'And did Victoria believe the PA...about Jennings? I mean, if she'd been sacked, could it have been sour grapes on her part?'

Townsend lit yet another cigarette and took a long drag before exhaling as he spoke. 'The whole way she was sacked was dodgy. I don't know the full details, but apparently, during a cost-cutting exercise a while back, Claire was asked to work for Jennings as well as Vicky. His own PA was retiring and they were looking at consolidating roles. Claire had initially just reported to Vicky, but seemed fine with taking on Jennings too. I don't think Vicky was too happy about it, because she liked having Claire to herself, but she understood the need to save money. So, everything moved on and seemed to work ok for the next twelve months or so. Then, out of the blue, Claire was sacked after twenty years' service. She left in a hurry and wouldn't tell Vicky why she had been dismissed. When Vicky pushed Jennings on it, he said it was to do with financial irregularities and it needed to remain confidential. Vicky was furious. Having been Claire's direct line manager for so long, she demanded to know what was going on, but Jennings threw policy in her face and told her it wasn't up for discussion.'

'Did Vicky ever get to the bottom of it?' asked Phillips.

'No. Claire dropped off the radar and wouldn't answer her calls or emails. Vicky even went round to her house to have it out with her, to see if they could work it out and get her her job back, but Claire wouldn't let her in and told her she couldn't speak about it for legal reasons. That really hurt Vicky. They'd worked together for a very long time and she'd thought they were close. Anyway, after that final snub, Vicky gave up trying and they hired someone new into the role. I think her name was Shaw.'

'Cindy Shaw. I've met her,' said Phillips. 'When I went to see Jennings, she was there.'

'Vicky hardly ever spoke about her. She was Jennings's hire, so I don't think Vicky was all that taken with her, to be honest.' Townsend stubbed out his cigarette and folded his arms. 'So where do we go from here?'

'Well, you should get back to work and I need to get back to Ashton House,' said Phillips, 'see what I can find on Jennings.'

31

Back at Ashton House, Phillips strode into the squad room with purpose, but was stopped in her tracks when confronted by her team, slumped at their desks looking sorry for themselves. Jones in particular, with his gaunt features and bloodshot eyes, looked exhausted and mentally drained.

'Well, you're a sorry bunch, aren't you?' said Phillips as she dropped into the chair at the spare desk.

'Sorry, Guv, I'm just knackered,' said Jones. 'This jet lag is killing me.'

Bovalino rubbed his face with his thick hands, causing the skin to redden. 'We're getting nowhere with this case, Guv. This Zhang Shing fella is like a bloody ghost; there's nothing on him anywhere.'

Phillips rapped her knuckles on the desk. 'Well, keep looking. He's involved in Carpenter's murder, I'm sure of it.'

'But look where?' said Bovalino. 'I've tried everywhere.'

'What about Interpol?' said Phillips. 'Have you tried them?'

'Er, no.'

'Well you haven't look *everywhere* then, have you?'

Bovalino's cheeks flushed slightly.

Phillips turned her attention to Entwistle. 'Who do we know at Interpol?'

'No one currently, Guv. My contact moved on recently, over to Intelligence.'

'Well, it's time you made some new friends there, then. Get onto Interpol and get reconnected. And call your mate in Intelligence. You never know, they may have something on Shing that could help us.'

'Consider it done,' said Entwistle.

'Bov and Jonesy, I want you to dig into Eric Jennings's background.'

'As in, Jennings from the Council?' asked Jones.

'That's the one. Carpenter's old boss. I've just caught up with Don Townsend, and he claims that Victoria believed he was on the take, accepting bribes to get projects and developments signed off in the city centre.'

'I can believe that; he seemed like a slippery bugger when we met him,' said Jones.

'That's how Townsend described him too – or words to that effect. If Carpenter *was* killed because she got in the way of the St John's development, as the leader of the Planning Department, he could very well be connected to this whole mess. So, let's see what his life looks like. You know the drill: career history, finances, known associates, etc., and see if you can track down his movements on the night Carpenter was killed. If he drives a car, what is it and where was it that night? The same with his mobile phone.'

Jones and Bovalino nodded in unison as their postures straightened, their focus renewed.

'Shout up as soon as you have anything,' said Phillips as she stepped up from the chair and headed for her office.

It was well after 8 p.m. when Bovalino knocked on Phillips's office door. She glanced up from her laptop. 'What have you got for me?'

'You'd better come and have a look at this, Guv,' he said with a grin as he beckoned her out into the squad room.

Phillips followed him to his desk where he retook his seat, then angled the computer monitor in her direction. 'I checked the DVLA records as you asked. Jennings is the registered owner of a four-year-old black Volvo XC60, registration Whisky Bravo 66, Tango Charlie November. I ran that through the ANPR database on the night of the 11th of August, and guess where it shows up?'

'Outside Carpenter's house?' said Phillips, praying they could be so lucky.

'Not quite, Guv, no. But it *was* caught on camera in Didsbury – which is only half a mile away – half an hour before, and again ten minutes after the estimated time of death.'

'Jesus. That's bloody brilliant, Bov!' exclaimed Phillips as she slapped him on the shoulder.

'Well, that's no coincidence is it, Guv?' said Entwistle.

'No it's not,' said Phillips with a knowing smile. The fact she didn't believe in coincidences, and would constantly remind people of that fact, had become a great source of amusement to the team over the last few years. 'Is there any footage that might put him near the house at the time Carpenter was killed?'

'Nothing that I can see,' said Bovalino. 'His car was captured on the ANPR cameras on Wilmslow Road, in the heart of the village, heading towards Parrs Wood at 7.45. We don't see it again for forty minutes, and then it reappears at 8.25, going back towards Withington, before turning left on Barlow Moor Road towards Chorlton. We pick it up again as he goes left down Palatine Road, at which point we lose it.'

'So where did he go during those forty minutes?' asked Jones.

'There are any number of back roads around that area that he could have used to double back towards Withington,' said Entwistle.

'What about his phone? Do we know where that was?' said Phillips.

Jones shook his head. 'No. I've identified his number, but I can't get access to the mobile-tower records until the morning. There's nobody in at this time of night that deals with that sort of information.'

'There's something else, Guv,' said Bovalino.

Phillips eyes widened with anticipation. 'Yeah?'

The big Italian opened a file on the screen. 'The ANPR database also pulled up a car using plates taken from a SORN vehicle. This red Vauxhall Astra is carrying plates from a Volkswagen Golf.' He tapped the screen with his pen.

Phillips stepped forwards to take a closer look at the number plate. With the proliferation of CCTV and ANPR cameras actively tracking car registration plates, more and more criminals had resorted to using plates taken from cars with the statutory off road notifications, making it impossible to trace them after the fact.

Bovalino continued, 'I mean, what are the chances of a car fitted with dodgy plates travelling through Didsbury around the time of Carpenter's murder, *and* at the same time as Jennings's car was seen there?'

'Slim to very slim,' said Phillips.

'Totally,' said Bovalino.

'This is great work, Bov, really great.' Phillips looked at her watch; it was coming up for 9 p.m. 'It's late and there's nothing more we can do tonight. Let's go home, get some rest, and get back on it tomorrow first thing. Jonesy, I want you to come with me to see Jennings in the morning.'

'Ok.' Jones nodded.

Phillips continued, 'Entwistle, you pick up where Jonesy left off with the mobile phone companies. I want to know where he was during that forty minutes, preferably before we talk to him. So get onto them as soon as they're operational.'

Entwistle made a note in his pad. 'Will do.'

'Bov, you keep digging into Jennings's background. See what his finances look like. His salary should be a matter of public record. Check his incomings for anything that looks unusual. What's his mortgage like? Has he bought any fancy toys recently?'

'On it.'

Phillips clapped her hands together and headed for her office. The case was starting to open up. She could feel it in her bones. She was back in the squad room a moment later, wearing her jacket. The team had begun to shut down their various laptops and PCs.

'Well done guys,' she said with a wide grin. 'I think we're finally getting somewhere.'

32

Early next morning, as Phillips and Jones made their way across Albert Square towards Manchester Town Hall, Phillips put a hand on Jones's arm. He stopped. 'Before we get any deeper into this whole thing, I just wanted to check how things are with you and Sarah?'

Jones's shoulders sagged. 'Not great. I spoke to her last night on the phone and we ended up having a blazing row.'

'What about?'

'That's just it,' said Jones. 'It was over something and nothing. One minute we were fine, and the next thing I know, she said something about how many hours I've been working lately...and I lost my temper.'

'Oh dear.'

'The reality is, what she was saying was right, but I couldn't control my anger.'

Phillips nodded. 'Look, I'm not gonna get all Dr Phil on you, but what we saw in Hong Kong when Wong was murdered, that was incredibly traumatic. It might have affected you more than you realise.'

Jones ran his hand through his hair and exhaled loudly. 'To

be honest, Guv, I don't know what the fuck's going on in my head at the minute. I can't seem to get anything straight. My moods are up and down like a yo-yo.'

Up close, Phillips could smell last night's alcohol on Jones's breath. 'Are you drinking?'

'More than I should, yeah. It's the only way I can get to sleep at the minute.'

After her own battles with anxiety and high levels of stress, Phillips recognised that kind of relationship with alcohol only too well. 'Maybe you should take that time off that we talked about?'

'There's no point.,' said Jones. 'All I'd be doing is sitting at home stewing or drowning my sorrows. I'm better off at work; at least there I can keep busy.'

Phillips watched him for a moment as she pondered the best way forwards. She was conscious of him being exposed to too much stress, but at the same time she knew how dangerous it could be to send him home where he would be alone with his demons. 'Ok. But if you get to the point where you're feeling overwhelmed or things are becoming too much, you've gotta tell me, right?'

Jones nodded. 'I will, Guv. I promise.'

At that moment Phillips's phone began to vibrate in her coat pocket. She fished it out. 'What have you got, Entwistle?'

'I've spoken to Jennings's phone provider. The last time it registered on the network as being used was at 6 p.m. on the day Carpenter died. It connected with the city centre transmitter on the top of the CIS building at 5.58, then disappeared.'

'What do you mean it disappeared?' Phillips asked as she walked slowly towards the Town Hall.

'It stopped transmitting a signal, Guv, so it was either switched off or it ran out of battery.'

Phillips stopped, and Jones followed suit. 'That's convenient, isn't it?'

'That's what I thought,' said Entwistle.

'So when did it reappear on the grid?'

'Seven a.m. the following morning, at his home in Northenden.'

Phillips took a moment to process the information. 'There's no way any of this is coincidental. Jennings is involved. I can feel it in my bones.'

'I think you may be right,' said Entwistle.

'Is there anything else I need to know before we go in and see him?'

'One more thing, Guv. My mate in Intelligence came back to me. Sadly for us, Zhang Shing is not a person of interest. In fact, my mate had never even heard of him.'

Phillips blew through her lips. 'Bugger, that's disappointing.'

'Sorry, Guv,' said Entwistle.

'Don't worry about it. It was always going to be a long shot. Just make sure you get onto Interpol as a matter of urgency, ok?'

'It's my next call, Guv.'

Phillips rang off, and brought Jones up to speed as they continued walking towards the Town Hall. As they reached the main entrance, she placed a firm hand on Jones's shoulder. 'Right, Jonesy. I think it's time to get in there and scare the shit out of Jennings, don't you? Let's see what information we can shake out of the slimy bugger.'

Jones grinned and followed her as she stepped inside the old building.

Jennings looked less than pleased to see them as his PA, Cindy Shaw, ushered Phillips and Jones into his office. His thin face twisted with disdain as he cleaned his glasses with a cloth. 'So what can I do for you?' he asked without getting up from his desk.

Phillips wasted no time in getting to the point as she took a seat opposite him. Jones pulled out his notepad as he took the seat to her right. 'What were you doing in Didsbury on the evening of the 11th of August?'

Jennings stuck out his chin, barely masking his sneer. 'The 11th of August? I don't remember. Why, *should I*?'

'It was the night Victoria Carpenter died, so yes, I'd say you should.'

His brow furrowed. 'Oh yes. Of course.'

'So, what were you doing in Didsbury?'

Jennings reached inside his suit jacket pocket and produced a small diary. He took a moment to flick through to the relevant page, then peered over the top of his glasses as he inspected the contents. A look of recognition flashed across his face. 'Oh, yes. I was picking up some wine from the specialist wine merchant, Bartholomew's. I go there once every couple of months.'

'You live in Northenden, don't you?' asked Phillips.

Jennings's eyes narrowed. 'Er, yes.'

'So why shop in Didsbury for your wine?'

'Well, it's hardly a million miles away from Northenden, Chief Inspector, and besides, as the name suggests, they're *specialists.*' His tone was more than a little patronising. 'I happen to be very fond of their Croatian wines; in particular their Dingač from Pelješac. I buy a case of twelve each time.'

'And they can vouch for you, can they?' said Phillips.

'Vouch for me? I'm sorry. Have I done something wrong?'

Phillips ignored his question. 'Can they vouch for you?'

'I'm sure they can, but why would they need to? What is it you think I've done?'

Again Phillips ignored his question. 'How long were you in the wine merchant's?'

Jennings shifted in his seat. 'Er, I don't know. About twenty minutes, maybe half an hour.'

'That's a long time to buy just one case, isn't it?' said Jones.

'They were busy, and I like to browse whilst I'm there. They have a lot of guest wines that come in each month, and I enjoy seeing what's new.'

'Do you have the receipt for the wine?' asked Phillips.

'No. I pre-order online, so I just go in and pick it up.' Jennings was clearly getting agitated. 'Look, are you going to tell me what this is about?'

Refusing to answer his questions was part of Phillips's strategy to unnerve him. She changed tack now. 'Why was your phone switched off that night?'

Jennings recoiled. 'My what?'

'Your phone? It was switched off at exactly 5.58 p.m. that evening. Why?'

'How do you even know that? And why on Earth do you want to know about my phone?'

'Answer the question, Mr Jennings,' said Phillips.

'I have no idea. It probably ran out of battery. It's ancient.'

'Don't you have a charger?' asked Jones, playing his part in their carefully planned strategy to put Jennings on the back foot.

'Yes, but it's at home.'

'Do you have your phone with you now?' asked Phillips.

Jennings swallowed hard as a bead of sweat appeared on his large forehead. 'Yes, it's in my coat pocket.' He stood and retrieved it, then handed it to Phillips.

Inspecting it, she could see it was indeed ancient – a gold and grey Nokia 6310i.

'Jesus,' said Jones, 'did you get that on the Ark?'

Jennings appeared affronted. 'I'm not interested in technology. A phone is for making calls, and that does it just fine for me.'

Phillips handed it back and changed tack again. 'Do you know why anyone would want to kill Victoria Carpenter?'

Jennings's mouth fell open. 'Kill her? She committed suicide, didn't she?'

'We believe she was murdered – around the time your car was seen in the area,' said Phillips.

Jennings protested. 'Now wait a minute—'

Phillips didn't let him finish. 'Did anyone ever try to bribe you or Victoria in order to pass planning or rezoning applications?'

'I beg your pardon?'

Phillips pressed on. 'In particular, around the rezoning of St John's Gardens to facilitate a twin tower development worth £700 million?'

Jennings's face flushed. 'If you're accusing me of taking bribes, you'd better have evidence Chief Inspector.'

Phillips remained stoic and stared into Jennings's eyes. 'And let me assure you, Mr Jennings, if you have been taking bribes, *I'll find it*.'

Jennings's eyes bulged. 'Am I under arrest?'

'No, not yet.'

'Then I think you'd better leave.'

Phillips stared at Jennings in silence for a long moment, then flashed a thin smile. 'Very well,' she said as she stood. 'Bribery is a very serious crime, Mr Jennings, and murder? Well, the consequences are very grave indeed.'

Jennings was now standing, his eyes dancing in his head. 'I want you out of my office this minute!'

Phillips nodded, and headed for the door. As she opened it, she turned back to face Jennings. 'We'll be seeing you again, Mr Jennings. I'm sure of that.'

She stepped out of the room, Jones just behind her.

33

Back in the car, with Jones driving, Phillips called Entwistle and debriefed him on the meeting with Jennings, then tasked him with checking out the wine merchant alibi. As ever, Entwistle promised to get straight onto it, and Phillips ended the call.

She sat in silence for a moment and stared out the window as they made their way to Claire Peacock's address in Urmston, which Jones had programmed into the Sat Nav.

Twenty minutes later, they pulled up outside the semi-detached house on Cedarwood Street. From the outside it looked smart, with a well-maintained garden – walled on all sides – recently fitted double-glazed windows and a bright red door with a polished chrome 22 taking pride of place in its centre.

Phillips got out of the car with Jones behind her. As she pushed open the black metal gate, her eyes were drawn to the bright pink hydrangeas, in full bloom, in the flower bed beneath the front window. This house is loved, thought Phillips as she rang the doorbell. A moment later, the door opened and a petite woman with jet black hair and wearing heavy-rimmed glasses peered out.

'Hello?'

'Claire Peacock?' said Phillips.

'Yes. Who are you?'

Phillips produced her credentials. 'Chief Inspector Phillips and Detective Sergeant Jones, Major Crimes Unit. We'd like to talk to you about Victoria Carpenter's death.'

Peacock's eyes widened. 'Oh, right. Well, you'd better come in then.'

Phillips and Jones followed Peacock into the front room, where she took a seat in an armchair and offered them the two-seater sofa; a small glass coffee table was positioned between them.

'How can I help?' asked Peacock when they were all seated.

'Can you tell us why you left your position as PA to Eric Jennings and Victoria Carpenter?'

Peacock's brow furrowed. 'I thought you wanted to talk to me about Victoria's death?'

'We do,' said Phillips. 'The circumstances of your dismissal may have a bearing on it.'

'I fail to see how my leaving could have had anything to do with her suicide.'

'We believe Victoria was murdered,' said Phillips flatly.

Peacock's eyes bulged. 'I beg your pardon?'

'Her death wasn't suicide.'

Peacock stared at Phillips, eyes wide, mouth hanging open.

Phillips continued, 'So, with that in mind, can you tell us why you left your position at the Town Hall?'

Peacock remained silent for a long moment and appeared lost in her thoughts, then shook her head. 'No. I'm afraid I can't.'

'Can't, or won't?' asked Jones.

'Can't. I signed a non-disclosure agreement. If I talk about the circumstances of my exit, the Council could claim back my severance pay. I simply can't afford for that to happen.'

Phillips sat forwards. 'I understand your reticence, but by talking to us, you could help us find Victoria's killer.'

Peacock folded her arms tight across her stomach and shook her head. 'No, I'm sorry. I'd like to help of course, I really would. Victoria was very good to me, but I just can't take the risk.'

Phillips was beginning to lose patience. 'Ok, but let me explain the other risk you're facing if you *don't* answer our questions. We're investigating the murder of a young woman you were connected to. *You* may have information that could help us establish a motive as to why she was killed, but currently you refuse to share that with us. That is what's called obstruction of justice, which means I have the right to arrest you and compel you to tell me what I want to know. Ultimately, we'll get the information one way or the other; the only difference is, if you go down the second route, it'll take slightly longer and *you'll* spend a night in a police cell under caution and may face criminal charges and prison time.'

Peacock swallowed hard.

'So, which route would you prefer?' said Phillips, unrelenting. 'Tell us what we want to know here and now, or come back to Ashton House and tell us during your taped interview, tomorrow morning?'

Peacock's mouth fell open and she stuttered slightly. 'Er...er...'

Phillips continued to press, her eyes locked on Peacock's. 'What's it going to be?'

There was a long moment of silence before Peacock answered. 'What do you need to know?'

'We understand you were fired. Why?' said Phillips.

'I was accused of misappropriating funds.'

'And did you?'

'Certainly not! I've never stolen anything in my life.'

'So how did you get caught up in that?' asked Jones.

'I was set up,' said Peacock firmly.

'By who and why?' said Phillips.

'Well, I can't prove it, but I believe Jennings did it because I wouldn't share certain information with him.'

'What information?' asked Phillips.

'He wanted me to give him access to Victoria's emails and main computer drive. I had access to both, and he said he wanted full transparency within the department. I told him I would need Victoria's permission, but he said that it had to remain confidential between just the two of us. Well, that hardly sounded like transparency to me, so I refused. He didn't seem too pleased with my response, but at the time he said he understood my position. He asked that I keep the conversation between us two. As nothing had been shared, I agreed and thought nothing more of it. Then, a week later, I was called into his office and confronted with a sales invoice for electrical items that had been paid for using a Council account I had access to. The delivery address was here.'

'This house?' said Phillips.

Peacock nodded. 'I'd never seen that invoice before in my life. I had nothing to do with it and I told him so, but he had a letter printed out that terminated my contract; said he had no choice, based on the supposed misappropriation of funds. However, because of my long service and unblemished record up to that point, he told me he had managed to agree a severance package of three months' salary and let me keep my pension. He also offered to give me a glowing reference, but only if I signed an NDA and left that day. I'd worked there for over twenty-five years. I was devastated.'

'Was there a member of HR in that meeting?' said Phillips.

'No. Just the two of us.'

'And did he explain that you should've had the NDA checked by a solicitor?'

'No. Nothing like that. He just told me to sign it if I wanted the money, my pension and the reference.'

Phillips shook her head. 'None of that sounds kosher to me. He can't just fire you. Even if you had used that account to buy something for yourself—'

'But I didn't!' Peacock cut her off.

'I'm not saying you did,' replied Phillips. 'In fact, from what I've seen of Eric Jennings so far, I can well believe you *were* set up. But, whatever the case, you, as a full time, long-serving Council employee, should have had the chance to defend yourself with proper representation from Human Resources. You had nothing of the sort, which makes it look to me like a total stitch-up.'

Peacock's face softened and tears welled in her eyes. 'It's been horrendous, feeling like everyone thinks I did something wrong, and not being able to talk to anyone about it. Victoria came round one day. I was desperate to tell her what had happened, but I had no choice but to send her away. We never spoke again after that, and now she's dead.' Tears streaked down her cheeks now.

Phillips leant forwards and placed a reassuring hand on Peacock's wrist. 'This isn't over, I can assure you of that. And I promise, if Jennings did set you up, we'll make sure he's brought to account for it.'

Peacock reached forwards and pulled a tissue from a box on the coffee table, then dabbed her eyes. She smiled. 'I can't tell you what a relief it is to tell someone what really happened.'

Phillips returned her smile. 'Before you left the Council, had you ever heard rumours that Jennings might be taking bribes to approve planning and rezoning?'

'Nothing that I'm aware of.'

'And how would you describe his relationship with Victoria?'

Peacock chortled. 'Fractious to say the least. They didn't see eye to eye.'

'Why was that?'

'They were like chalk and cheese. He believed a lot of the planning restrictions were outdated and wanted them changed, and she was the total opposite. She wanted to protect the heritage and history of the city from greedy developers and overseas investors. I mean, you only have to look at the Manchester skyline now to realise just how much has changed in the last ten years. It's unrecognisable.'

'Did Jennings ever threaten Victoria?' said Phillips.

'Not that I know of, no.'

'But you say he wanted access to her files and drives?'

'Yes,' said Peacock. 'Like I said, he told me he wanted transparency, but I think it was more likely that he wanted to know what she was doing. She had told me on many occasions that she only told Jennings what he needed to know. She didn't fully trust him and because of that, neither did I.'

Phillips took a moment to digest the information. 'Is there anything else you can tell us that might be useful?'

Peacock shook her head. 'I'm sorry, I don't think so.'

'Ok. Well you've been very helpful, and think we have what we need for now.' Phillips stood up and made ready to leave, but Peacock stopped her in her tracks.

'You said it wasn't suicide?'

'We don't believe so, no.'

'But I don't understand. Victoria was a lovely, kind woman. Why would anyone want to kill her?'

'That's what we're trying to find out,' said Phillips, then headed for the front door.

As she and Jones got back into the car, her phone rang.

Answering it, she activated the speaker function. 'Entwistle, please tell me Jennings's alibi doesn't stack up.'

'Well, Guv, it does and it doesn't.'

'Go on.'

'The wine merchant remembers seeing him and talking to him that evening but he can't be sure of the time. So he was in there, but—'

'—maybe not at the time he said he was,' Phillips finished his sentence.

'He confirmed Jennings pre-paid and that there's no till receipt, which again makes it hard to ascertain the exact time he was in there that night.'

'What about CCTV?'

'They have cameras, Guv, but they're dummies.'

'Bugger,' said Jones.

'Bloody dummies again!' said Phillips, Then she brought Entwistle up to speed on their conversation with Peacock.

'So what now, Guv?' asked Entwistle.

Phillips checked her watch. It was after 6 p.m. 'Well, first thing in the morning, me and Jonesy are going to pay Mr Jennings another visit. I think it's fair to say he has a lot more questions to answer.'

'What do you want me to do?' said Entwistle.

'Get onto the Council's HR department and see if you can find out how Jennings reported Peacock's dismissal. It sounds like he bent the rules more than just a little, so let's see how he explained it away officially.'

'Will do, Guv.'

'Right. I think we've all had enough for one day. Let's get off home on time, for once.' Phillips winked at Jones and ended the call.

34

'This is harassment!' said Jennings from behind his desk as Phillips and Jones strode into his office just after 9 a.m. the next morning. His face was flushed and his eyes were wild. 'I've a good mind to call security.'

'We supersede them, so I wouldn't waste your time,' said Phillips without emotion as she and Jones took seats. 'So, what can you tell me about Claire Peacock?'

'Claire Peacock?' said Jennings, then cleared his throat. 'Why on Earth do you want to know about her?'

'She was fired for stealing from a Council bank account, wasn't she?'

Jennings smoothed his grey tie. 'In a manner of speaking, yes.'

'So, if she was caught stealing, why wasn't it reported to the police?' asked Phillips.

'I didn't feel that was necessary. Losing her position was punishment enough.'

'How very noble of you,' said Phillips, hardly able to mask her sarcasm.

Evidently Jennings hadn't noticed Phillips's tone. 'Well, she'd been with us for over twenty years and it felt fairer to let her go quietly.'

'As I understand it, you organised a severance package for her?'

'Yes, I did.'

'That again seems very good of you, considering she'd effectively broken the law and stolen from the taxpayer.'

'We all make mistakes and, despite hers, I liked Claire. Because of the theft, I had no option but to let her go, but I also wanted to make sure she was looked after.' Jennings sounded almost smug.

Phillips smiled thinly. 'Could you tell us which of the Council's HR team managed her dismissal?'

Jennings flinched. 'I'm sorry?'

'I'd like to talk to the person in your HR team that processed her dismissal for you.'

'Erm.' Jennings coughed. 'I, er, didn't involve anyone from HR. I handled it myself.'

'Why was that?' asked Jones.

'Well, you know. As I said, I liked Claire and I didn't want to put her through undue stress, so I felt it was best handled quietly.'

'So what you're saying is, you brushed it under the carpet?' said Phillips.

'No. That's not what I'm saying.'

'But that's what you did, isn't it?' said Phillips. 'I mean, she's caught stealing, you find out and tell her to leave, but you don't share the reasons with your HR team. Surely that's not following proper Council protocols?'

Jennings's jaw clenched. 'I did what I thought was *right* given the circumstances.'

'Like getting her to sign an NDA forbidding her from speaking to anyone about what had happened?'

Jennings's mouth fell open.

Phillips pushed on. 'And in return she got a reference, her pension and three months' salary? Is that what you mean by doing the right thing?'

'Well, erm...' Jennings appeared lost for words.

'DS Jones, what does all that sound like to you?' said Phillips.

'Blackmail, Ma'am,' said Jones, playing his part to perfection.

'Blackmail, that's just what I was thinking. And why would you need to blackmail Ms Peacock?'

'This is preposterous!' shot back Jennings.

Phillips stared into his eyes. 'Was it because you needed Ms Peacock out of the way and silenced? So you could get access to Victoria Carpenter's files, which she had already refused to give to you?'

'You're talking nonsense. I did nothing of the sort.'

'So why did Ms Peacock tell us you did?'

'Because she's a liar and a thief!' said Jennings, almost shouting now.

Phillips feigned surprise and allowed his words to echo around the large room. 'But a moment ago, you said you *liked* Ms Peacock and wanted to help her. Now you're saying she's a liar and a thief?'

'You're twisting my words.'

'I don't think I am, Mr Jennings. More like you're catching yourself in your own lies,' said Phillips.

Jennings visibly snarled. 'I know my rights, Chief Inspector, and I am no longer happy having this conversation. Unless you wish to caution me in an official capacity, I would like you to leave.'

Phillips ignored his request and changed tack. 'What time were you in the wine merchant's the night Carpenter was killed?'

The question seemed to catch Jennings off guard. 'I don't know, I can't remember specifically.'

'And how long were you in there?'

'Again, I don't remember.'

'I see,' said Phillips as she stared at Jennings for a long moment in silence, a deliberate ploy to unnerve him.

It clearly worked, as he shifted uncomfortably in his seat.

Finally, Phillips stood. 'Well, we won't keep you. Thank you for your time, Mr Jennings.' She and Jones left the room in a hurry; another deliberate ploy to shake him up.

Phillips waited until she and Jones were outside of the building before speaking. 'He's in this up to his neck somehow,' said Phillips as they made their way back across Albert Square to the squad car.

'Proving it, Guv. That's the issue,' said Jones as he walked alongside.

'Townsend was right; he's a slippery fucker,' said Phillips, then exhaled loudly as she considered their next steps. Every fibre in her body was telling her that Jennings was crooked and somehow involved in Carpenter's death. She was also convinced Zhang Shing was involved too, but so far they had nothing at all on either of the men that she could take to the CPS in relation to Victoria Carpenter's murder. And without approval from the Crown Prosecution Service, she had no case.

'Damn it, we're going round in circles here,' said Phillips as they reached the car.

Jones nodded.

'There must be something we're missing, Jonesy.'

'If there is, I'll be buggered if I can see it, Guv.'

Phillips jumped in the passenger seat as Jones took up his usual position as driver. 'Let's get back to Ashton House and see what Bov and Entwistle have come up with. Maybe they've found something that can finally open this case up.'

A moment later, Jones pulled the car into the road and gunned the engine as they made their way back to Failsworth and the Greater Manchester Police HQ.

35

As the last one into Phillips's office, Bovalino closed the door and took a seat next to Jones and Entwistle, opposite Phillips. After running through the events of the meeting with Jennings, it was Entwistle and Bovalino's turn to debrief on their findings with regards to Zhang Shing and Jennings.

Entwistle went first. 'Seriously, Guv, there's so little on Shing in the system, it's frightening. Like I said the other day, my mate in Intelligence had never heard of him, and my new contact at Interpol has next to nothing either.'

'So what did he have to say?'

'*She*, Guv. Her name's Olivia Gilbert. She connected me with their Organised and Emerging Crime operatives, who have access to the Royal Hong Kong Police database. Based on your concerns that your contact, Senior Inspector Billy Li, might somehow be involved with – or influenced by – Gold Star Trading's connections, I asked that they keep our enquiry off the books. They didn't have an issue with that, but it did limit the amount of data they could access.'

'So what *could* they tell you?' asked Phillips, wishing he'd get to the point.

'Pretty much what we already suspected; that Zhang Shing has been linked to multiple murder cases in Hong Kong where the victims were essentially assassinated. He's been arrested multiple times by the RHKP, but each time the charges were dropped when witnesses either recanted or themselves died.'

'So he was tampering with witnesses?' said Jones.

Phillips nodded. 'Or someone else was on his behalf. We've seen first-hand how ruthless the Triad gangs can be.'

Entwistle continued, 'There are over fifty cases of murder which Shing is connected to, but not a single conviction. In fact, not one of the cases ever made it to trial.'

'Jesus,' said Phillips. 'This guy's a piece of work, isn't he?'

'I also checked on Wong to see if his name came up as connected to Shing,' said Entwistle.

'And?'

'Nothing directly in Hong Kong, Guv, although they did confirm he was believed to be part of the same organised crime family as Shing—the Lui family.'

'Well, we know for certain that Wong was there when Carpenter died, so if he and Shing were connected through the Triads, then surely, with his reputation, Shing has to have been his accomplice that night,' said Bovalino.

Phillips nodded. 'I'm certain of it, Bov, but how do we prove it? All the DNA we found at the house has been accounted for, and there was nothing at all in the house that connects Carpenter to Shing in any way.'

'Judging by what he's believed to have done in Hong Kong, he's clearly too clever to leave anything behind,' said Jones.

'Anything else?' asked Phillips.

'No, Guv.'

Phillips remained silent for a moment as she digested the

information, then turned her attention to Bovalino. 'What about Jennings? Anything on him?'

Bovalino passed across a folder, which Phillips opened on her desk. 'What am I looking at?'

'Jennings's life in print. He's fifty-eight and a career Council official,' explained Bovalino. 'He started out as a junior clerk in the Housing Department in 1980 at the age of eighteen, and has steadily worked his way up through the ranks to his current position as Head of Planning. He earns ninety grand a year, with a large government pension to look forward to when he turns sixty. He lives alone in Northenden in a three-bed, semi-detached house that he bought in 1993 for eighty thousand pounds, and is now worth over three hundred grand. His mortgage was cleared two years ago, and he has ten grand in a high-interest savings account.'

'Sounds deeply unremarkable,' said Jones.

Bovalino nodded. 'Yeah.'

'What else?' asked Phillips.

'He also owns a two-bedroom holiday home in the Lake District, not far outside the village of Grasmere.'

'All right for some,' said Phillips. 'Grasmere's a beautiful place. That wouldn't have been cheap.'

Bovalino continued, 'He got it for nothing, actually.'

'You what?' Phillips was incredulous.

'He inherited it from his mother a couple of years ago,' Bovalino explained. 'As far as I can see, Eric Jennings's accounts are clean.'

Jones shook his head. 'But the man's dodgy as fuck, Guv. It's written all over his ratty little face.'

'Even if he is, Jonesy,' said Phillips, 'without evidence, we can't prove a thing.'

'There has to be *something* we can throw at him, leverage to get him talking,' said Jones.

Phillips remained silent for a moment as she crystallised

her thoughts. 'According to Carpenter's original PA, Claire Peacock, Jennings was trying to force her to give him access to Vicky's files and emails, right?'

Jones nodded. 'Right.'

Phillips continued. 'And not long after she refused to do that for him, she was sacked. Swiftly followed by Cindy Shaw; a young, far more impressionable character than Peacock...'

'Who was far more likely to give him the access that he wanted,' said Jones.

'Exactly,' said Phillips with a wide grin. 'I think it's time we paid her a visit, Jonesy, don't you?'

Jones returned her grin.

'Whilst we're doing that, Bov,' said Phillips, 'for completeness, see if you can find out who the Council banks with. It'd be good to get an audit on any accounts Eric Jennings has access to. It might come to nothing, but you never know, it might just turn up something.'

Bovalino scribbled down the instructions.

'Entwistle, I want you to run a background on Cindy Shaw. See what we can find out about her. How she lives her life, finances, previous convictions, known associates, anything and everything, ok?'

'On it, Guv,' said Entwistle.

Phillips stood, indicating it was time for everyone to get moving. 'So then, Jonesy,' she said with a wry smile, 'looks like you and I are heading back to the Town Hall,'

Jones feigned surprise. 'The Town Hall, really, Guv? That'll make a nice change. I've not been there in ages.'

36

As Jones pulled the squad car onto Princess Street, Phillips spotted something out of the corner of her eye. 'Pull over,' she barked, then jumped out. She walked briskly, and stopped just before the entrance to a coffee shop and bakery. Peering inside the busy space, she saw who she was looking for before stepping back out of sight. Turning, she signalled for Jones to remain in the car, then waited. Five minutes went by before her target walked back out onto the street carrying a paper bag of hot drinks.

Phillips stepped to her shoulder, 'Cindy?' she said firmly.

Cindy Shaw turned, and her eyes widened as she caught sight of Phillips.

'We need to talk,' said Phillips.

Shaw looked left, then right. 'What do you want?'

'Come with me and I'll explain.' Phillips held her arm up in the direction of Jones and the squad car. 'I'm parked over here.'

'I need to be getting back,' said Shaw as she retreated, pointing over her shoulder towards the Town Hall. 'I've only nipped out for some coffees.'

Phillips held her gaze. 'This won't take long. Or we can always do it at the station, if you'd prefer?'

Shaw's eyes widened further as she scanned her surroundings, then nodded reluctantly.

Phillips led her towards the waiting car, opened the back door and ushered her inside, then walked round to the other side of the car and jumped in the back seat behind Jones. 'You've met DS Jones before, haven't you?'

Jones glanced at Shaw in the rear view mirror and she nodded.

'I'll get straight to the point, Cindy,' said Phillips, as she half turned to face her. 'When you were working for both Eric Jennings and Victoria Carpenter, did you have access to their files and emails?'

Shaw swallowed hard. 'Why do you want to know?'

'Yes or no,' Phillips said firmly.

Shaw opened her mouth for a moment, then finally nodded. 'Yes.'

'And is that common in the Council – for support staff to be able to see what their bosses are working on?'

'It was a general directive put in place before I joined, but as I understand it, the leader of the Council was trying to reduce the amount of admin the executives were doing each day. He felt their time was better served getting on with their actual jobs. So that meant I had sight of both their emails and various drives on their profiles.'

'And do you know if Jennings *himself* had access to Victoria's email and files?'

Shaw's brow furrowed. 'What's this about?'

Phillips ignored the question. 'Just answer the question, Cindy. Did Eric Jennings have access to Victoria's email and files?'

Shaw's breathing had become shallow and her neck flushed

red. 'Not that I'm aware of, no. Her documents were private. Like I say, aside from Victoria, I had access, but only me.'

Phillips stared at Shaw in silence for a long moment. 'Did Eric Jennings ever ask you to share Victoria's emails or files with him?'

Shaw let out a nervous laugh. 'Why would he do that?'

Phillips didn't respond, and instead stared at Shaw.

'No. He didn't,' said Shaw, finally.

Phillips changed tack. 'Are you aware of an ongoing investigation into the misappropriation of funds within the Council's Planning Department?'

There was, of course, no such investigation in place, but Phillips wanted to check Shaw's reaction to the suggestion there might be.

Shaw's eyes bulged as the question landed. 'I don't know what you're talking about.'

Phillips continued with the lie, 'Yes. Apparently, someone from within the Council has been syphoning off public money into private accounts.'

'Well, I can assure you I know nothing about that,' said Shaw, looking anywhere but at Phillips.

'Really? Because if you do, we will find out about it and it would be much better for you to tell us sooner rather than later.'

Shaw made a point of checking her watch. 'I really do need to be getting back. Mr Jennings's coffee is getting cold.'

Phillips had rattled Shaw's cage and suspected she – like Jennings – wasn't telling the whole truth. Something irregular was at play in the Planning Department and she sensed Shaw was the weak link. In an attempt to unnerve her further, Phillips stared in silence at Jones's eyes, reflected in the rear view mirror, then nodded and turned her attention back to Shaw. 'Well, we don't want you getting on the wrong side of Mr

Jennings, now do we?' she said through a thin smile. 'Off you go, then.'

Shaw couldn't get out of the car quick enough.

Phillips stepped out and made her way back round to the passenger door.

Shaw was already walking away as Phillips called after her. 'Cindy?'

Shaw stopped and turned.

'If you do remember anything about the misappropriated funds, you will let us know, won't you?'

Shaw nodded without speaking, then turned on her heels and set off across the road.

Phillips dropped into the passenger seat once more and closed the door. 'She's definitely hiding something, Jonesy.'

'One hundred percent, Guv. She was like a deer caught in headlights sat back there. I actually felt sorry for her at one point. She's a terrible liar.'

Phillips nodded. 'Did you see the way she reacted to my questions about Council money being stolen?'

Jones chuckled. 'Yeah, she almost shit her pants.'

'We should call Entwistle and see if he's found out anything on her, but first...' Phillips reached for the door handle. '...I need one of those coffees.'

37

Phillips returned with a black coffee for her and Jones's favoured mint tea. 'How's your jet lag?' she asked as she passed over the hot drink.

Jones took the cardboard cup. Steam billowed from it as he removed the plastic lid. 'I still can't sleep properly. I'm wide awake in the middle of the night and then ready for bed at lunchtime. I didn't think it'd last this long.'

Phillips took a sip of her hot coffee. 'I've had it before where it's hung around for well over a week. We've only been back a few days, so it's still kicking my arse too.'

'A week? Jesus. I hope it doesn't take that long.'

Silence descended on the car as they both took drinks.

'Any news from Sarah?' said Phillips, a few minutes later.

Jones let out a frustrated sigh. 'Nothing much, no. A couple of texts, but she doesn't want to speak on the phone. She says we need a proper break from each other.'

'And what about the kids?'

'Typical moody teenagers with their heads glued to their phones. They don't want to talk to their old man,' said Jones with a sad chuckle.

'So how are you feeling about it all?'

'I'm trying not to think about it, if I'm being honest. I can't imagine life without Sarah and the kids in it every day, and the thought of having to start all over again terrifies me. I'll be that sad lonely old copper who sits in the corner working late every night and never goes home.'

'No change there, then,' said Phillips with a chortle.

Jones shot her an incredulous look, then burst out laughing. 'Kick a man when he's down, why don't you?'

Phillips grinned. 'Sorry. Too soon?'

'With friends like you, who needs enemies,' said Jones as he returned her grin.

'I'm the last person to be dishing out relationship advice, but give her time, mate. I'm sure she'll realise what you guys have.'

Jones nodded without conviction. 'Yeah. Maybe.'

Just then, Phillips's phone began to ring. She answered it and switched on the speaker function. 'Entwistle, I was just about to call you.'

'I've found something on Shaw's finances that looks dodgy to say the least, Guv.' He sounded excited.

'Go on.'

'Well, she has a number of bank accounts, one standard current account that looks after all her bills, etc., another that appears to be a savings account that's empty, and then another one under her married name of Cindy Hunter.'

'She's married?'

'Divorced. Two years ago, but it appears that she and her husband had a joint savings account whilst they were together.'

'Ok, and why is that important?' asked Phillips.

'Because in the last nine months, just under twenty grand has been deposited into that account; two grand each month.'

'Could that be from the ex-husband? Alimony, maybe?'

'Possibly, but that seems excessive considering they were married for

less than a year and have no kids – and besides – I've traced the account number that made the deposits and its registered to a bank in Macau.'

'Macau, China?' Jones said.

'That's the one,' said Entwistle.

'And when did you say these payments started?'

Entwistle was quiet for a while. *'Er, last November.'*

Phillips remained silent as she worked the dates over in her mind. 'Entwistle, when did Shaw start working for Jennings?'

Again, Entwistle took a moment to find the information. *'According to the Council's HR records, her first day was the 14th of September.'*

Phillips looked at Jones and nodded.

'What you thinking, Guv?' he said.

'Jennings asked his old PA Claire Peacock for access to Carpenter's files. She refused, and was sacked last August. Jennings then hired *another* PA, Cindy Shaw, in September – who Victoria described to Don Townsend as Jennings's hire – then two months later, Cindy Shaw started receiving payments from a bank in China.'

'Money to look the other way, perhaps?' said Jones.

'It would make sense,' said Phillips. 'Shaw started her new job in September. Jennings sussed her out for a month before making his offer in October, and by November the money started appearing in Shaw's account.'

'I can buy that,' said Jones.

'And are you totally sure, Entwistle, that the money doesn't have anything to do with her ex-husband?' asked Phillips.

'As far as I can tell, it doesn't. I've run a check on his finances and from what I can see, just after the divorce, he withdrew half of the one thousand pounds that was sitting in the joint account. Since that withdrawal, Steven Shaw has never once deposited funds in either the joint account or Cindy's account. In fact, after the divorce, the joint account lay dormant for over a year. That is, until last

November, when the monthly payments of two thousand pounds started.'

Phillips felt her pulse quicken. 'She's involved in all this too. She has to be.'

'Do you wanna go and talk to her again?' Jones asked.

'No. Not at work; not near Jennings. I want her on her own and feeling as vulnerable as possible. She's weak, and with the right pressure, she'll cave. Is Bov there, Entwistle?' asked Phillips.

'Yeah, he's next to me.'

'Put him on, will you?'

'Sure.'

A moment later, Bovalino appeared on the line. *'Guv?'*

'You got any plans this evening?' asked Phillips.

'No, Guv. I was just gonna do a bit of work on the car. I've got a race coming up.'

'Well, leave the rallying alone for one night, will you? I want you and Jones to go and put the fear of God into Cindy Shaw for me.'

'As in Jennings's PA?' said Bovalino.

'That's the one.'

'Ok. I'll need to call Izzie and let her know, but that won't be a problem.'

'Great,' said Phillips. 'Jones and I are heading back to the office now. Shaw should be home by 7 p.m., and that's when I'd like you to go round and do your thing.'

'Jones and Bovalino, the dream team back in action,' said Jones with a chuckle.

Bovalino laughed along. *'Looking forward to it, partner!'*

'Right. We're just outside the Town Hall now, so we'll see you in half an hour,' said Phillips and ended the call.

Jones pulled the car away from the curb and slipped into the late afternoon traffic.

'Sorry, I should have asked,' said Phillips. 'You're all right working late tonight, aren't you?'

Jones shrugged his shoulders. 'Yeah. I mean, I've got nothing else to do have I? Better than sitting at home on my own.'

38

The journey from Ashton House in Failsworth to Shaw's home in Droylsden took just over ten minutes with Bovalino at the wheel, driving with the usual aggressive style he had honed on the weekends as an amateur rally driver.

As a densely populated suburb situated four miles east of Manchester City Centre, many people still found it surprising that Droylsden actually had its own marina, home to over twenty narrowboats and their moorings. Shaw's small apartment was located on the top floor of a three-storey block that overlooked the water.

As Bovalino turned off the engine, Jones opened the file on his knee and checked the contents were all in place. Satisfied, he closed it and stepped out of the car along with Bovalino.

'I'll take the lead, but jump in as and when you want,' said Jones as they approached Shaw's front door.

'Got ya,' replied Bovalino.

In the absence of a bell, Jones rapped his knuckles on the door three times and waited. A moment later, the door opened on the chain and Cindy Shaw peeped out through the gap.

Jones held up his credentials and deliberately spoke in a voice that was louder than necessary. 'DS Jones from Major Crimes; we spoke earlier today with DCI Phillips.'

'I know who you are,' said Shaw.

Jones continued, 'This is my partner, DC Bovalino. May we come in?'

'What's this about?'

Jones glanced left towards the neighbouring flat – purely for effect – then back at Shaw. His voice remained loud. 'I think you'd prefer it if we explained the reason for our visit *inside*, Miss Shaw.'

Shaw stared out in silence for a long moment, nodded, then closed the door in order to release the chain before she opened it wide. 'Go on through to the lounge.'

Jones did as directed, with Bovalino in tow, and stepped into the small, but smartly decorated, lounge room. He took in the view of the water and the boats through the large window in front of him.

Shaw joined them. 'Can I offer you gentlemen a hot drink?'

Jones turned to face her. 'No, thank you. Would you mind taking a seat?' He gestured, with his arm outstretched, towards the small IKEA-style armchair.

Shaw followed his instruction as Jones and Bovalino squeezed together into the petite sofa that matched the armchair. Both men remained silent as Jones made a show of opening the folder on the small glass coffee table in between them.

'How much do you earn in your job at the Council?' Jones asked.

The question appeared to catch Shaw off guard. 'I'm sorry?'

'What's your annual salary, currently?'

'Why do you want to know?'

'Because we're police officers, Miss Shaw, and it's important.'

Shaw's neck flushed. 'I really don't see how what I earn could be important to the police?'

'Oh it is, I can assure you,' said Jones through a thin smile.

'Erm, well, I'm on twenty-five thousand pounds if you must know.'

Bovalino made a note in his pad.

'I see,' Jones nodded. 'And when was the last time you spoke to your ex-husband?'

Shaw recoiled in the chair. 'I beg your pardon?'

'I think you heard my question just fine.'

Shaw stared open-mouthed for a moment. 'Why? Has Steven done something wrong?'

'You tell us, Miss Shaw,' said Jones as he locked eyes with her.

'I really wouldn't know. I haven't spoken to Steven since the divorce came through.'

'And when was that?'

Shaw shrugged. 'I dunno. Probably eighteen months ago, now.'

'Was it amicable?'

'Well, considering he cheated on me, not really, no.'

'He was seeing another woman?' Jones asked.

'Another *man*, actually,' said Shaw, her tone acerbic. 'It turns out I was Steven's beard.'

Jones felt his cheeks flush slightly at the unexpected revelation, and the room fell silent for a moment. Regaining his composure, he continued, 'Do you receive any payments from your ex-husband as part of the divorce settlement?'

Shaw scoffed. 'You're kidding, aren't you? He's broke. All I got was full responsibility for the mortgage on this place when he buggered off with his boyfriend.'

'And how much *is* that mortgage each month?'

Shaw rubbed the back of her neck as her brow furrowed.

'Look, why are you asking me all these questions about money?'

Jones didn't respond, and instead deliberately took a moment to locate the PDF file he was searching for. He held it in his hands for a few seconds before passing it over to Shaw. 'Is this your account?'

Shaw took the file, and her eyes widened as she stared down at the statement.

'You and Steven had a joint account whilst you were married; a copy of which you have in your hands right now. As far as we can tell, Steven withdrew five hundred pounds around the time your divorce was finalised in 2018, and he's not touched that account since. You did the same, at which point it sat doing nothing. Until last November, when someone suddenly started paying two thousand pounds a month into it.'

Shaw's breathing had become rapid. She held her clenched fist up to her mouth and began to shake her head.

Jones pushed on. 'We've traced those payments and they're coming from a bank in Macau. So, who's sending you two grand a month from China, and why would they want to do that?'

'I need a glass of water,' said Shaw as she got up out of the chair.

'Please sit, Miss Shaw,' Jones said firmly. 'DC Bovalino will get you a drink. We don't want you running off now, do we?' He forced a smile.

Bovalino disappeared into the kitchen for a minute as Jones and Shaw sat through an awkward silence. The big man returned with a tall glass of water from the tap and carefully placed it on a coaster on the glass table in front of Shaw. She picked it up and took a couple of mouthfuls. Jones sensed she was playing for time, trying to figure out how to explain the money, so he pushed on. 'Once again, Miss Shaw, who is sending you two grand a month from China, and why?'

Shaw began to cry, quietly at first, and then tears streamed down her cheeks. Jones and Bovalino had already discussed this as a possible outcome of the interview, so were prepared. It was vital that they remained aloof until she admitted what was going on. Then they could support her if needed.

'If you come clean, Cindy,' said Jones, deliberately using her first name to disarm her, 'it will look a lot better for you than if you stay silent on the matter. We'll find out in the end. We always do, and it could mean the difference between a suspended sentence or prison time.'

'Oh God,' said Shaw as she placed her face into both hands and began to sob.

Jones continued unabated. 'Are you receiving money in exchange for favours within the Planning Department?'

Shaw's face remained covered, but she nodded slowly.

'And is Eric Jennings the man who offered you the money?'

Shaw lifted her head and noisily wiped her nose on her sleeve, then folded her arms across her stomach. 'Yes.'

'When did he first propose this arrangement?'

Shaw shook her head and shrugged. 'I dunno. A month or so after I started at the Town Hall, I guess.'

Bovalino stepped in for a moment. 'What made him think you'd be receptive to such an offer?'

'He must have overheard me talking to one of the girls in the office about money one day; how I was struggling to pay for this place on my own after Steven left. About a week later, he asked me to work late for a couple of hours, and when everyone had gone home, he called me into his office and asked if I wanted to earn some extra money – *off the books*. The other girls in the offices had told me he was a bit creepy and lived alone, so at first I thought he was going to ask me to sleep with him. I remember actually being quite relieved when he told me it involved me acting as signatory on one of the corporate accounts. All I had to do was co-sign the transactions and he would do the rest.'

'You must have known what he was asking was illegal, though?' said Bovalino.

'I had my suspicions, but I needed the money, so I didn't ask too many questions. I mean, he's the head of the Planning Department and a clever bloke. I assumed he had it all under control and there was no real danger of anyone finding out.'

Jones took the lead once more. 'So, who is the money coming from?'

'I honestly have no idea,' said Shaw. 'Mr Jennings knew I'd been married before, and asked if I still had access to any accounts in my married name. I hadn't bothered to close the joint account, so I gave him that and the money started coming in the next month, regular as clockwork.'

'Do you know what he's doing with the funds you're signing off?' said Jones.

'No. He makes a point of covering up the document itself; "plausible deniability" he called it. All I do is sign and print my name.'

Jones exhaled loudly. 'You do realise you could have opened yourself up to serious fraud with this caper of yours, don't you?'

Shaw's bottom lip trembled, and she nodded.

'You could be in serious trouble; looking at a custodial sentence.'

Shaw broke down again.

Jones watched her for moment. As a father, his heart went out to her. It was evident for all to see, she was no criminal mastermind; rather, a naive young girl who'd made a terrible mistake in a desperate moment. This time he grabbed a box of tissues from the side and handed them over. 'Look. Whatever mess you've gotten yourself into, if you help us, we can make sure the CPS know about it. That will stand for a lot when it comes to the level of charges you could face.'

Shaw blew her nose into the tissue and attempted to control her breathing.

'Is there anything else you can tell us about Jennings that might help us?' asked Jones.

'Like what?'

'This afternoon – when DCI Phillips asked you if he'd asked for access to Victoria Carpenter's emails and files – you said he hadn't. Is that true?'

Shaw's shoulders sagged and she appeared to shrink in the chair. 'No, it's not.'

'So he *did* ask you for access?'

'Yes.'

'And did you give it to him?' said Jones.

'Yes, I did. I said no initially, but by then I'd already started receiving the extra money. At that point he made it quite clear that I had no choice but to give him what he wanted.'

'I see. And did he ever ask for anything else regarding Carpenter?'

Shaw took a deep breath and exhaled loudly. 'He asked me to take a photocopy of her personal diary each week. She kept it in her desk drawer, and because I knew her movements at work and was in and out of her office constantly, it wouldn't look suspicious if anyone came in and found me there.'

Jones sat forwards now. 'Did you give Jennings a copy of her personal diary the week that Victoria was killed?'

Shaw nodded.

'Were you aware Victoria was having an affair?'

'Yes.'

'And how did you find out?'

'Mr Jennings told me. Said he had it on good authority.'

'I see.' Jones moved forwards on the small sofa. 'Cindy, did you call Aaron Carpenter to tell him about Victoria's affair?'

'Yes. Mr Jennings told me to do it or he'd tell everyone about the money I'd been getting.' Tears began to well up in Shaw's eyes again before she dropped her face into her hands once more.

Jones glanced at Bovalino; they both knew these revelations needed to be on the record.

A few minutes later, when Shaw had composed herself and sat upright, Jones changed his approach, adopting a soft, supportive demeanour. 'Look, Cindy, we want to help you out of this mess, we really do. But to do that, we'll need you to come to the station and make a formal statement about what you've just told us.'

'The police station?'

'Yes. Ashton House in Failsworth. You'll need to come in first thing in the morning.'

Shaw exhaled and rubbed her face so the skin reddened to match her tear-stained eyes. Mascara ran down her cheeks.

'How does 10 a.m. suit you?' said Jones.

'That's fine.'

Jones produced a warm smile. 'Good. We can leave you in peace, now.'

As they made their way to the door, Shaw stopped them. 'Will there be an investigation into what I've done, Sergeant?'

Jones turned to face her. 'It's highly likely, but you've helped yourself a lot by being so open about it. That'll go a long way with the CPS.'

Shaw forced a weak smile. 'Well, that's something, I suppose.'

Jones offered her a faint smile and then headed for the door.

39

She had never met him before, so there was no way she would recognise him. Still, as a precaution he wore the hood of his jacket pulled up tightly over his head, along with a pair of large black sunglasses, perched on the bridge of his nose, that covered the majority of his face. The city centre was awash with CCTV cameras – as was the tram that would carry her towards Manchester – and it was imperative he remained covered and unrecognisable at all times.

He had been waiting for her, out of sight opposite her tiny flat, since the early hours of that morning. Finally, just over an hour ago, she had emerged before making her way on foot off the small housing estate and five hundred metres down the main drag towards the tram stop. He had followed her at a safe distance the whole way before eventually boarding the tram through a door that was positioned behind her. She had not noticed him – or anyone else, it would seem – appearing lost in whatever it was that was playing through the small headphones secreted in her ears.

The tram was destined for the city centre where, he suspected, she would alight at St Peter's Square, then wait for the connecting tram to Rochdale. With each passing stop, more and more rush-hour commuters piled into the carriage, each of them lost in their own little world, focused on the phone in their hand, or the free morning papers handed out along the route.

Thirty minutes later, the tram rolled slowly across St Peter's Square, and came to a stop. The doors opened and passengers leaving the tram pushed and shoved their way past those who remained, as well as impatient commuters keen to board.

As she stepped up from her seat and headed for the exit, he leapt to his feet and followed her out, moving quietly within the crowd behind her as she made her way across the tramlines to the opposite platform.

Careful to position himself with his back to the CCTV camera above him, he watched as she stood staring into space in the direction of the oncoming trams.

It wouldn't be long now, he thought.

40

When Jones and Bovalino had left Cindy Shaw's apartment the previous evening, they hadn't expected to be back again so soon. She had been a no-show for her 10 a.m. appointment at Ashton House and, after unsuccessfully trying to reach her for an hour on the phone, they had returned to her home.

This time it was Bovalino who rapped his knuckles on the door whilst Jones cupped his hands to the side of his face as he looked in through the small kitchen window at the front of the residence. After five minutes of continued knocking and still no response, Jones crouched down and opened the letterbox to peer inside. From his viewpoint, he had sight of the majority of the flat, including the hallway and most of the lounge. There was no sign of Shaw anywhere.

Next, they tried the neighbour's door, which was answered by an elderly woman who Jones put in her mid- to late-seventies.

'Yes?' she said, opening the door without the use of a security chain.

'We're from the police, ma'am,' said Jones as they both

presented their IDs. 'Do you know your neighbour, Miss Shaw, at all?'

'Cindy? Oh yes, she's a lovely girl,' said the lady with a warm smile.

'We're trying to contact her but there's no answer.'

'She's probably at work. She usually sets off about eight each morning.'

'She was supposed to meet us for an appointment first thing, but she didn't show. We just want to check she's ok.'

The old lady raised her finger. 'I have a spare key. I won't be a second.'

She returned a moment later, holding the Chubb-lock key in her grip with purpose. 'She gave me it in case of emergency. She was burgled not too long since, and I think she felt safer knowing someone else could get in if she was in trouble.' The lady moved the short distance to Shaw's front door and rattled the key in the lock. 'Now, I'll have to stay with you. I wouldn't feel right letting you in on your own.'

Jones opened his mouth to protest but, seeing the steely look in the woman's eyes, he decided against it. 'Very well, Ma'am, but for your own safety, we'll need you to stay out here by the front door.'

She nodded her agreement and opened the door.

Jones stepped inside and took point.

The flat was deadly silent. As they moved through the various rooms, they found no sign of Shaw – but no indication of foul play either.

'Do you think she's done a runner?' asked Bovalino.

'Check the bedroom, see if any of her stuff is missing,' said Jones.

'Got ya.'

'Is this to do with her husband, Steven?' asked the lady in a loud voice, from her position by the front door.

Jones made his way back to speak to her. 'Why do you ask that?'

'Well, I'm not one for gossip,' said the lady in hushed tones, as she glanced behind her to check if she was being overheard. 'But as I understand it, he was one of *those*.'

'One of *what*?' asked Jones.

'*You know*.'

Jones shook his head. 'I'm afraid I don't. One of what?'

'A ho-mo-sex-ual,' said the lady, her voice barely audible now as she broke the word down into its syllables.

Jones felt his eyes roll. 'Oh, I see. Yes I believe he is, but no, that's not why we're here. You see, that's not been a crime since 1967 so I think we're all *quite* safe now,' he said, his tone sarcastic.

Bovalino returned from the bedroom. 'Doesn't look like anything's been taken.'

'Well, where the hell is she?' said Jones.

At that moment, Entwistle called through on Jones's mobile. He answered it quickly. 'What's up?'

'Have you found Shaw yet?'

'No. She's not at the apartment. Why?'

'I've just seen a report that a young woman was hit by a tram this morning in the centre of town, at St Peter's Square.'

A shot of adrenaline coursed through Jones's body. 'Tell me it's not Shaw?'

Bovalino raised an eyebrow and moved closer.

'The woman's not been identified but she matches her description – and the tram from Droylsden passes through that stop,' said Entwistle.

'Which hospital was she taken to?'

'The MRI Accident and Emergency Department. The incident happened at about 8.30 a.m. She was treated at the scene for over an hour before they transferred her.'

'Right, we're heading there now,' said Jones, then ended the call.

Bovalino's face was filled with concern. 'What's happened?'

'I'll tell you on the way to the car,' said Jones as he turned to face the old woman. She remained in position by the front door, her eyes wide and expectant. 'I'm afraid we need to be going now. Are you ok to lock up?'

The woman seemed slightly affronted, as if she too was hoping for a full debrief on Jones's call. 'Oh right. Well of course, yes.'

Jones offered a fleeting smile and headed out of the flat. Bovalino was hot on his heels as they marched towards the car.

Bovalino's voice brimmed with tension as he caught up to Jones. 'What the fuck's going on? Who's in hospital?'

Jones continued walking at pace. 'A woman's been hit by a tram in St Peter's Square this morning. Entwistle's not one hundred percent sure, but the victim's description matches that of Shaw.'

'You're kidding?'

'I wish I bloody was,' said Jones as they reached the car. 'She was taken to the MRI A&E. Sounds like a bad one.'

'Don't worry,' said Bovalino. 'With the lights on, I'll get us there in no time.'

TRUE TO HIS WORD, Bovalino snaked through traffic and made it to the MRI in just ten minutes. As they strode through the automatic doors to the A&E Department, Jones noted the time on the wall clock: 12.44 p.m. Jones quickly explained the reason for their visit to the receptionist, who immediately called one of the doctors.

He appeared a few minutes later, a grave look across his face.

Jones was prepared, holding his ID ready. He wasted no time. 'We need to speak the young woman who was hit by the tram.'

'I'm afraid that won't be possible—'

'Look, we won't stay long, but we need to speak to her,' Jones cut him off.

'She died an hour ago,' said the doctor.

Jones felt his face contort. 'What?'

The doctor nodded. 'Her injuries were extensive. There was nothing we could do. I'm sorry.'

'Has she been identified?' asked Bovalino.

'Yes, we found her driving license in her purse.' The doctor looked down at his notes. 'Her name was Cindy Shaw.'

Bovalino continued, 'Was it a suicide?'

'We can't say for sure, but her injuries were consistent with jumpers that I've dealt with before. The pathologist will be able to tell you for certain.'

Jones was suddenly overwhelmed by a sense of guilt that smashed down over him like a wave; he pictured her breaking down in tears the previous evening as he and Bovalino interrogated her. He turned to his partner now. 'This is my fault, Bov, I was too hard on her last night. I could see she was upset. I should have been more careful.'

Bovalino placed his large hand firmly on Jones's shoulder. 'That's bullshit. I was there, mate. You weren't too hard at all. She was in the shit and she obviously didn't want to face up to it. Don't you dare blame yourself.'

'If there's nothing else, I'm afraid I must be getting back,' said the doctor.

'Yes of course, thank you,' said Bovalino.

Jones said nothing. He felt numb all over. 'I need some air,' he mumbled as he made his way back outside.

41

After hearing the news about Shaw's untimely death, Phillips had agreed to meet Jones and Bovalino at her apartment. Wearing latex gloves, she worked her way slowly around the lounge room, looking for anything that might help explain her death. She'd been there for about five minutes when Bovalino walked in alone, a grim look on his face.

'Where's Jonesy?' she asked.

Bovalino pointed over his shoulder. 'He's outside, Guv, having a fag.'

Phillips did a double take. 'Jones is smoking again? Since when?'

'Since we found out Shaw was dead. He's taken it personally.'

'Seriously? Why?'

'He reckons he pushed her too hard when we were here last night, and that's why she killed herself. I've told him that's bullshit; he did everything by the book, Guv.'

Phillips frowned. 'I'm sure he did. And besides, who's to say it *was* suicide.'

'What? You think she might have been pushed?'

'With everything that's happened with this case up to now, Bov, I'm not ruling anything out. In fact, Entwistle is looking at CCTV footage at the tram stop as we speak.'

Phillips pushed past Bovalino and headed outside, where she found Jones stubbing out his cigarette. 'What the fuck's this all about?'

Jones frowned. 'I just needed a cigarette.'

'After two years without them?'

Jones pulled the packet from his jacket pocket and reached for another smoke.

'Where the hell did you get *those*?'

'I made Bov stop at the garage on the way over here.'

Phillips checked to see if they were alone, then stepped forwards, out of Bovalino's earshot. Her voice was low, her tone irate. 'Do you *really* think this is gonna help you get Sarah back? Feeling sorry for yourself and chain-smoking?'

'Oh come on, Guv. I think that after everything I've been through in the last couple of weeks, I'm entitled to a little self-reflection. You said yourself that I needed some time off.' Jones placed the cigarette between his lips.

'Yeah and I meant it. If the job's getting on top of you, then go home and get your head straight. But if you're at work, then you're on your game, not hanging outside potential crime scenes smoking yourself silly like a moody teenager.'

Jones removed the unlit cigarette and stared open-mouthed at Phillips.

'Bov tells me you've taken this case personally.'

'Did he, now?'

'Yes he did.'

'Well, he's a fine one to talk; he's not exactly firing on all cylinders either,' said Jones petulantly.

'And what's that supposed to mean?'

Jones's shoulders sagged and he looked away. 'Nothing. Ignore me. I'm just venting.'

Phillips stared at Jones in silence until he turned back to face her. She could see the pain etched on his face, and she softened. 'Look, I know you think you were too hard on Shaw last night and that caused her to jump in front of a tram this morning, but I know you too well to believe that. You're the best copper I've ever worked with and you know where the line is. If she did jump, then her state of mind had to be incredibly fragile in the first place. People don't do something like that after just one police interview, no matter how tough it might have been.'

Jones closed his eyes and exhaled loudly. 'God, what a mess.'

Just then, Phillips's phone rang. She pulled it from her pocket. 'I want you to hear this,' she said as she answered it. 'You're on speaker, Entwistle. I'm here with Jones. Have you found anything?'

'Yes, but only from one camera at the moment, which is part of the main Council CCTV system in St Peter's Square. I've requested footage of the tram stop platforms from Metrolink, but that'll take a couple of hours to come through.'

'So what can you see on the stuff you've got?'

'The angle's not great, but it captures her falling from the platform onto the track, just as the tram pulls into the stop.'

'How does she fall?' asked Phillips.

'How do you mean?'

'Does she fall forwards, backwards, head-first?'

'Oh right, I see. Head-first with her arms out in front of her, kind of like she's lost her balance at the edge of a pool.'

'How many jumpers have you ever seen dive in front of a train like that? They always jump up and out,' said Phillips. 'Was there anyone behind her?'

'A few people actually. It's hard to see for sure, but there was defi-

nitely a surge of movement from one guy right behind just before she fell.'

Phillips continued, 'If you had to bet money on it Entwistle, would you say she jumped or she was pushed?'

'Like I say, it's hard to say for sure, but from this angle, it looks to me like she could have been pushed.'

Jones's posture seemed to straighten in an instant and his features softened. 'So, maybe it wasn't my fault?'

'What wasn't your fault?' asked Entwistle sounding confused.

'Nothing. Never mind,' said Phillips. 'Look, we're going to be here for a while, so make sure you chase up the Metrolink footage and find out who was behind her when she dived off the platform. Call us the moment you find anything.'

'Will do, Guv.'

Phillips ended the call and smiled at Jones. 'Bet you wish you hadn't started smoking again now, don't you?'

Jones chortled. 'What? Like a moody teenager, you mean?'

'Yeah. Sorry about that. I—'

'You were right, Guv.' Jones cut her off. 'I'm the one that should be sorry. I made it all about me and I wasn't pulling my weight.'

Phillips pulled out two pairs of latex gloves and handed one to Jones. 'I've got extra large for the gorilla in there,' she said, lightening the mood.

Jones laughed. 'For Bov and his banana fingers, you mean?'

'Yeah,' chuckled Phillips, then led the way back into Shaw's apartment.

For the next hour, the team painstakingly searched the small apartment, trying to piece together Shaw's last hours in her home. Frustratingly, they found nothing out of the ordinary whatsoever.

Dejected, they gathered at the edge of the lounge, where it connected with the small semi-open plan kitchen. Phillips blew her lips. 'Does it look any different to last night?'

'Tidier maybe, but not by much. I mean, it was hardly a mess or anything,' said Jones.

It was getting pretty warm in the small space with three bodies moving around.

'I'm bloody roasting. I could do with a breather,' said Bovalino as he stepped to one side and squeezed past Jones towards the narrow hallway. As he did, his broad shoulder caught a picture frame, causing it to fall to the floor and smash. He looked down and then back at Jones and Phillips, his expression like that of a child caught up to no good. 'Ooops!'

'What was it you said about banana fingers, Jonesy?' joked Phillips.

Bovalino stepped into the kitchen and grabbed the small waste bin, then bent down to pick up the broken pieces. Something stopped him in his tracks. 'What's this?' he said as he stood up and inspected the back of the frame.

'What have you found?' asked Phillips.

'I dunno, but it looks electrical.'

Phillips moved to get a closer look at the small circular object that had been attached to the frame. It had a tiny piece of wire hanging out of the base. Bovalino handed it over and she squinted, holding it up to the light for a long moment as Jones moved next to her. Her voice was a whisper. 'Maybe it's me being paranoid,' she whispered, 'but is this a listening device?'

Jones brow wrinkled. 'As in a *bug*?'

Phillips nodded as they both continued to stare at it, then took a photo of it on her phone and sent it through to Entwistle with the message:

Any ideas what this is? An audio bug, maybe?

Next, she turned her attention to Bovalino. 'Pass me an evidence bag will you, Bov?'

She placed the picture frame inside and handed the bag back to Bovalino. 'Get that over to the Digital Surveillance

Team. See if they can identify it.' She turned to Jones. 'In the meantime, I want a forensic team to go through this place with a fine-toothed comb.'

'Jesus, Guv,' said Jones as he pulled out his phone. 'This case gets weirder by the minute.'

'Doesn't it?' Phillips chewed her bottom lip as she considered what they had potentially uncovered. 'And I have a horrible feeling it's only gonna get worse!'

42

Whilst Bovalino and Jones hightailed it over to the Digital Surveillance Team on the second floor at Ashton House, Phillips stayed behind at Shaw's apartment to wait for Andy Evans and the rest of his forensic team. After debriefing Evans outside the apartment on the events of the morning – and explaining her own paranoia regarding the potential listening device – she left him and the team to their work, with strict instructions to call her immediately if they found anything else.

Thirty minutes later, the full team reconvened in the conference room of the Major Crimes Unit. Entwistle had connected his laptop to the big screen in readiness for the debrief.

Phillips took a seat at the head of the large conference table, facing the projector screen. 'How did you get on with Digital Surveillance?' she asked looking at Jones and Bovalino.

'They're pretty sure it's a bug of some kind,' said Bovalino, 'but not something commonly used in the UK,'

'That would make sense,' Entwistle said as he activated his

laptop screen. 'I had a look online and I couldn't find the exact match to the picture you sent me, but it definitely looks like this kind of stuff being sold from Russian and Chinese sites.'

A web page filled with devices similar to the one found in Shaw's apartment appeared on the big screen.

Phillips stared at the screen and her brow furrowed. 'Why would Wong or Shing, or anyone, for that matter, want to bug Cindy Shaw's apartment?'

'She was Carpenter's PA, so surely it had to be something in connection to her. Maybe she was working with her, trying to stop the development, somehow?' said Jones.

'Playing both sides, you mean?' Phillips said. 'Unless she was an amazing actress, I can't see it. And besides, according to Don Townsend, they weren't close at all. In fact, he said Carpenter considered Shaw to be Jennings's hire.'

The team fell silent for a moment as they each processed the information so far. Then Phillips's phone rang. She answered it eagerly. 'Evans, have you found another one?'

'Yes, Ma'am, we have. In fact, we've found five more – one in each of the rooms – positioned in the same way as the first, behind picture frames.'

'My God,' said Phillips, drawing raised eyebrows from the team.

'This place is wired for sound. There isn't a single spot in the whole apartment that doesn't have one.'

'Right. I want a full forensic sweep of the whole house; you're looking for fingerprints, fibres, DNA, footprints, anything that might help us identify who put the devices in there.'

'I thought you might say that,' said Evans. *'We've already started.'*

'Excellent work, Evans,' said Phillips.

'Thank you, Ma'am.'

Phillips ended the call and briefed the team. 'There's bugs in every single room.'

'You're kidding?' said Jones.

'No, I'm not. Evans has found five, so that's six including the one Bov discovered.'

'That's hardcore,' said Entwistle.

'Whoever put them in had to have had free rein of the flat in order to install them, so it had to have been when she was out for a long period of time,' said Phillips.

Jones nodded. 'Like all day at work?'

Phillips continued, 'So whoever it was would've known her routine.'

'Could it have been Jennings?' asked Bovalino.

'I'm not sure I see him as an espionage kind of guy, Bov, but he may well have helped whoever it was by telling them Shaw's movements. He would have known them better than anyone.'

Jones's eyes narrowed. 'The neighbour, Bov.'

Bov recoiled. 'You think the old lady is responsible?'

'No, you daft bugger. I'm thinking what she said about Shaw being burgled recently. Could that have been when the bugs went in?'

Phillips sat to attention. 'Aaron Carpenter said that they had been burgled too. A few months before Carpenter was killed.' She pulled out her phone and called Evans back.

He answered promptly. *'Ma'am?'*

'When you did the sweep of Victoria Carpenter's house, did you ever find anything that resembled one of those listening devices?'

'I'm sorry, Ma'am, remind me which one was Carpenter's? We see so many crime scenes.'

'The hanging in Withington.'

'Oh, yes. No, nothing. But, now you mention it, I do remember finding sticky residue on a number of picture frames at the house. We tested it, but it was nothing more than glue and matched the kind of

adhesive you'd find on picture hooks you'd stick to the wall. It went in my report, but it seemed of no consequence.'

'How are the bugs fixed to the frames?' asked Phillips.

'Hang on a minute,' said Evans. He moved the phone away to talk to one of his team. A few moments later, he returned. *'We've just removed one, and the mark left behind is almost identical to what we found at the Carpenter house.'*

'She was bugged too,' said Phillips in a low voice. 'Thanks, Evans,' she added, then rang off.

Jones's eyes were wide. 'What did he say, Guv?'

'It looks like the Carpenters' house was likely bugged too, but they must have been removed before she was killed.'

'Have we stumbled into an MI5 operation here?' said Entwistle, half joking, just as his laptop pinged and an email icon appeared on the big screen. 'I think this is the CCTV footage from Metrolink.'

The team watched the big screen as Entwistle opened the link within the email and downloaded the files, which opened automatically.

'Shaw went under the tram around 8.30 this morning,' said Phillips as Entwistle searched the footage for the correct period of time. 'Start at 8 and let's see what comes up.'

Entwistle found what he was looking for and pressed play.

For the next twenty minutes, the team watched the video in real time as people filed onto the platform and trams came and went every few minutes. At 8.19 a.m., Shaw could be seen clearly as she walked onto the north-bound platform and stood with her arms folded. She was carrying a large handbag over her shoulder and, wearing wireless headphones, stared off into space. The Rochdale tram approached at 8.27 a.m. and Shaw turned to face it, along with those around her, as it drew closer to the platform edge. Suddenly someone wearing a hooded top rushed to her back, and a second later, Shaw fell head-first in front of the tram.

'That's him!' shouted Phillips.

Entwistle stopped the video and stared in silence at the screen.

'Fuck,' Jones said, shaking his head.

'Play it again,' said Phillips. She got up from her chair and moved to take a closer look. She turned to Entwistle. 'Do you have video from the south-bound platform?

Entwistle scanned through the file names, then nodded and pulled up the video. They watched in silence as footage from the opposite platform played out. Once again, they could see Shaw standing, arms folded, then stepping forwards in readiness for the Rochdale tram's arrival. From this angle, they had a better view of the hooded man, but, frustratingly, his face remained covered by the hood as he moved in behind Shaw, then shoved her in the back and rushed away without waiting to see the outcome of his actions.

'See where he goes,' said Phillips.

Flip-flopping between Metrolink cameras and Council CCTV, they were able to track him until he disappeared down a small alleyway. After that, they could find no trace of him.

'He's vanished, Guv,' said Entwistle.

'Damn it!' Phillips slammed her hand on the desk in frustration. 'How the hell can he just disappear in a city with CCTV on nearly every corner?'

'Maybe he knows the blind spots?' said Jones.

Phillips dropped back into her chair and stared in silence at the frozen image of Shaw falling from the platform. 'We need to find this guy now. Entwistle, I want every camera across the city checked.'

'Got it.'

'I'll head over to see Aaron Carpenter, find out more about their burglary,' said Phillips. 'Jonesy and Bov, you guys go back through ANPR and CCTV in Withington and Droylsden the nights Carpenter died and Shaw was burgled. See if you can find anything to connect the two.'

'Yes, Guv,' said both men in unison.

'Right. I know it's late and we've all got places we'd rather be, but let's get to it,' said Phillips as she picked up her car keys and headed for the door.

43

Aaron Carpenter looked like a haunted man as he opened the front door. In just over a week, he appeared to have aged ten years; the dark shadows that framed his eyes were in stark contrast to his almost opaque skin; his posture reminiscent of a frail geriatric.

'I'm sorry to bother you, Mr Carpenter, but could I have a quick word?'

Carpenter nodded and led the way into the house and through to the lounge room. An array of fast food cartons and boxes littered almost every available surface, and a half-empty bottle of whisky sat in the middle of the smoked-glass coffee table. He flopped down onto the sofa and muted the large television in the corner of the room, which was showing a classic Manchester United football match.

Phillips took a seat in the armchair nearest to him. 'How have you been?' she asked softly.

Carpenter scoffed and appeared intoxicated. 'How do *you* think I've been?'

'Is your sister still checking in on you?'

Carpenter nodded. 'Every few days. She comes in, tells me off for drinking too much, cleans up and leaves.'

'And when was she last here?' said Phillips, casting her eyes around the filthy room.

Carpenter shrugged. 'Dunno. I can't remember.'

It was clear Phillips would struggle to get much from him in this mood, but she pressed on regardless. Even the slightest detail right now could be the breakthrough they were looking for. 'When we last spoke, you said you suffered a burglary a couple of months ago.'

Carpenter nodded again.

'You said you thought they'd been disturbed, as nothing much had been taken. Can you remember any details of what *was* actually stolen, other than Vicky's laptop?'

'Not really. A bit of cash, I think, that we use to pay the window cleaner. It was on the side near the microwave, as he was due the next day.'

'Anything else?' asked Phillips.

Carpenter's head lolled back against the sofa and he stared at the ceiling for a long moment. She couldn't tell whether he was thinking hard or struggling to remember through the booze. 'I honestly can't recall,' he said eventually.

Phillips took a deep breath as she attempted to control her mounting frustration. It was time for a different approach. 'Would you mind if I take a look around the house?'

'Be my guest,' said Carpenter as he leaned forwards and poured himself a large whisky, then unmuted the TV.

Phillips got up from the armchair. 'Thank you.'

Leaving him to his drink and the football, she made her way into the kitchen. It was even filthier than the lounge; plates and dishes strewn across the worktops, with yet more used food cartons lying around. 'What a mess,' she mumbled under her breath as she walked through. Pulling on a pair of latex gloves, she soon found what she was looking for: a large replica Kandinsky print within a heavy frame, secured to the wall. She lifted it off and inspected the back. Sure enough, she came across a sticky circular residue like Evans had described. She took a photo on her phone, then returned it to the wall. Next, she moved into the hallway, where she removed a number of pictures for inspection. The first three were clean, but the final frame, situated close to the front door and above the landline phone, boasted another sticky circle on its reverse. Again, she took a photo and hung the picture back up. For the next ten minutes, Phillips worked her way through all the rooms on the ground floor, finding yet more evidence that listening devices had potentially been removed. She took a seat inside Carpenter's study and called Jones.

'Guv?'

'I'm at Carpenter's house. So far, I've found four picture frames with what looks like evidence of there having been listening devices on the backs of them. And that's just *downstairs*.'

'Bloody hell. Whoever put them in wasn't taking any chances, were they?' said Jones.

'You're not kidding.'

'We think we may have found something significant ourselves, Guv,' said Jones.

Phillips's pulse quickened. 'Go on.'

'You'll recall the night Carpenter was killed, we spotted a cloned vehicle in Didsbury?'

'Yeah.'

'Well, that same car was also picked up in Burnage the night of the Carpenter burglary, as well as on Ashton New Road – about half a mile from Shaw's home – on the night she claimed to have been burgled, too.'

'They have to be linked,' said Phillips.

'No doubt about it.'

'But how do we connect them?'

'Therein lies the problem,' said Jones.

Phillips sat in silence for a moment as she cast her eyes around Carpenter's study and considered her next move. Her attention was drawn to a newspaper cutting on the desk, of Victoria and Eric Jennings standing on a building site wearing hard hats and high-viz vests over their suits. The article was entitled *'MANCHESTER'S SKYLINE – IN SAFE HANDS.'*

'I think we need another run at Jennings; see how he's taken Shaw's death,' said Phillips.

'Not a bad shout. Do you want me and Bov to pay him a visit?'

'No. I'm only ten minutes from his. I can do it. You guys get off home and we can reconvene first thing tomorrow.'

'Well, do you want me *to come with you? I can be there in half an hour and I've got nothing else on.'*

'No,' said Phillips. 'I'll get nothing more from Carpenter tonight. I'm pretty sure he's hammered, so I'll say my goodbyes and head over to Jennings now.'

'Seriously, Guv. After what's happened in the past, I'm not happy about you going into a suspect's home alone.'

'I'm touched, Jonesy, but I'm sure I can handle Jennings on my own. He can't be more than eight stone wet through. Don't worry, I'll be fine. Look, if it makes you feel better, I'll call you when I'm done, ok?'

'Ok, Guv. Just be careful.'

'I will.' Phillips ended the call and made her way back through to the lounge room, where she found Carpenter snoring loudly on the couch. She watched him for a moment. Her heart went out to him. She was sure that battling grief with whisky would not end well, and hoped his sister could get through to him sooner rather than later.

Tiptoeing out of the room, she moved quickly to the front door and let herself out.

~

PHILLIPS DROVE at a steady pace down Palatine Road towards Northenden. As she approached Withington Golf Club on her left, her phone began to ring through the in-car speaker system; a landline number she didn't recognise appeared on the digital display on the dash, but she accepted the call. 'DCI Phillips.'

'Phillips. You have to help me! My life is in danger!' said the agitated male voice.

'Who is this?'

'Eric Jennings.' The words sounded slurred.

'Have you been drinking, Mr Jennings?'

He ignored the question. *'You have to protect me. Someone's trying to kill me.'*

Phillips continued on towards his house. '*Who*'s trying to kill you?'

'I can't say over the phone.'

'Are they an immediate threat to you?'

'I don't know. I can't see anyone at the moment, but that doesn't mean they're not watching me.'

'Lock the doors and get away from the windows. I'm on my way to your house as we speak. I'm five minutes out.'

'In Northenden?'

'Yes, I'm just passing along the High Street.'

'I'm not there.'

'Well, where are you?'

'The Lake District.'

'The Lakes?'

'Yes. I have a house here.'

'Right. Let me call the Cumbria Police for you—'

'No! I'll only deal with you.'

Phillips was certain Jennings *was* drunk. 'With respect, Mr Jennings, if you feel you're in imminent danger, then the safest and quickest thing to do is to call the Cumbria Police.'

'I'm not putting my life in the hands of the local plod! I need you.*'*

'Eric. I'm almost two hours away. If you ring the local pol—'

'I know who killed Carpenter and Shaw,' Jennings cut her off.

Phillips pulled the car over to the side of the road and brought it to a stop.

'What did you say?'

'I know who killed Victoria Carpenter and Cindy Shaw, and I'm scared that they're coming for me next.'

'Who is?'

'I want to go into witness protection!' ranted Jennings.

'Witness protection? That's not a simple thing to arrange, Eric. I need to know why you think your life is in danger to organise something as complex and costly as that.

'Because I know too much about their illegal operations, just like Cindy did – and they killed her.'

'Who did?,'

'The Triads! The Triads are gonna kill me.'

'Why Eric? Why would the Triads want to kill you?'

'Because of the rezoning of St John's Gardens,' slurred Jennings. *'They're the ones that have been pulling the strings, and now it's been approved—'*

'It's been approved?' Phillips cut him off. 'Since when?'

'Since yesterday's meeting, and less than a day later, Cindy was murdered. I'm telling you, they're removing all the loose ends, and I'm next on the list.'

Despite Jennings's obvious drunken state, his story certainly fit with Phillips's theory that Gold Star Trading were behind the St John's development. There was no way she could risk leaving him in the hands of the local police if the Triads *were* after him. 'Ok. I'll drive up to your place, now.'

'Oh, thank God,' said Jennings. *'I'll give you the address.'*

'I have it on file. It'll probably take an hour and a half to get to you. So, like I said before, lock the doors, stay away from the windows, and whatever you do, do not call anybody else until I get there. Understood?'

She heard as Jennings swallowed hard on the other end of the line. *'Ok, whatever you say. But please hurry.'*

Phillips reassured him she would be there as soon as she could, then hung up.

Next, she called Jones.

'That was quick, Guv,' he said cheerfully.

Phillips wasted no time. 'There's a been a change of plan. Are you still in the office?'

'Yeah, I was just about to head off.'

'What about Bov and Entwistle?'

'They left a couple of minutes ago. They'll be heading downstairs as we speak.'

'Go and get them – then find me Jennings's address in the Lakes and call me back.'

'What's going on Guv?'

'I don't have time to explain, Jonesy. Just get the guys and that address, and call me back. I'll tell you everything then. *Hurry.*'

44

Ninety minutes later, Phillips pulled her car onto the gravel drive outside Jennings's holiday home, located on a small, dark lane about half a mile outside of Grasmere. The nearest neighbour was a few hundred meters away, and for a fleeting moment, as she gazed up to the small, single-storey cottage cast in darkness, she wondered if Jennings had made a run for it. She sat in silence, feeling suddenly tired; the jet lag was stubbornly refusing to leave her system. Exhaling loudly, she straightened her ponytail and refreshed her spectacles.

A moment later, she approached the front door and tried the handle. As expected, it was locked. Pulling out her phone, she returned Jennings's call, but the signal was weak because of the surrounding terrain, so it failed. She tried again a couple more times, and as it finally connected, she could hear his landline ringing inside the house. After what felt like an age, he answered.

'*Hello?*' His voice was low and tentative.

'It's Phillips. I'm out front.'

Jennings ended the call, and a few seconds later she could

see his silhouette through the small glass panel in the middle of the front door. The lock released, and he opened it on the chain and peered out into the darkness.

'Are you gonna let me in, then?' asked Phillips impatiently.

Jennings removed the chain, then opened the door, standing behind it as though it was a shield. She stepped inside and waited for him to lock it. The whole place smelt stale, like it had been locked up without being used for a sustained period of time.

'Are you alone?' said Jennings, his speech more slurred than on their earlier call.

'Yes, but my team is en route as we speak. They should be here in twenty minutes or so.'

'Can they be trusted?' he said as he walked past her and made his way to the rear of the house, still wearing his work shirt and trousers over stockinged feet.

Phillips couldn't help but feel slightly affronted that a man of Jennings's supposed questionable behaviour would question the integrity of *her* team. 'Yes, they can be trusted. They've saved my arse on more than one occasion, I can tell you.'

'Well, let's hope they can do the same for me,' Jennings said as they made their way through to the small kitchen at the heart of the house. A single table lamp lit the room, and Phillips noted the layout from where she stood; one hallway ran from the kitchen to what she assumed were the bedrooms, and a narrow, windowless corridor appeared to lead to a rear door.

Jennings took a seat. In front of him was a bottle of brandy with a large measure poured into a glass, and a metal golf club was positioned against the wall to his left. Phillips glanced at it and wondered what damage – if any – it could do in the hands of a scrawny man like Jennings. At this moment in time, with booze coursing through his veins, he looked as if just picking it up would be a challenge.

Phillips took a chair at the table opposite him. 'So, who killed Vicky and Cindy, Eric?'

Jennings took a gulp from the brandy, then winced and made an unnecessary amount of noise after swallowing it. 'Once I'm in witness protection, I'll tell you everything, but not before.'

With her head fogged from jet lag and fatigue, Phillips bit her lip as she stifled her growing irritation. She had never warmed to Jennings, and his current drunken state and dramatic performance was getting on her last nerve. 'Look, if you really *do* know who killed Cindy, then you need to tell me, now.'

Jennings was defiant. '*Not* until I'm in witness protection.'

Phillips exhaled loudly and folded her arms. 'I'm curious. What exactly do you think witness protection looks like?'

Jennings drained his glass with the same dramatic flair as before and poured himself another large measure. As he placed the bottle back on the table, Phillips grabbed it and moved it out of his reach, much to his apparent chagrin.

'Well, you put me in a remote house somewhere with armed police to protect me,' said Jennings.

Phillips nodded. 'I see, and what gave you that idea?'

'I've seen it on the TV enough times.'

Phillips opened her mouth to respond when her phone began to ring. It was Jones, and a welcome relief from Jennings. She stepped away from the table and into the hall to take it. 'How far away are you?'

'Just a couple of minutes, according to the Sat Nav.'

'Wow, that was quick.'

'Bov's driving, Guv.'

'Say no more,' chuckled Phillips.

'So, any sign of the Triads?'

'Not so far.'

'And how's Jennings?'

Phillips lowered her voice. 'Pissed and bloody annoying. He's acting like he's turning States Evidence in an episode of "Law and Order".'

'Has he given up anything on the Triads yet?' asked Jones.

'No. He point blank refuses to tell me anything of value until we get him into a safe house with armed guards stationed along the perimeter,' said Phillips sarcastically.

Jones chortled. *'Been watching American TV, has he?'*

'Yep. He's one of *those*. An armchair litigator.'

'God. That's all we need.'

'And like I say, he's pissed, so not making much sense at all.'

'Do you think he's telling the truth about all this, Guv?'

'I dunno, Jonesy. He's so drunk it's hard to tell.'

Jones was quiet for a moment, before answering. *'Looks like we're here, Guv. I can see your car.'*

'Good. Tell Bov to park up on the road with a clear view of the house. I want Entwistle to stay in the vehicle and watch for anyone coming or going. You and Bov check the gardens, then come inside. I'll let you in through the back door. I'm gonna make some coffee, see if we can't sober up our star witness'.

'No worries. We'll see you in a few minutes.'

Walking back into the kitchen, she watched Jennings for a moment, hunched in the chair cradling his brandy, his eyes barely open. It took all her strength not to slap him into sobriety. She prayed he was telling the truth, otherwise she'd have some explaining to do to Superintendent Fox. Her boss would want to know why she had dragged her already overworked and expensive team a hundred miles out of Manchester in the middle of a murder investigation. Staring down at him as his head lolled forwards, she was beginning to think she had made a mistake.

A few minutes later, she heard the rattle of thin glass from the rear outside door and moved along the corridor to let Jones and Bovalino into the small porch. Both men carried heavy-duty torches in their hands, and the big Italian was forced to bend down to stop his head from cracking on the ancient door lintel.

'They didn't make these houses for people who were six-feet-four, did they, Bov,' chuckled Phillips, as she gestured for them to follow her through to the kitchen. 'Is Entwistle ok?'

'Yep, sat on the street watching the house as you asked,' said Jones from behind her.

'And what about the gardens?'

'All clear.'

By now, Jennings was asleep at the table, chin resting on his chest and breathing heavily.

'You weren't kidding about him being drunk, were you, Guv?' Jones said.

Phillips shook her head and blew her lips, pointing at the brandy on the side. 'I reckon he must have demolished half of that tonight.'

Jones moved to pick up the bottle and inspected the label. 'Supermarket's own brand. He's hardly a connoisseur, then?'

'Having seen him throwing it back like it's water, I don't think he's drinking it for the taste,' said Phillips.

'So what's the plan of action?' asked Bovalino.

'Well, first up, we need to sober him up.'

Bovalino moved to Jennings's left shoulder, his eyes glistening in the low light. 'You want me to chuck him in a cold shower?'

Phillips smiled at the thought for a moment, but decided to try a less drastic approach initially. 'Let's try coffee first, shall we?' she said, eliciting a disappointed look from the big Italian. '*But*, if that doesn't work, Bov, you have my full permission to dunk him in the bath!'

Bovalino grinned. 'I'll put the kettle on, then,' he said, taking off his coat.

45

Patience had always been the watchword of his work. He never rushed, and always ensured he'd done a thorough recce of a kill site before he made his final move. However, tonight he cursed himself for not taking full advantage of the target being alone when he had arrived an hour earlier.

Since then, he had taken his position amongst the trees in the rear garden and watched Eric Jennings sitting in almost total darkness through the window with the aid of his night-vision goggles, which cast everything in green. He had taken his time to suss out the floorplan of the building, as well as the surrounding land. Noting that Jennings was drinking heavily had initially given him a false sense of security that this would be a simple hit. That had all changed the moment the police-woman had knocked on Jennings's door thirty minutes earlier. His first instinct in that moment had been to take them both out. However, reinforcements had arrived just a few minutes later, and entered the house through the rear of the building. For a moment he considered aborting, but that would not be acceptable to the family. Jennings had become a liability that needed to be eradicated. The additional bodies made things problematic, but not impossible; the kill had to happen tonight. With so much at stake, there was no way Jennings could be allowed to live to share what he knew.

Reassessing the house, which now contained four targets, he made the necessary adjustments to his plan. He checked his weapons for the final time before securing them about his person, and noted the time; it was approaching 11 p.m.

Phase one of his plan involved taking out the lookout stationed in the car on the street. In his experience, attacking a man in a vehicle was not without complications – something he could live without tonight, what with four other targets to neutralise. So he decided the best option was to lure him out. Pulling a small micro-torch from his pocket, he switched it on and pointed it in the direction of the man in the car. Then, he began to tap out S-O-S in Morse code, over and over. A few seconds later, the car door opened and the driver got out.

From his position within the canopy of leaves, he watched as the bright green glare of a torch lit up the pathway to the side of the house, bobbing and weaving in the right hand of a young-looking man. He held a phone in his left hand and appeared athletically built and muscular.

For a brief moment, his pulse quickened as his adrenaline spiked and his body prepared for the fight. It was a chemical reaction he had experienced a hundred times before. His training kicked in automatically, allowing him to access well-practiced techniques to slow his racing heart in a matter of seconds. With his nervous system soon back under control, he stared out at the young man as he stepped closer to his position.

He held his hands out in front of him – the tips of his thumbs touching in readiness – as the young man came to a stop on the other side of the bushes, virtually on top of him. The torch beam arced left and right across the canopy.

He watched on; ready to pounce.

The young man was just inches from his face now and staring straight at him, blissfully unaware that his opponent lurked before him.

He would wait for the exact moment to strike. Swallowing gently, he took a deep breath in and let it out silently as his fingers flexed in front of him.

The young man took one last glance at the bushes before he turned back towards the house.

In that split second, he pounced, thrusting his open hands out through the leaves, clamping them around the young man's throat, then yanking him backwards into the darkness.

46

With Jennings onto his second cup of coffee, he showed no signs of either sobering up or sharing the name of Carpenter's or Shaw's killer, much to Phillips's mounting frustration. As the time passed 11.15 p.m., the headache that had been building from the base of her skull for the last hour became unbearable. She felt sure it was partly due to the stress of the stalled investigation, and partly due to her lack of sleep over the last week. After checking Jennings's cupboards for pain killers – without luck – she took her leave and headed back to her car. As a seasoned detective who'd spent most of her life under pressure, she was no stranger to headaches. As such, she always carried a pack in the glove compartment. In truth, she was glad of the break from Jennings and his drunken rambling. She stepped out of the house and filled her lungs with the fresh country air, then made her way along the driveway lit by the full moon.

The car beeped as she released the central locking, which in turn activated the lights within the car's interior. Her footsteps crunched on the gravel as she approached it. Dropping down into the passenger seat a moment later, she pulled open the glove box, retrieved the pack of pain killers and slipped a couple of tablets into her mouth. Washing them down with a swig of water from the half-drunk bottle in the central console, she breathed heavily through her nose as she dropped her head back onto the headrest and stared at the house through the car's windscreen. The inside was fully lit now, with the team having conducted a full sweep of the interior on arrival. Unlike Shaw's and Carpenter's houses, they had found no signs of listening devices. Phillips had a gnawing feeling that, rather than being at genuine risk, Jennings was simply drunk and being dramatic. As Phillips replayed the strange events of the last few weeks in her mind, her own paranoia began to kick in. Was this whole night just an elaborate ruse? Had Jennings drawn them away from Manchester for a reason? Nothing was beyond the realms of possibility. This was, after all, an investigation like no other she had encountered.

Sliding out of the car, she stepped up and closed the door, casting her eye in the direction of the squad car. To her amazement, the car looked empty. Entwistle knew better than to leave his post.

Phillips's pulse quickened as she moved at pace towards the car and yanked open the door in one movement. With no sign of life, she pulled her phone from her pocket and dialled Entwistle's number, but the call failed. Inspecting her phone, she realised she was struggling for signal once again, and began to move back towards the house in search of a connection. As she returned to the gravel drive, she spotted a couple of signal bars on the home screen and dialled again. This time it connected, and to her surprise, she could hear his phone ringing somewhere in the nearby garden. 'Entwistle!' she shouted. No response. 'Entwistle! Where are you?' she repeated as she ran in the direction of the phone. A second later, she found it lying on the grass next to Entwistle's torch. There was no sign of her detective.

Every fibre in Phillips's body told her something was seriously wrong. She charged back into the house through the front door.

At that exact moment, the entire house was plunged into darkness.

~

'Entwistle's missing!' Phillips said as she raced into the kitchen, where she found Jones and Bovalino standing motionless in the dark. The only light flooded through the windows from the moon.

'What the fuck's going on?' whispered Jones.

'He's here! He's come to kill me!' Jennings wailed with the pitch and volume of a banshee.

'Shut up, you idiot!' growled Phillips in a low voice.

'You have to protect me. I don't want to die,' Jennings continued a high volume.

Phillips grabbed him by the shoulder. 'I'll bloody kill you *myself* if you don't fucking shut up.'

Bovalino flicked the light switch on and off on the wall next to him. 'It's dead, Guv.'

Jones stepped into the hallway and tried the switch out there. 'Same here.'

Both men turned on their torches, and Jones handed his to Phillips.

Bovalino arced the beam of his torchlight to scan the room.

'I think it's time we got you out of harm's way,' said Phillips as she pulled Jennings up from his chair.

The sound of smashing glass coming from the direction of the back door stopped everyone in their tracks. Bovalino swivelled and stepped forwards to see down the small corridor that led to the back door. He shone his torch down towards the rear porch.

'Bov. Go and check that out,' whispered Phillips.

Bovalino didn't respond. Instead he stood rooted to the spot, his eyes fixed on the beam of light ahead of him.

'Bov!' said Phillips, as loud as she dared, but still he didn't respond.

'I'll go,' said Jones, and stepped past the big Italian, grabbed the torch out of his hand and disappeared down the corridor.

'Bov. What's going on?' growled Phillips as he remained static.

Jones's footsteps bounced off the walls as he edged across the ancient stone slabs of the cottage floor.

'Bov!' said Phillips again.

Bovalino appeared to snap back into the moment, glanced quickly at Phillips, then headed off after his partner along the narrow corridor.

Phillips turned to Jennings now. 'Does your bathroom have a lock on the door?'

Jennings nodded frantically.

'Where is it?'

'Down the end of the hall,' he said, pointing behind Phillips's head in the direction of the bedrooms.

'Take me to it, now.'

As Jones stepped tentatively towards the back door, he could see shards of broken glass on the ground, glistening like diamonds in the light from his torch. The door itself was ajar and, aside from the missing glass, appeared to be intact. He swallowed hard as he moved closer. A moment later, Bovalino appeared at his shoulder.

'Is there anyone there?' the big Italian whispered. Jones could hear the fear in his voice.

'I dunno,' Jones said as they edged forwards together until they reached the door.

Jones trained his torch directly onto the broken pane of glass and slowly wrapped his finger round the door handle. His heart beat like a drum as he pulled it open.

In that instant, there was a flash of light as someone rushed from the darkness towards them. Instinctively, Jones raised his arms to protect himself. Something razor-sharp sliced through his wrist, over and over again. He cried out in agony as he dropped backwards to the floor. He could feel hot blood escaping from his body. From above him came a loud, buzzing noise, and a second later, Bovalino crashed in a heap on top of him, trapping him against the cold stone slabs.

WITH THE TORCH lighting their way, Phillips was following Jennings along the hallway towards the bathroom when a blood-curdling scream caused her to stop and turn back in the direction of the kitchen. Jones and Bovalino shouted, followed by the sounds of a scuffle, a heavy thud, then nothing but deathly silence. Pulling her phone from her pocket, she attempted to call 999. But, thanks to the thick walls in the belly of the house, there was little chance of a signal. 'Damn it!' she growled, but tried the number again, in the vain hope the call would be diverted to another network. After two failed attempts, she gave up.

She turned back to face Jennings, who stood at the bathroom door behind her. He was about to step inside when she stopped him. 'Wait! Let me check it first,' she said in a low whisper, then moved past him.

Arcing the torch around the small space, she noted it had a bath, a toilet and an ancient hand basin with a metal frame. Much to her relief, it was empty. She signalled for Jennings to step inside and pushed the door closed behind them before drawing him closer. 'Are there any other ways in or out of this place besides the main doors?' she whispered.

Jennings's eyes were wide with fear. He swallowed hard. 'Just the main bedroom. A set of patio doors.'

'Which is the main bedroom?'

Jennings pointed towards the bathroom door behind Phillips's head. 'It's the room directly opposite.'

'Ok. I want you to lock the door, lie down in the bath and keep hold of this.' She handed him her phone. 'Keep trying 999. If you get through, tell them you're with the police and have a Code Zero. Get them to send armed police immediately, ok?'

Jennings nodded frantically. 'Where are *you* going?'

'Jones and Bovalino could be seriously hurt. I can't just leave them there.'

'What about *him*?'

Phillips locked eyes with Jennings eyes now. 'Who's out there, Eric? What am I up against?'

Jennings was visibly shaking now, his breathing shallow. 'I only know him as Shing,' he whispered.

'*Zhang* Shing?'

'I don't know. I just call him Shing.'

'Did Shing kill Vicky?'

'Yes.'

'And Cindy?'

Jennings nodded.

Phillips had been right about Zhang Shing all along. Now all she had to do was stay alive long enough to tell someone about him. Easier said than done right now, she thought.

She took a deep breath in as she attempted to slow her heart rate. 'Are you ready?'

'I think so,' said Jennings.

Phillips placed her finger to her lips, then turned and tentatively opened the door.

Casting her flashlight down the corridor, she saw nothing and no one, so stepped out into the hallway and turned to face Jennings, her voice barely audible now. 'Remember, lie in the bath and don't come out. And if you get through to the police, it's Code Zero and we need an armed response, ok?'

Jennings repeated it back to her.

'Now, lock the door behind me.'

Jennings nodded. Then suddenly his eyes bulged as he stared at something over Phillips's shoulder. She swivelled back to face the bedroom and an icy chill ran the length of her body as her eyes landed on the silhouette of a man standing before an open door ahead of her. In that instant, the man's right hand shot upwards. A blinding flash, followed by the terrifying sound of a silenced gun, filled the air.

Phillips felt the bullet whip passed her head before it tore through Jennings's shoulder. Acting on instinct, she threw herself backwards, pushing him back into the bathroom, where they both fell onto the hard tiled floor. Another muzzled shot rang out, shattering the mirror above their heads. She could hear Shing moving closer as he continued to fire. Scrambling across the floor, she swung her leg and kicked the door shut. The bullets continued to come. Careful to stay as close to the ground as possible, she reached up and turned the lock in the door just as Shing thrust his boot hard into it.

Phillips crawled to where Jennings lay moaning, dark blood pooling under his back from the hole in his shoulder. 'You're gonna be ok, Eric. Stay with me. I'll get you out of this,' she said, as she grabbed a towel and wrapped it around his shoulder.

Shing continued to kick the door but the lock held true.

Phillips prayed it would hold.

Just then, she heard a different sound. Turning towards the door, she watched in horror as the narrow wood panel above the handle splintered and a large metal blade appeared, then immediately disappeared. A second later, there was another thud as the wood began to disintegrate in the frame. The blade came through farther this time. Phillips froze as she recognised it as the kind of metal butcher's cleaver used to execute Wong in Hong Kong.

Trapped, she frantically scanned the tiny bathroom for a weapon. Something, *anything,* that she could use to fend Shing off. She found nothing but the torch.

The blade continued to slice through the wooden panel, and soon a maniacal-looking Shing appeared on the other side, hacking the door with the razor-sharp meat cleaver.

Phillips jumped to her feet and prepared to face him, holding the heavy torch in both hands like a baseball bat.

Shing reached through the broken panel, then unlocked the door. He turned the handle and opened it slowly, a demonic grin spreading across his face as he stared at his quarry. He finally spoke. 'Si wú duì zhèng!' His eyes bulged as he moved the cleaver to his left hand and pulled the pistol from his shoulder holster. 'Si wú duì zhèng!' he repeated as he stepped inside.

Phillips took a swing at him with the torch, but he dodged it with ease and whipped the pistol across her face, catching the muzzle agonisingly on the bridge of her nose. The blow forced her backwards and she fell painfully to the floor, next to Jennings.

Disorientated, and bleeding heavily from both nostrils, she tried her best to shield Jennings. 'Armed police will be in here any moment,' she lied through bubbles of blood.

Shing stepped over Phillips now and placed the muzzle of the gun against the top of her head. 'Si wú duì zhèng!' he said again, before adding 'Goodbye,' in broken English.

Phillips closed her eyes and waited for death.

'Fuck you, you piece of shit!' Bovalino roared as he charged in behind Shing. The big Italian shoved him forwards into the broken mirror above the handbasin with immense force, which caused the cleaver to fall from his hand.

Phillips attempted to get out of the way.

Above her, a rampant Bovalino grabbed Shing by the back of the head, then rammed his forehead down onto the sink with a sickening thud.

'You-fucking-bastard!' he raged, using the words to punctuate each time Shing's head connected with the sink. 'I'll fucking kill you!' he yelled, then grabbed the cleaver from the floor and raised it high into the air.

'Bov! Stop!' shouted Phillips, as she jumped up between him and Shing, who had slumped unconscious to the floor.

Bovalino's eyes danced in his head as he struggled for breath.

'It's ok, Bov. It's over,' said Phillips softly.

Bovalino's eyes remained like saucers, but his breathing slowly began to stabilise.

'It's over, Bov. Stand down. Stand down, mate.'

The big Italian appeared suddenly aware of his surroundings. He lowered the cleaver and stumbled backwards before dropping heavily onto the edge of the bath.

Phillips took a knee and checked Shing's pulse. It was weak and, judging by the state of his face and head, he clearly needed urgent medical attention. Taking no chances, she rolled him into the recovery position, then handcuffed him to the metal frame of the hand basin. 'Where's Jonesy?' she asked.

'Shit! Jonesy,' said Bov, as he dropped the cleaver in the bath, then jumped up and ran out of the room.

Phillips followed close behind. Her heart almost stopped when she spotted Jones lying face down by the back door, soaked in blood.

Bov took a knee and rolled him onto his back. 'Jonesy! Talk to me.'

Jones's skin was almost grey from the massive blood loss. Phillips knelt down and checked his pulse. It was there, but very weak. His left arm had been heavily lacerated by the cleaver in what looked like defensive wounds.

Just then, Entwistle appeared at the back door, looking dazed and confused.

'Where the hell have you been?' shouted Phillips angrily.

'Sorry, Guv. I've just come round in the trees,' he said. Then he spotted Jones's prostate body. 'Jesus. What happened?'

'Shing cut him up with a meat cleaver,' said Bovalino.

'I'll go and get help,' said Entwistle.

'The signal's shit, so you'll need to use the radio in the car. Tell Cumbria Control we need urgent medical support immediately.'

'Got it,' said Entwistle.

'And make sure they send the Air Ambulance!' Phillips shouted after him. 'Because if they don't, Jonesy will bleed out.'

47

MANCHESTER ROYAL INFIRMARY, SURGICAL WARD

THREE DAYS LATER.

Phillips knocked on the door of Jones's private room and leaned through the doorway so she could see him.

'Guv,' he said with a broad smile. He sat up in bed as his wife, Sarah, turned to face the door.

'I'm not disturbing you, am I?'

'Of course you're not,' said Jones.

Sarah got up from the chair. 'Actually, I think I'd better be going. I need to get the kids their tea.'

'Please don't leave on my account,' said Phillips.

Sarah bent down to kiss Jones on the forehead, then turned back to face Phillips. She appeared slightly embarrassed. 'Nice to see you again, Jane,' she said, then headed for the door.

Phillips watched her leave, then turned back to face Jones. 'Was it something I said?'

Jones looked coy. 'More like something *I* said.'

'What do you mean?'

'I told her you knew about the separation and I think she feels embarrassed about it, considering what happened to me.'

Phillips dropped into the seat next to the bed. 'You mean being attacked with a cleaver and almost bleeding to death?'

Jones nodded solemnly, before a wide grin spread across his face. 'I tell you what, though. He hasn't half done me a favour.'

Phillips frowned, causing a surge of pain from her broken nose. She grimaced slightly. 'How does Shing slicing up your arm do you a favour?'

'Got me my wife back,' said Jones with certainty.

Phillips blew her lips and then chuckled. 'So it's all good again then, is it?'

Jones nodded. 'Totally. When she found out I'd been seriously injured, she suddenly realised what life would really be like without me, and she says she couldn't stand the thought of it. She's now talking about renewing our vows next summer in the Maldives.'

'Bloody hell. Shing *did* do you a favour, then.'

'I know, right,' said Jones, his grin even wider now.

'I don't mind telling you though, Jonesy, I thought we'd lost you at one point.'

Jones produced a slow smile. 'The surgeon reckons that, without the Air Ambulance, I'd have bled out.'

Phillips nodded silently.

'So, how's your nose?' asked Jones, appearing keen to change the subject.

Phillips instinctively touched her nose at the point of impact. 'Broken and sore, but I'll live. It's a good thing my job doesn't rely on my looks,' she said with a smile.

'And what about Shing? What's happened to him?'

'He's still in intensive care with a swelling on the brain,' said Phillips. 'Bovalino knocked the shit out of him.'

Jones laughed nervously. 'Even a Triad assassin is no match for the Italian Stallion.'

Phillips laughed too for a moment, then caught herself. 'Seriously, though, I've never seen Bov like that. If I hadn't been there to stop him, he'd have killed Shing.'

Jones nodded sagely.

'I need to ask you something,' said Phillips, 'about Bov.'

'Go on.'

'Last week, outside Shaw's apartment, when I was giving you a hard time for smoking—'

'And feeling sorry for myself,' said Jones with a wry smile.

'That too, yeah. Well, during that exchange you told me that Bov wasn't firing on all cylinders. What did you mean by that?'

Jones took a deep breath and let it out with a sigh. 'Look, I shouldn't have said anything.'

'Maybe not, but you did. So, what did you mean?'

'You should ask him, Guv. I wouldn't feel right talking about him behind his back.'

'Look, Jonesy. I watched Bov – our very own gentle giant – almost beat a man to death on a sink. Because of that, he's facing an investigation for use of excessive force, and if he's found guilty he'll be gone. So if there were mitigating circumstances that led to it, as his boss, I need to know,' said Phillips.

'They can't throw him out for protecting us!'

'They can and they will if they feel Bov overstepped the mark. Don't forget, Fox is in the running for Chief Constable. If she thinks making an example of one of her own will help her get the job, she'll have him out in a flash. So, for Bov's sake, tell me what you meant that day.'

Jones rubbed his mouth and nodded. 'Ok. I'll tell you, but only because it might help him.'

'Go on.'

'It was something he said on the train down to London when we went after Wong. He mentioned that he was struggling a bit.'

'Struggling? With *what*, exactly?'

'He'd lost his bottle. After the Hawkins case. Said he was frightened of getting hurt again. He'd cheated death once and he was wondering if he could carry on. Izzie was constantly worried about him and that was playing on his mind too.'

'Jesus,' said Phillips. 'I had no idea.'

'None of us did. I mean, who'd have thought a big guy like Bov would get scared?'

'No wonder he froze at Jennings's house.'

Jones nodded. 'That's why I went out the back first. I knew he couldn't face it, and I didn't want you to find out.'

Phillips processed the information for a moment.

'Come on, Guv, they won't kick him out, will they? If he hadn't taken Shing out, we'd *all* be dead.'

'I hope not. I really do,' said Phillips, 'but you can never underestimate Fox's ambition either.'

'Is there anything we can do to help him? You know, speak on his behalf?'

'I'll be doing that,' said Phillips. 'Don't you worry. I promise you, if I have anything to do with it, he's not going anywhere.'

The room fell silent for a time before Jones spoke again. 'So, what's the score with Jennings, then?'

'He's in here with you. Will be for about a month, they reckon. The bullet shattered his shoulder and made a right mess inside, so he's gonna need a couple more surgeries before they'll let him out.'

'And what then?'

'Then?' said Phillips. 'Then, I'm gonna throw the book at the slimy bastard. I want him on conspiracy to murder, fraud, embezzlement, bribery, the lot. Entwistle's going through the Planning Department's accounts as we speak. If Cindy Shaw was right, then I've no doubt we'll unravel his false accounting. By the time I'm finished with him, he'll wish Shing had bloody killed him.'

Jones cackled. 'Poor bugger won't know what's hit him.'

Phillips chuckled and said nothing for a moment before stepping up out of the seat. 'Right, well, I don't know about you, but I'm knackered. Time for me to go home and get some sleep.'

Jones nodded. 'I can't be sure if it's the meds they've put me on, or the jet lag has finally buggered off, but I slept like a baby last night.'

Phillips recoiled playfully. 'What? You mean you shit your pants and cried all night?'

'Ha-bloody-ha,'

'I'm only kidding,' said Phillips. 'Mine's gone too, and all I want to do right now is slip into a hot bath, have a glass of wine and go to bed. I'll leave you to it.'

'Thanks for coming by, Guv. It means a lot.'

'Take care, and I'll speak to you tomorrow,' said Phillips and headed for the door before stopping in her tracks and turning back to Jones. 'You won't have heard him saying it, because you were out for the count that night, but as Shing was about to kill us, he kept repeating a phrase, over and over. It was bloody eerie, and I remembered hearing it just before Wong was killed.'

'Oh, what was that?'

'Si wú duì zhèng!' said Phillips, trying her best to pronounce the Cantonese.

'What does it mean?'

'I had no idea, so I got googled it.'

'*And*?'

'"The dead cannot testify; dead men tell no tales,"' said Phillips.

'Jesus. We really are lucky to be alive, Guv.'

Phillips nodded. 'Yes, we are.' She left the room.

48

ASHTON HOUSE, MAJOR CRIMES UNIT, INCIDENT ROOM

ONE MONTH LATER.

Phillips drained the remaining coffee from her mug and took a moment to sit back in her leather chair as she mentally prepared for the interview she was about to conduct with Eric Jennings. After three weeks in hospital and several surgeries, he had finally been allowed to go home. Phillips and Entwistle had wasted no time in getting around to his house, and promptly arrested him on suspicion of conspiracy to murder and fraud. The CPS was confident of convictions on the fraud charge, but far less so on conspiracy to murder. However, Phillips had been keen to include it in the hope that the added pressure might scare Jennings into incriminating himself in the interview. It was a long shot and she knew it, but it was worth a go. And that was the one charge she *really* wanted to get him on.

The Digital Forensics team had quickly recovered the fraudulent documents he had co-signed with Cindy Shaw, plus a host of evidence that he had been doctoring official documents in an attempt to force through the rezoning of St John's Gardens. It was hardly the crime of the century, and, if convicted – at best – Phillips knew he would serve a minimal amount of time in a Category C prison for small time offenders.

In her gut, she truly believed Jennings had been involved in Carpenter's murder and, in doing so, had robbed her and her unborn baby of their future – not to mention the heartbreak her death had caused for both Aaron Carpenter and Don Townsend. Phillips was determined he should receive justice in line with the crime, but she knew only too well that justice and the rule of law were not always great bedfellows. Unless she could secure a confession, she had little evidence to convince the CPS the conspiracy to murder charge would stick.

She checked her watch – 10.50 a.m. – then closed her leather portfolio case on the desk and made ready to leave. At that moment, there was a knock at her door.

'You got a second, Guv?' asked Entwistle, his laptop balanced on his left arm.

'Can it wait? I'm due downstairs with Jennings in ten minutes.'

'It's *about* Jennings. I've found something I think you'll want to see before you go in.'

Phillips eyes widened. 'In that case, I have all the time in the world.'

Entwistle walked to the side of her desk and placed the laptop down. 'So, I took the bus last night for the first time in years because my car was in for a service.'

'Right.'

'Yeah, I sat downstairs near the front.'

'Ok,' said Phillips, wondering where this was going.

'And totally by chance, I noticed that the bus company uses cameras to monitor their drivers.' Entwistle showed her his phone. 'See – I took a photo of it.'

Phillips glanced at the image. 'Is there a point to this, Entwistle?'

'Stay with me. You'll be glad you did.'

Phillips was still not convinced.

Entwistle continued, 'Anyway, it suddenly dawned on me that when we trawled the bus company CCTV outside Carpenter's house on the night she died, we only ever saw footage from the passenger-focused cameras – *not the driver cams.* So this morning I contacted the bus company and asked for all the footage from the driver cams for every bus that passed the murder scene. Specifically, from two hours either side of the time of death.'

Phillips's pulse quickened with anticipation.

'And look what I found at 7.30 p.m.,' said Entwistle opening a large image on the screen.

Phillips took a moment to focus, and then her eyes widened. 'Jesus Christ. We can't be that lucky?'

'We can, Guv, and we are!'

A wide grin spread across her face as she grabbed her leather case. 'Can you print those off for me.'

'I'll do it now,' said Entwistle.

'And then I want you to observe the interview from the video suite.'

'You got it.'

Ten minutes later, Phillips walked into Interview Room Four and took a seat opposite Eric Jennings and his legal aid solicitor, David Thorogood. Jennings's right arm was in a sling and he looked like he'd lost a lot of weight during his time in hospital. He held a plastic cup of water in his left hand.

After explaining the finer details of the interview process and the various recording devices that would be in use, she got straight to it. 'Eric Jennings, you've been arrested on suspicion of conspiracy to murder Victoria Carpenter as well as fraud—'

'My client categorically refutes being involved in any way in the death of Victoria Carpenter,' Thorogood cut her off.

Phillips fixed him with an icy glare, which he returned. 'You have nothing to tie my client to Carpenter's death, and I would like that noted on the record. Mr Jennings fully intends to cooperate with the investigation into the fraudulent actions of Cindy Shaw, and is keen to see justice prevail.'

Phillips turned her attention to Jennings and flashed a thin smile. 'That's very noble of you.'

Jennings remained stoic.

'Can we just go back to the night Victoria Carpenter was murdered?' said Phillips.

Thorogood rolled his eyes. 'Really? Do we have to go over this again?'

'Humour me,' said Phillips, as she focused on Jennings. 'Your car was seen near to the Carpenters' home around the time Victoria died. About half a mile up the road in Didsbury, wasn't it?'

'Yes. Like I told you at the time, I was buying wine in the village.'

'And you only stopped at the wine merchant? Nowhere else?' said Phillips.

'That's what I said,' said Jennings, clearly irritated.

'And you were nowhere near the Carpenter house that night?'

'No. I wasn't. I left work, drove to the wine shop, had a quick chat, picked up my order and went home.'

'You're completely sure of that?'

'Yes!'

'I see,' said Phillips, before changing tack again. 'At your cottage, the night we were both attacked by Zhang Shing, you told me that *he* had killed Carpenter. How did you know that?'

Jennings took a sip from the water and swallowed hard. 'I just assumed he had.'

'Also on the night in question, you rang me and said you knew who Vicky and Cindy's killer was, and you were worried that that same person was going to kill you. You even offered to tell me their name in exchange for witness protection.'

'I'd had half a bottle of brandy. I can't recall what I said.'

'Well, I'll remind you, shall I? You told me that Zhang Shing had killed Cindy Shaw and Victoria Carpenter, and that he had come to kill *you* because you knew too much about the Triads' illegal operation – in particular the rezoning of St John's Gardens, which you had forced through the Council. Any of that ringing a bell?'

'Like I said, I was drunk. I don't even know the man.'

'Well, if you'd never met him, how did you know his name when we spoke that night?'

Before he could answer, Thorogood drew Jennings close and whispered in his ear for a moment.'

Jennings nodded, sat upright, and stared at Phillips. 'No comment.'

Phillips smiled slowly and nodded, then pulled the prints from Entwistle's bus camera footage from her leather file. She placed them face down on the table. 'Are you familiar with the 6A bus that passes through Withington?'

'No,' said Jennings.

'Well, you might like to know that the 6A travels right past the Carpenters' house every fifteen minutes. In fact, there's a bus stop right across the street.'

'I don't use public transport.'

'No, I'm sure you don't – but if you *did* – you'd know that they have CCTV cameras on them, some of which point at the door and capture footage out on the street as they travel along or sit at stops.'

'What has any of this got to do with my client?' asked Thorogood, sounding impatient.

Phillips glanced at Thorogood, then back at Jennings. 'After Carpenter was murdered, we checked the CCTV footage of every bus that travelled or stopped along that route the day she died, and we found nothing,' said Phillips. 'Not a thing...but then one of my team – who's a bit of a whizz with technology –

spotted the fact that buses also have cameras trained on the drivers. One can see them, but also what's happening over their right shoulders. You see – we had no idea those cameras existed, so we'd never checked them.'

'Is there a point to this?' said Thorogood.

Phillips ignored him. 'So, armed with this new information, we went back and checked the drivers' cameras that day, too.' She stared at Jennings now, unflinching, then turned one of the images over. 'And look what we found.'

Jennings's eyes flashed to the printout in front of him and Phillips noticed he flinched, as Thorogood's brow furrowed .

Phillips tapped the picture with her index finger. 'We took these images from a bus sitting at the stop on Wilmslow Road, across from the Carpenters' house. You'll have to excuse the round edges of the images – the camera uses what's called a fish-eye lens – but even so, you'll recognise that as Carpenter's front drive. Notice the timestamp on this one says 7.37 p.m.'

Jennings shifted in his seat.

Phillips continued. 'Here we can clearly see two men, one with his back to the camera staring directly at Carpenter's front door, and the other looking back to the road.' Phillips tapped the man's face. 'A suspected Triad henchman known to the police as Jimmy Wong.' She turned over the next image. 'In this one, we can see *you, Mr Jennings*, opening Carpenter's front door to them from inside the house...'

Jennings's mouth fell open, and Thorogood's eyes bulged.

'Now, why would you be opening the door to Vicky's house?'

Jennings said nothing and instead stared at the images on the table.

Phillips continued and turned over the last image. '...and in this last picture, the third man has turned to the side and we can finally see his face. Surprise, surprise, it's the one and only...' She paused for effect. '...*Zhang Shing!*'

'I never thought they'd actually kill her!' The words tumbled from Jennings's mouth, 'I swear!'

'What were you doing there that night?' asked Phillips.

Thorogood reached for Jennings's arm to stop him from answering, but he was too late. It seemed as if Jennings couldn't get the words out quick enough. 'I went round to Vicky's one last time to try and talk her into signing off the rezoning, but she was having none of it. Shing and Wong were waiting outside. I had no choice but to let them in.'

Thorogood grabbed Jennings's wrist tightly now. 'That's enough,' he said firmly, then turned to face Phillips. 'I need a moment with my client.'

'Do you know, I had a feeling you might,' said Phillips, then smiled to herself as she gathered the images and returned them to the folder. 'Take all the time you need. Your client's not going anywhere. I'm suspending this interview at 11.29 a.m.,' she added, then stood up and left the room.

She'd got the bastard.

49

The next morning, Phillips took a seat in Fox's empty office and waited for her boss to arrive to update her on the investigation into Bovalino's actions. It was very unusual for Fox's PA, Ms Blair, to allow anyone access to the 'inner sanctum' alone, but Phillips sensed the vibe on the fifth floor was very different today. Quite why, she couldn't put her finger on, but there was definitely something going on. Ms Blair had even prepared her a coffee, which was unheard of.

As she sat cradling her steaming mug now, she glanced around the room. Her eyes fell on Fox's 'Hero Wall', where she'd hung an array of framed photos of her with so-called VIPs: politicians, dignitaries, even the odd TV star. Phillips had studied it many times during their meetings and noted that a number of photos were missing today. She wondered why.

At that moment, the office door burst open and Fox strode in. 'Ah, DCI Phillips.' She was in an uncharacteristically good mood as she walked round the desk, then dropped into the large leather chair. 'How are things?'

Phillips placed her mug on a coaster on the glass desk. 'Good, Ma'am. Very good, in fact.'

'That's what I like to hear.' Fox's Cheshire Cat grin seemed even wider than usual. 'So, where are we at with the Carpenter case?'

'After yesterday, I think we're just about over the line.'

'Yesterday? Why so?' asked Fox.

'Entwistle discovered CCTV footage that puts Zhang Shing, Wong and Eric Jennings at the scene of the crime around the time she was murdered.'

'Excellent work, Jane. Top notch.'

Jane? thought Phillips. Fox really was in a good mood. 'Faced with that evidence, Jennings has been singing like a canary in the hope of getting leniency from the CPS. He's given us full disclosure on Victoria's murder; how he went round to the house that night to persuade her to accept a bribe to rezone St John's Gardens. When she wouldn't, he let Shing and Wong into the house and they murdered her. He claims he didn't *know* that's what they were going to do – and wasn't there to see it – but his testimony, plus the audio recordings of Carpenter's and Shaw's homes, along with the theft of Carpenter's laptop – which we found in Shing's flat – means he's going down for life.'

'Has Jennings explained how he came to be involved with the Triads? I mean, he's hardly gangster material, is he?' said Fox.

'No, he's not. He insists it was a one-time deal and he did it to get his own back on his bosses at the Council.'

'For what?'

'"Retiring him,"' said Phillips, making inverted commas in the air. 'Apparently his bosses wanted a more dynamic Planning Department with Victoria Carpenter as the new boss. They pretty much told him he was no longer needed. Well, as you can imagine, a man like Jennings didn't take kindly to being "thrown on the scrapheap," as he put it. So, when he was approached by Gold Star's representatives, the thought of getting one over his bosses and Carpenter – plus a nice addition to his pension pot – was too good an opportunity to turn down. He claims they offered him a brand-new apartment in the St John's Tower Development, and in return he would ensure a successful outcome for their rezoning application.'

'An apartment in the city centre? That could be worth close to half a million pounds.'

'Depending on its size, yes, Ma'am.'

Fox shook her head. 'Bloody fool. Instead of going quietly and enjoying his government pension in his holiday home, he'll spend most of his retirement in Hawk Green Maximum Security Prison.'

Phillips nodded.

'And what about Zhang Shing,' said Fox. 'Is he talking yet?'

'No. Nothing. But that's not an issue, now we have Jennings's evidence. As well as Shing, he's also implicated Gold Star Trading for attempting to bribe a government official. Sadly, it's not enough to warrant us going after them ourselves, but we intend to share what we know with the Ministry of Commerce and Customs Administration, as well as the World Trade Organisation.'

'And what will that do?'

'Well, it'll hopefully mean that any future deals they attempt to do in the UK will come under intense scrutiny. Whether that will actually happen, who can say, but their plans to rezone St John's Gardens have been overturned. Plus, thanks to a campaign Don Townsend is running through the *Manchester Evening News*, the site is expected to fall under a preservation order, meaning it can never be built on no matter who's in charge of the Planning Department. There's even a discussion about a memorial garden being created for Victoria.'

'That really is a *wonderful* idea. Good for Vicky,' said Fox.

The new-look 'happy Fox' was starting to unnerve Phillips. 'Yes, Ma'am. And the Council's licensing team is also undertaking an investigation into Gold Star Trading's investment into the Belmont Casinos. As I understand it, they'll be shut down for the duration of that investigation, and the word from inside the Town Hall is they'll do whatever it takes to make sure they never reopen.'

'Hit them where it hurts: in the pocket,' said Fox.

'Quite, Ma'am.'

'So, what about Senior Inspector Li? You mentioned the Royal Hong Kong Police had launched an investigation into his conduct regarding the death of Jimmy Wong. Any news?'

'Officially, they're keeping their own counsel on it, as you'd imagine, but according to my contact on the island, Jonny Wu, it looks like they've linked him to the Lui Triad family. It seems he's been taking payments to look the other way for many, many years. Based on that, I'm pretty sure he was the one that led them to Wong in Chungking Mansions.'

'But why get you and Jones involved in that mess? Why not just tell the Triads where to find Wong?'

'I'm guessing because it would kill two birds with one stone – no pun intended,' said Phillips. 'Eliminate Wong, and scare us into giving up the investigation and leaving Hong Kong.'

Fox leaned back in her chair and cast her eyes to the ceiling. 'You can almost admire his cunning, in a way,' she said wistfully.

Phillips stared at her in silence. Fox's cheerful demeanour was really confusing.

'So, what will happen to Li now, do you think?'

'I'm told it all depends on how it's viewed by mainland China. They're looking to make an example of anyone with connections to the Triads, so if he's found guilty – which looks likely, according to Jonny Wu's insiders – Li could end up front page news and facing a life sentence in general population. Not a safe place for a disgraced copper.'

'Serves the bastard right,' said Fox with a grin.

Phillips shifted in her seat. 'Er, Ma'am. On another note, I've been meaning to ask: has a decision been made on Bovalino and his return to work?

'Of course, Jane. Fully exonerated,' said Fox. 'And rightly so.'

Phillips let out a loud sigh of relief. 'Oh, thank God!'

Fox continued, 'The email came through last night. The panel found that he did what he needed to do under extreme circumstances. In fact, considering his actions saved the lives of four police officers and a civilian, I've recommended him for a commendation.'

'Oh, wow. He'll be over the moon.'

'He's a bloody good copper, Jane. *You all are.*'

The room fell silent for a moment, and Phillips took a drink from her coffee to distract her from the strange atmosphere. 'Is everything all right, Ma'am?' she asked finally. 'You seem...different.'

Fox nodded eagerly, then leaned forwards across the desk, beaming with delight. 'I have news,' she said in a low, conspiratorial tone.'

'Oh?'

'But it's strictly confidential. I only found out last night.'

'Found out what?'

Fox looked left and right, as if checking no one was eavesdropping. 'I'm to be the new Chief Constable.'

Phillips eyes widened. 'Oh God...I mean... er, that's amazing news, Ma'am.'

'Isn't it? The Divisional Commander called me last night to tell me. I'm over the moon.'

Everything suddenly fell into place. Blair's unusual cheerfulness was on account of the fact she too was being promoted, by proxy. She had already begun to pack away Fox's office in readiness for their move to the biggest office suite in Ashton House.

'Credit where credit's due, Jane,' said Fox. 'MCU's results over the last few years played a big part in me getting the job over Broadhurst. Your conviction rate is the best in Greater Manchester. Naturally, Broadhurst's totally pissed off, but tough titties. This is *my* time.'

Phillips wasn't sure how she felt about Fox getting the top job, but right now she had a more pressing concern. 'So, do you know who your replacement will be, Ma'am?'

'Why? Fancy it yourself, do you, Jane?' said Fox grinning.

Phillips shook her head vigorously. 'God, no. I couldn't cope with the bullshit and the politics.' The words left her mouth before she could stop them, and she held her breath for a long moment as she waited for the repercussions.

Instead, Fox's grin remained in position. She was obviously too happy to notice. 'I must admit, I've never seen you in the higher ranks, Jane. Not your world, is it?'

Phillips wasn't sure whether to be offended or take it as a compliment.

Fox continued, 'Well. It's a good job you *don't* want it, because they've already offered it to someone.'

'Who?' said Phillips, eagerly.

'I'm afraid I can't say. You see, they haven't accepted it yet, so until they do, it's confidential. I'm not about to make my first action as Chief Constable be breaking protocol.'

'Well, can I at least get a clue, Ma'am?'

The trademark Cheshire Cat grin enveloped Fox's face. 'Let's just say, you've worked with *him* before.'

Phillips's stomach turned. 'Oh God. It's not Brown is it?'

Fox chuckled. 'Now, now Jane. That would be telling.'

ACKNOWLEDGEMENTS

This book was planned, researched and written during the COVID-19 pandemic, and I have never felt more grateful for the level of support I received whilst creating *Deadly Betrayal.*

It has not been easy navigating such strange times for anyone, and I am so blessed to have the unwavering belief of my amazing wife Kim, who ensured I was able to escape the noise of our home during lockdown and write my daily chapters.

My gorgeous boy, Vaughan. I'm sorry I wasn't always available, locked away in my office at times. 'Daddy Working!'

Estelle and James Ramsey, my eyes and ears in Hong Kong, who helped me bring such an amazing city to the page.

Carole Lawford, ex-CPS Prosecutor. What you don't know about British Law isn't worth knowing.

My coaches, Donna Elliot and Cheryl Lee, from 'Now Is Your Time.' You are truly amazing and never fail to inspire me.

My publishers, Brian and Garret, and my editor, Laurel. Thank you for your focus, belief and incredible attention to detail.

And finally, thank you to my readers for reading *Deadly Betrayal.* If you could spend a moment to write an honest review on Amazon, no matter how short, I would be extremely grateful. They really do help readers discover my books.

Best wishes,

Owen

www.omjryan.com

ALSO BY OMJ RYAN

The DCI Jane Phillips Crime Thriller Series

(Books listed in order)

DEADLY SECRETS (a series prequel)

DEADLY SILENCE

DEADLY WATERS

DEADLY VENGEANCE

DEADLY BETRAYAL

DEADLY OBSESSION

DEADLY CALLER

DEADLY NIGHT

DEADLY CRAVING

DEADLY JUSTICE

DEADLY VEIL

DEADLY INFERNO

DCI JANE PHILLIPS BOX SET

(Books 1-4 in the series)

Published by Inkubator Books
www.inkubatorbooks.com